CURSED

OF

MOON

BOOKS BY KRISTA STREET
SUPERNATURAL WORLD NOVELS

Fae of Snow & Ice

Court of Winter
Thorns of Frost
Wings of Snow
Crowns of Ice

Supernatural Curse

Wolf of Fire
Bound of Blood
Cursed of Moon
Forged of Bone

Supernatural Institute

Fated by Starlight
Born by Moonlight
Hunted by Firelight
Kissed by Shadowlight

Supernatural Community

Magic in Light
Power in Darkness
Dragons in Fire
Angel in Embers

Supernatural Standalones

Beast of Shadows

Links to all of Krista's books may be found on her website.
www.kristastreet.com

CURSED

OF

MOON

paranormal shifter romance

SUPERNATURAL CURSE
BOOK THREE

KRISTA STREET

PREFACE

Cursed of Moon is a paranormal shifter romance and is the third book in the four-book *Supernatural Curse* series. The recommended reading age is 18+.

CHAPTER ONE

I stared at the hunter, blinking, unable to believe what I was hearing. Kaillen thought he'd potentially turned me into a werewolf and that I'd be the first female supernatural to ever *shift* into a wolf.

The devastated expression on Kaillen's face grew. Behind him, the pearly moon shone brightly through the bedroom window in his Montana home. It was only one day away from the midpoint of the lunar cycle.

My heart pounded more. "Do you really think I'm going to shift tomorrow night?"

He stared back at me, so many emotions reeling through those fiery amber eyes that I couldn't decipher them. "I don't know, but it's possible."

"But *how*? How did this happen?"

"It must be because of my blood. When you drank from me on that night you nearly died, and I spelled it so I could always track you—" His throat bobbed in a swallow. "That spell must have also activated the wolf traits in my blood, and since you consumed so much of it, it changed you. It's the only explanation I can come up with, because when human men are made into wolves, the process is similar."

I scoffed. "So you knew this was a possibility when you did it?"

"No." A muscle ticked in his jaw. "I never thought making you a werewolf was a possibility. No woman has ever been made into a wolf."

"Right." So it was only me. I inhaled sharply. Disbelief, anger, and the feeling of betrayal hit me all at once, because I knew, *knew* to the depths of my core that I would shift, and *I'd never freakin' agreed to this.*

The scent of ash, or fiery timber, filled my nose. But nothing was burning. I sniffed, then sniffed again. "What's that smell?"

"What smell?"

I wiped at my tear-filled eyes. "It smells kind of like ash, but nothing's burning."

"Emotions, they . . . have their own scents."

My lips parted. "Wait, I'm smelling an emotion? *Your* emotion?" 'Cause I sure as shit didn't think I could smell my own. Or at least, I hoped I couldn't.

He gave a small, nearly imperceptible nod. "Most likely."

"What emotion smells like ash?"

His eyes burned. "Guilt."

So Kaillen was feeling *guilty*. My teeth snapped together. He damn well should feel guilty for turning me into something I never consented to. Not to mention, he'd also bound me to him with his blood, so now the dude could find me anywhere I roamed. Talk about an astronomical breach of privacy.

My nostrils flared. Even though his blood had saved me when I'd nearly died during Jakub's first abduction attempt on me, the hunter hadn't needed to spell his blood when he'd given it to me. Nope, that was his newly born mate bond driving him to do that. Because with a blood bond, he could always sense me—something every mated werewolf male would crave. So, because of *his* choice, I was now bound to him and would most likely turn all furry tomorrow night.

I scrubbed a hand down my face. *Ugh.* It was beyond infuriating since Kaillen hadn't needed to spell his blood to save me. His blood alone would have healed me after that three-story fall, but since he'd spelled it, I was now this female werewolf-witch-otherworldly power-hybrid. Whatever that even was . . .

The hunter took a step closer to me. "It's possible that I'm wrong and you won't shift tomorrow night." His gaze turned pleading, as though wishing he'd never been more wrong in his life.

I crossed my arms, those damned tears still clouding my vision. "Can female werewolves normally scent emotions?"

"No."

I gave a slow, resigned nod. "Then that confirms that I'm not a normal female werewolf, because I think I can scent your guilt." I scoffed. "Your brother was right. I am an abomination."

A low growl tore from his throat. "What the fuck did my brother say to you?"

"Nothing. It doesn't matter." I gave my back to the hunter, then crawled across the bed, intent on fleeing him. But I knew that was pointless. Where would I go? Out in the field to admire the moon? I blanched. I'd probably start howling at it, or dancing naked, or doing something else that would be equally mortifying and completely foreign. Something that was no longer *me*.

My pulse sped up, and for the first time, I heard my heart beating. It thundered in my ears, in time with the blood whooshing through my veins.

I slammed my hands over my ears, but it did nothing to drown out the sounds.

"Tala? What is it, *colantha*? What's wrong?" The hunter's muffled questions came through my lousy attempt at stifling these new sensations.

Gods, when had they grown so strong?

But I already knew the answer to that. They'd been growing steadily stronger during the last two weeks, ever since I'd drunk his blood. My body was slowly adjusting to its first shift that would apparently happen tomorrow night under the full moon. And now, as though recognizing what was imminent, the sensations had increased a hundred-fold.

Kaillen still stood by the window, the glowing night sky

at his back, as the snowy white moon beckoned me to join it.

Trembling, I stood on shaky legs on the other side of the bed. "I think I'm gonna shower or maybe get something to eat." I shook my head. "Or not. I just don't know about anything anymore. Maybe I should go home."

I still had an apartment in Chicago and a comfy bed to sleep on, even though my life in the windy city felt like it was eons ago. My trembling increased. The last time I'd slept in that bed, I'd nearly been abducted.

"You can't go home," Kaillen said softly, reminding me of something I already knew. "It's not safe there. You'll stay here in Montana . . . with me."

"Right, 'cause *here* is so safe." I didn't even care when his face fell, because I was so sick of surprise after surprise being sprung on me.

I was supposed to have been safe in Oak Trembler, Ontario, but then Cameron—Kaillen's sadistic oldest brother—had betrayed me and handed me over to two sorcerers who worked for Jakub. Even though that wasn't Kaillen's fault, this was all so much. *Too* much.

I sighed in defeat. "Fine. I'll stay here, but can I have some privacy?"

His face wiped clean, the guilt, anguish, and anger disappearing in a veiled mask of nothingness.

It was a look I'd seen so many times on the hunter. He was a master at hiding everything. Or, at least, he had been. I supposed I had an edge now since I could scent what he was feeling.

I snorted bitterly at that thought.

Kaillen walked on silent footsteps to the door. I watched him go, wondering if I would eventually be able to move like that—so silent and still—the walk of a predator.

"Answer one thing for me," I called to him.

He stopped at the doorway and turned, his broad shoulders tensing.

"When did you begin to suspect that I was transitioning into a female werewolf?"

He didn't reply, but instead simply watched me, and I knew he was aware of my anger and distrust. Who knew what *those* emotions smelled like. "About ten days ago."

That statement slammed into me with so much force that I actually stumbled back onto the bed. Ten days ago we'd been training my new awakening power daily. We'd been together every single minute of every single day, and he'd still kept his suspicions from me?

My chest lifted in a shaky breath, then another, as cold hurt washed through me. Another coating of tears filled my eyes. "Were you ever going to tell me? Or were you just gonna let me shift and figure it out?"

He pushed away from the door.

"Don't come any closer."

He stopped mid-stride. "I was hoping I was wrong."

"Right. You *hoped* you were wrong." I shook my head. "Goodnight, Fire Wolf."

He stiffened, those words no doubt casting a blow. I hadn't called him Fire Wolf since that night in his bed, when I'd nearly slept with him and he'd asked me to start calling him Kaillen.

His face tightened, before he snapped his spine upright and all of his emotions vanished. "Good night."

He dipped out of the room and closed the door.

I sighed again, but instead of getting up to shower and eat, I lay down on the bed.

Too much. Too much. Too much was happening.

In the past twenty-four hours, I'd admitted to the hunter, while we were still in Ontario, that what we had between us wasn't real because his feelings were all mate bond driven. It was something I'd known ever since his wolf had shown an interest in me. So that conversation had been bad enough, even though we still hadn't finished it. But right now, I couldn't stomach even the thought of another heavy emotional discussion, so who knew when or if we would broach that subject again.

My shoulders fell when I remembered that contentious conversation. *Gods, was it really only yesterday?* Kaillen had disappeared after I'd told him we could never be together because his feelings for me weren't real, that his interest in me was manufactured by his wolf. Following that, I'd escaped to the bathroom, and Kaillen had stormed off. So when Cameron had come calling, I'd been easy prey since I'd been so distracted.

I didn't blame Kaillen for that, though. My distraction wasn't his fault. Nope, that was one hundred percent on me. I shouldn't have let my guard down around Cameron. It still infuriated me that he'd tricked me so easily.

The only good thing that had come out of my abduction was that I'd possibly met Jakub, the fucker who was after my power. I'd also learned that I could combine my witch powers with my otherworldly ones to be hella strong, something I hadn't known I was capable of. And that was all before I'd been knocked unconscious by some ax that was bound to hell and which I'd only just woken up from.

I crawled under the sheets again. Any burst of energy I'd felt earlier had vanished.

I lay there and tried to sleep, but that feeling, that tug, that *pull* throbbed again in my chest. *Don't do it. Don't look.*

But I was helpless to resist it.

My gaze coasted again to the moon, to that beautiful heavenly body that hung in the sky. It owned me now, commanded and *called* to me.

Without a doubt, I knew that tomorrow night, I would be the first female in the history of the world to shift into a wolf.

"Fuck my life. Seriously." I pulled the covers up and slammed a pillow over my face. More than anything, I just wished all of this would go away.

I MUST HAVE FALLEN asleep at some point because the next thing I knew, bright sunlight was spilling into the room and sharp scents were assaulting my senses.

Without opening my eyes, I already knew that the

hunter was awake and in the house, because after a sharp inhale, it wasn't just the smell of coffee, bacon, and eggs that hit me. I also smelled *him*.

His citrusy cedar fragrance wafted into my room, not as strong as the sizzling food cooking downstairs that I could not only smell—as if it were being cooked in the same room as me—but also hear.

The scrape of a pan. The flickering flames of a gas stove. The crack of eggshells. All of it swirled together, yet I could detect all of those sounds individually too.

So last night wasn't a nightmare.

I jolted upright in bed, the movement so fast that for a second, I wondered if my actions had been blurred.

I brought a hand to my head. My head ached. Absentmindedly, I scratched my arm, then realized I felt itchy all over, and something felt *off* in my chest, like there was something inside of me.

I tentatively felt around within. My witch magic was there, swirling as it always did in my chest. And deeper and lower, near my navel, was my forbidden power—my power that enhanced another supernatural's magic. And just to the side of it, in the dark, invisible cave that I'd come to recognize as a void that wasn't actually a void, was where my new awakening power lay—my newly born power that sucked another's magic from them and gave it all to me.

But now there was something else.

Something new.

Something pulsing just beneath my skin that wasn't fully there but was still *there*.

If that made any sense.

"Gods," I mumbled. "I'm a mess." I rubbed my hand on my breastbone, then clawed again at my limbs, trying to dispel the itching feeling, but the sensation that I was going to crawl out of my skin remained.

Or maybe *I* wasn't going to crawl out of my skin but a wolf was.

I shuddered, then finally gave up. I didn't even want to think about what all of this meant. Because tonight was the night of the full moon, the true test to see if I would indeed shift.

"Not thinking about that. Definitely *not* thinking about that."

With slow movements, I stood from the bed, expecting to wince or feel sore from the beating I'd taken in the past twenty-four hours, but—

I stretched. My arms moved freely and easily. I lifted my knees, pumping them up and down. They moved just as quickly, as though my joints were perfectly lubricated hinges.

I figured it could be from the healing potion the hunter had given me the night prior, or it could be from . . . my newly awakening werewolf powers.

My heartrate picked up a staccato beat as the scents rolling up from downstairs continued to assault me. My nose twitched. Because underneath the scent of bacon and eggs, I detected other things, too. Subtler things.

The scent of icy water dipped in soil with a wash of ozone—it was the fragrance of . . .

My brow puckered, and I glanced outside.

Snow.

A light sprinkling of snow fell from the sky, coating the pastures and fields which stretched for miles to those endless mountains in the distance.

Sniffing, I padded closer to the window. The pull of the moon was gone, thank the lord baby Cheez-Its, but in its place was a myriad of new smells. I sniffed again, detecting those crisp snowflakes.

There were other scents too, some I could only guess at. Soil. Perhaps dust. Laundry detergent. Spiderwebs, maybe? Carpet. I had no idea what was what, but the subtle undertones of all of those things came to me at lightning speed.

My heart beat faster, and I began to massage my temples.

A headache brewed, which was odd since werewolves rarely got them, but I figured this momentous shift in the fabric of my very essence seemed like an appropriate occasion to have one.

I pinched my nose shut, ignoring the throbbing in my skull, and tried to stop the bombarding onslaught of never-ending scents. At least I knew about my impending shift, 'cause if I didn't, I was pretty sure that right now I would be thinking I'd gone crazy.

Gritting my teeth, I stalked toward the corner door, assuming it was either a bathroom or a closet. Kaillen's Montana home was much bigger than the small cabin his father insisted on keeping for him in Oak Trembler.

A full bathroom greeted me when I swung the door

open. Hallelujah. I'd been hoping for that 'cause I did *not* feel like running into the hunter in the hallway while wrapped in a towel.

And the en-suite even had fluffy towels and a thick robe hanging behind the door. Seeing that reminded me of Kaillen's domestic streak.

Ignoring that thought, I hurriedly showered and did my best to ignore the pungent fragrances of the shampoo and soap. When I stepped back into the bedroom, toweling my hair off, I gaped when I saw my suitcases lining the wall.

From the looks of it, Kaillen had retrieved everything I'd brought to Oak Trembler. And given the lingering scent in the air, he'd just delivered them while I'd been showering.

I scowled. He'd no doubt used his yellow crystal to portal everything from one location to another, which probably meant it'd only taken him five minutes to grab it all since he was so freakin' powerful. Powerful enough to conjure his own portals, and powerful enough to turn me into a damned werewolf.

Grinding my teeth at the reminder of his betrayal, I threw on the first thing my hands touched in my bags— ripped jeans and a thick cable-knit cobalt-blue sweater. The sweater brought out the natural blue in my eyes and looked good against my golden hair. Normally, I would have appreciated that. But now, how I looked was the least of my concerns.

With damp hair trailing down my back, I pinched my nose again to stop the suffocating onslaught of scents that were enough to drive me mad, and finally went down-stairs. I passed a few closed doors on the second floor along the way, and I realized I hadn't seen any of his home beside the room I was in and his living area. I didn't even know where the master suite was.

But I was too hungry to explore. My stomach was growling so fiercely that I knew I couldn't put off an inter-action with the hunter any longer.

My stomach would probably eat itself if I did.

When I entered the kitchen, Kaillen was standing over the stove, scraping the bottom of a pan. His back was to me, his shoulders broad and rippling beneath his shirt. For a moment, all I could do was stare at the way his muscles bunched and moved, that familiar ache beginning in my core.

Gods. Really? You're thinking about fucking him even after what he's done?

I stomped my arousal down and made a beeline for the island. Two plates with ginormous portions of food sat steaming on it.

The tension in Kaillen's shoulders grew, and he began attacking the pan more, as if whatever was stuck on it was refusing to come free.

"Did you sleep okay?" he asked without turning around.

I slid onto one of the island's stools. Deciding to ignore him, I took in the large kitchen with its high-end appli-ances and sparkling granite countertops.

The color scheme in his permanent home was done in all neutrals: beige, white, light-gray, and cream. It was a simple design. Clean yet detached. In a way, it suited his personality perfectly.

And the impressive windows—which showcased the endless meadow that butted against the distant mountains —began in the living room and ran the length of the house. Sunlight poured in.

There was even a skylight above, which allowed additional natural light in. Since most of the first floor was vaulted with an open design, the light was so bright that lamps weren't needed at all during the day.

"Tala? Did you sleep?" he asked again.

Oh, okay then. It seemed like he was intent on talking. "Well enough," I replied curtly, then admonished myself, because the least I could do was act like a civil grown-up, but that was the extent of what our conversations would be, and I would not allow myself to notice how strong his forearms looked as he scrubbed the dirty pans. Yep, definitely ignoring that.

But speaking of dirty pans . . . "No fairy charms this morning?"

His gaze cut to mine, and my breath sucked in at the fire rolling through his irises, but more than that, I took in how *horrible* he looked. Unwashed dark hair stood on end from his head. Scruffy beard coated his cheeks. Blood lines shot through his eyes. He looked so tired, haggard almost.

I'd literally never seen him look anything but in control and strong.

But for a brief moment, that haggard appearance melted away and hope shone in his eyes. Pure, unadulterated hope. I figured it was because I'd made a joke about his fairy charms. It was the first attempt I'd made at joking with him in days, almost two weeks. Ever since I'd firmly committed myself to resisting him in Oak Trembler, not that *that* had turned out well. I'd still fallen in love with him despite my attempts not to.

And then the dude had turned me into a werewolf.

I shook my head. I wasn't going to think about my unwanted emotions. Kaillen had betrayed me, and I was still firmly pissed at him.

"No charms," he finally replied, his words thick. "Not this morning. I needed to . . . move."

I guessed that explained why his cookware had taken the brunt of his aggression.

My breathing kicked up a notch at the look on his face, so I eyed the food again just as my stomach let out another huge growl.

My cheeks heated. Gods, I hoped this wasn't my new norm, 'cause that sound was *embarrassing*.

And what the hell was up with how strong the food smelled? I swear I could practically taste the buttery eggs and crisp bacon that waited before me, even though I hadn't tasted anything yet.

My stomach let out another growl, and I slapped both hands over it sheepishly.

"You should eat." The hunter gave me his back again, but at least he'd stopped killing his cookware. "Since the full moon is tonight, your metabolism will be increasing with the impending shift. You'll find that you're going to have to start eating a lot more to meet your caloric needs."

I picked up a piece of bacon. "Did you sleep well?" I asked awkwardly as I bit into the crisp fat. My eyes widened at the burst of flavors that melted over my tongue. Gods, it tasted *amazing*. Before I knew what I was doing, I was inhaling the rest of it.

"No," he finally replied after he'd put the dirty pan that he'd near murdered onto the drying rack. "I didn't sleep."

I swallowed another mouthful of food. "At all?"

"No, not at all."

I frowned, remembering how he'd been awake after his demon-ax had rendered me unconscious. The ax's huge gush of magic had been needed to break through the glowing blue handcuffs Cameron had placed on me. But apparently, only I'd been affected by the ax since Kaillen had never fallen asleep. He'd also been sleeping poorly in Oak Trembler for the past week.

I cocked my head. "When did you last sleep?"

He shrugged. "I slept a few hours the night before you were—" He cleared his throat but didn't continue.

My eyebrows shot up. "The night before I was abducted?" What had that been, two days ago now? That was the night he'd drunk a bottle of whiskey in his living room and hadn't come to bed until the early hours of the morning. And the next day, we'd both woken up early and had our explosive interaction in which I'd accused him of not having real feelings for me. That had all taken place before

Cameron had overpowered me and delivered me to Jakub-Dipshit's sorcerers.

Obviously, it hadn't been a good morning for either of us.

Kaillen's jaw locked, but he didn't reply.

I picked up my fork again. "That was two nights ago."

"It was."

"Why aren't you sleeping?"

"I think you know why." He pushed the second plate toward me. I hadn't even realized I'd finished the first. "Eat."

I frowned. "Isn't that one yours?"

"No, it's for you. I already ate, and I couldn't fit all of the food for you onto one plate."

My cheeks heated, even more so when I saw that the amount of food on plate two was just as much as what had been on plate one. He'd probably cooked me a dozen eggs, two pounds of bacon, and toasted an entire loaf of bread.

And the crazy thing was that I wanted nothing more than to reach for plate two. My stomach felt like a clawing empty pit. It wanted more, more, *more*.

"Gods, this is going to do a number on my grocery bill," I grumbled as I reached for the damned plate anyway.

His lips twitched up, and for the briefest moment, the energy changed between us. It felt as it once had—before I knew of Jakub-Dipshit and before Kaillen's wolf decided that I was his mate. It felt like it had when we'd been hunting for Tessa, and bantering with one another had been our norm.

But that momentary lightening of his expression vanished when I plugged my nose and brought the fork to my mouth.

His lips tightened into a grim line. "You'll get used to the new, stronger scents and will learn how to filter them out. All pups have to learn that when they first shift."

My shoulders drooped. I was like a pre-pubescent boy about to go through his first shift. But despite that depressing thought, I began shoveling food into my mouth again.

"That's good to know," I replied while chewing. It seemed as though I could also kiss goodbye to any decent manners I'd once had, as apparently, I now talked with my mouth full. "Sounds like so much fun," I added sarcastically in between bites. "I'm now like a child who eats like a horse and has the manners of a troll."

I expected another lip twitch from him, but instead, his throat bobbed in a swallow. That ashy fragrance tickled my nose again, so subtle amongst the overpowering food smells that I almost missed it.

I swallowed and took another gulp of coffee. Kaillen's expression hadn't changed or wavered in the slightest, yet I could *scent* his guilt.

"It won't stay this bad. The initial shift evokes the biggest changes. You'll find that you'll need to eat a lot in the coming weeks, but in several months it shouldn't be as severe as this."

"Months?" I balked. I was going to be eating like this for *months*.

"Yes." Kaillen went to the sink and began drying the dishes. "By the way, Commander Klebus wants to meet us this morning."

That comment had me choking. I coughed and managed to swallow. "She does? Why?"

"She wants to interview us, since we may have encountered Jakub."

"When did she say that?"

"She called while you were showering."

I snatched the last piece of bacon. Gods, I'd finished the entire plate, and my stomach was so full now I could barely move, but at least that never-ending hunger in my gut had abated. "When are we meeting her?"

"As soon as you're ready."

"Is she coming here?"

He gave me a hooded look.

I rolled my eyes. "Of course not. Let me guess. She has no idea where you live."

"No, she doesn't. No one does."

"Not even Ocean?"

"No, not even my sister."

"What about your friends?"

"Nope. I usually go to them since they live in the fae lands."

I swallowed the last bite of bacon, my throat suddenly feeling dry. I'd already gulped down all of the coffee, but was I seriously the only other person on earth who knew where the hunter lived?

As if sensing what I was feeling, Kaillen filled a huge glass of water and slid it across the counter toward me.

My hand shook slightly when I picked it up, because despite his secretive, reclusive nature, the hunter had brought *me* to his hidden home.

I took a huge drink, then set the glass down. "Why did you bring me here?"

"I needed a safe place to take you."

"Why not take me to your man cave? I already know about that place."

"The wards here are stronger. You're safer here."

"Even so, could Jakub find this house?"

Kaillen's hands fisted, and a new scent rose from him. It was sharp and almost metallic smelling, like iron. Anger maybe? "He may be able to eventually, but the wards are thick and incredibly strong around the property. It will make it difficult for a seer to locate you, however, not impossible. And I can't guarantee the wards will keep him out. He's proven to be quite resourceful. But for the time being, you're safe."

But safe for how long? Klebus had specifically said before I'd gone to Ontario that wards couldn't be trusted to keep Jakub out. The others he'd abducted had wards in place, but he'd managed to get past them.

My nostrils flared as a deep, burning resentment began low in my gut. Because of Jakub-Dipshit, I'd been kicked out of my home, was barely able to manage my store, had basically abandoned my best friend and sister, and was now also running for my life.

And that dawning realization brought up another topic I hadn't even considered yet.

Where exactly was I going to stay now? If Oak Trembler was no longer an option and if this home would eventually be compromised, then what did that leave? An SF safe house?

Thinking about that made me consider what I'd said to the hunter last night, about how I was sick of being on the sidelines and wanted to hunt Jakub myself. It was either that or continue running and hoping I'd stay safe.

But that was before I knew that I was transitioning into a werewolf. Before I knew that the hunter had betrayed me.

Because I couldn't hunt Jakub on my own. Not only did I not have the skill set to do it, but alone I would be vulnerable. However, with the hunter at my side . . .

My chair scraped against the floor when I abruptly stood. I winced at the sound. I hadn't meant to move my seat that harshly, but the thought of hunting Jakub with Kaillen . . . how could I? Undertaking that would require trust and teamwork.

Before last night, I might have thought we'd be up to it, but now?

Now, I no longer knew what to believe and what was a lie. Although my newly budding gift of being able to scent emotions could help with that.

I took a deep breath, once again being reminded of how fucked up my life had become.

I glanced down, then gaped at the fresh gouges on the wood floor right where I'd pushed my chair back.

My jaw dropped. "Oh, shit. I'm sorry, but I apparently just scraped out part of your floor." I inspected the stool's legs, my heart quickening even more. "And I also shaved off the bottom of your stool." I set it down, my hands growing clammy at what the damage implied.

"It's fine," he said calmly.

But my heart just beat faster.

"Your increasing strength will also become something you'll have to learn to manage."

"You don't say," I replied dryly, bitterly, *angrily*. Because not only did I have my awakening power to contend with, but now this too? Just when I least needed it.

I took my dirty dishes to the sink on stiff legs.

Kaillen stood only two feet away, his body rippling with tension and the energy off of him soaring. That ashy scent again coated my tongue.

Shaking my head, I refused to meet his gaze. "I'll be ready in five minutes to meet with Klebus."

CHAPTER TWO

When I was ready to go, Kaillen conjured one of his portals in his living room. The golden void appeared as he whirled his yellow crystal.

"How come you can conjure portals in your actual home but not in your man cave in Portland?" I asked as I watched him.

"Different magic. I crafted the wards here from ancient tomes with more complicated spells." He put his crystal back into his pocket as his portal waited in front of him. "It takes more time to craft wards like these and it also takes regular maintenance, but they're stronger than the ones in Portland, and they allow me to move through them more easily, which is convenient when I want to get home in a hurry."

Home. He considered this place his home, not Oak Trembler. And I could hardly blame him. His older brothers had regularly bullied him, and his pack hated him.

Only his sister, Ocean, and his father had showed any kindness to him. I wouldn't call that place home either if I were in his shoes.

Shaking those thoughts off, I stepped forward.

Kaillen offered me his hand, like he usually did when the swirling yellow portal waited before us, but I brushed past him and leaped into it.

I welcomed the distracting sensations of jolting and popping, until I scented the hunter beside me. His scent was so potent and raw. *Ugh*, how was I ever going to get used to these new sensations?

His hand touched mine, then his fingers entwined around my fingers until he held me tightly. Holding onto me wasn't an absolute necessity, but I knew he felt better having close contact with me in his portals.

The portal plopped us out onto the sidewalk outside of the familiar SF office in Chicago. I removed my hand from his the second my feet touched solid ground, because I didn't want to think about how nice it felt to have him touch me again.

Crimson and marigold leaves fluttered on the sidewalk, their dry and decaying scents filtering through the air.

Looming ahead of us, the Supernatural Forces' office waited behind the mom-and-pop barbershop façade. I took a step forward, then came to a jolting stop.

I wasn't wearing my cloaking spell that hid the strength of my witch magic.

For the past two weeks, I'd lived as I was. No cloaking spell to hide my witch scent. No worries of anyone detecting how strong I was. But that had been in Ontario where nobody knew me, and this was Chicago where *everyone* knew me.

Grumbling, I whispered the spell to activate the shroud that would conceal my witch powers and hopefully my new werewolf scent too, then strode forward, not waiting for the hunter as I stepped over the threshold.

The SF's familiar illusion magic tugged at my skin, prickling my senses. A lemony scent tinged with a sharper, more noxious odor—almost like burnt plastic—assaulted me. The illusion spell that veiled the office vanished, and with a jolt, I realized that smell had been the spell. I'd just *scented* the illusion.

"Hi, Tala!" Shelley called from the front desk. Even though she was on the other side of the foyer, I could clearly read the name plaque in front of her.

Now, the sharpened eyesight from my impending shift I didn't mind, but the never-ending onslaught of smells? That I could do without.

Loosening a breath, I greeted Shelley when she came around her desk and handed over a bag with my cell phone. "Commander Klebus said you may want this since you're no longer at a safe house."

"Oh my gods, yes." I lunged for the bag. My turquoise cell phone case flashed in the light, but the second I pulled it out, my excitement vanished. My phone was dead, not surprising since I hadn't used it in weeks, but I itched to call Prisha. I hadn't spoken to her since going into hiding, and our only communication had been through old-fashioned letters that the SF had delivered.

The energy of a sudden presence looming behind me, along with the scent of citrus and cedar lacing it, told me that Mr. Silent Hunter was at my back, finally joining me.

Shelley's eyes widened, no doubt taking in the hunter's glare and haggard appearance. He hated this place about as much as one hated chlamydia.

"I'll take you back to meet with the commander." Shelley ushered us down the hall, bumping into her desk along the way before she resumed her brisk footsteps.

When we reached the back offices, Commander Klebus stood from behind her desk as Shelley waved us through the door. As usual, the vampire commander's blue eyes looked bright and astute, and her golden complexion—paled from her vampire transformation—shone in the overhead lights.

Klebus waved at the two chairs in front of her desk. "I was hoping you two would arrive shortly."

Neither Kaillen nor I replied as we sat.

The commander's expression turned grave after she'd settled back onto her seat. "I'm sorry to hear about what happened in Oak Trembler. I've spoken with your father." She inclined her head toward the hunter. "Paxton's dealing with those who betrayed Tala."

The hunter didn't reply, but his nostrils flared and that sharp metallic scent wafted up again. That scent had to be anger.

Despite Commander Klebus's assurances that Cameron

was being dealt with, I knew the hunter planned to deal with his oldest brother on his own. Kaillen had promised to kill him, although, I didn't know if he would actually go so far as eliminating his brother.

That threat had been made right after Kaillen had rescued me. He'd said it in the heat of the moment. But werewolf law would justify the hunter murdering his own brother. Because of Cameron, I'd nearly become enslaved to Jakub, and an atrocity like that against a wolf's mate was abhorrent. Pack law, and even the supernatural court's laws, would allow the hunter his retribution—if he chose to claim it.

I shuddered at the thought.

"Where are you staying now?" the commander asked me.

Her direct question snapped me back to our conversation. "With him." I hooked a thumb in Kaillen's direction.

She quirked an eyebrow. "Which is where?"

"None of your business," Kaillen replied smoothly. "You now have my phone number. That's all you need to reach us."

Oh, so he'd shared his digits with the SF commander? That was a first. But that also explained how she'd called him while I'd been showering.

The commander's icy eyes narrowed. "Twice in two weeks, Tala has nearly been abducted. For her safety, the SF needs to know her whereabouts."

"No, you don't," the hunter replied on a low growl. "I'll keep her safe."

The two stared at one another, the battle of wills commencing.

I rolled my eyes. "I was told you wanted to see us about Jakub. So, can we, like, get to that?" I was so *not* in the mood for their pissing contest.

The commander's lips pursed, but she broke eye contact with Kaillen and opened her drawer. "Very well." She extracted her magical crystal used for creating digital debriefs. "You know what to do."

I placed my hand on the crystal globe and let its magic tug at my mind, siphoning out the memories of my kidnapping, Cameron's betrayal, the two sorcerers commissioned to abduct me, the Philadelphia location, and finally, Maybe-Jakub.

The details flowed across the commander's tablet, as if being typed by invisible ghostly hands. Pictures appeared too, perfect 3D renditions of Jakub's face along with illustrations of other details—his vehicle, the blue cuffs he'd intended to put on the hunter, the spell he'd begun to weave that was frightening in its intensity, and of course, my head-butting.

Kaillen's lips curved when he watched that tidbit as the magical apparatus replayed it before us. The look of surprise on Maybe-Jakub's face during the replay, when I'd knocked him flat on his ass, filled me with dark satisfaction.

"It's almost as if you learned head-butting from someone," the hunter said under his breath.

"Really?" I replied just as dryly. "I wonder who that could possibly be."

His smile grew, a sparkle appearing in his amber eyes. A new sharp scent suddenly rolled through his natural citrus and cedar. It smelled of pineapple and sunshine. I had no idea what that new emotion was, but with a start, I realized that Kaillen and I had just spoken to each other as we used to . . . again. That made twice in one morning that we'd joked. It was as though I'd forgotten how much this man had betrayed me and hurt me.

I killed my smile even though inside, it felt so good to act as we once had. But I needed to remember what he'd done.

The pineapple and sunshine fragrance vanished from the hunter, and his expression wiped itself clean.

"All done," I said a second later and removed my hand from the crystal. The one thing I hadn't shared when my memories had been plundered was the colossal strength of my powers that had smashed through the binding and gag spells despite the magic-blocking cuffs. Call me crazy, but I was still hoping the extent of my powers wasn't common knowledge. A girl could hope.

Commander Klebus put the crystal sphere away, then picked up her tablet, studying the new report and mugshots that were more accurate than anything Chicago PD could ever come up with.

"So this is who Jakub possibly is." She stroked her chin as she stared at Maybe-Jakub's photo.

"Unless he was glamored," Kaillen said.

"Of course." She swiped to the sorcerers' photos, studying them too.

"Don't you have their bodies?" I asked, since she was spending just as much time studying the sorcerers' faces as she had Jakub's.

"No, only bloodstains."

I balked. "But we left them there, dead on the street."

The commander's sapphire eyes cut to mine, her dark hair brushing her shoulders. "As I've been informed. However, by the time we arrived, the scene had already been cleaned. But it had obviously been done in a hurry, since their blood remained."

I frowned at the hunter.

He shook his head. "I notified them within twenty minutes of our escape."

Commander Klebus nodded grimly, and a startling sense of the power Jakub's organization wielded made me shiver. How many people did he have on his payroll that he could have bodies removed that quickly? Before the SF even had a chance to arrive?

"Is there human security footage of the area?" I asked hopefully. Not that it would help. Our fighting had been cloaked under illusion spells, but maybe, just maybe, Jakub's cleanup crew had been sloppy. Perhaps forgetting to initiate an illusion spell or creating one too weak to hide all activity.

"We're looking into it."

I raised my eyebrows, but she didn't elaborate.

"So what are you going to do with this new info?" I

interlocked my fingers in my lap, trying to keep my nose from wrinkling. An underlying scent of decay had been tickling my senses ever since we'd walked into the room.

The commander leaned forward, and the stench grew.

Holy shit, it's coming from her.

"We'll run the evidence we were able to collect and these photos through our database to see if we can identify these three." She set her tablet down. "Now, the next question is what do we do with you?"

I began breathing through my mouth. "Actually, the next question is, what have you discovered so far? I'd like to know what your investigation has learned in the last two weeks."

Commander Klebus narrowed her eyes.

I huffed. "Are you still not going to tell me anything? Even after they tried to abduct me a second time?"

She sighed. "I told you, only if it's directly related to—"

"Yeah, yeah." I cut her off with a wave. "I get it. You're not going to tell me shit. Fine."

She bristled. "Now, as I was saying, we need to discuss where you stay moving forward. Since you're no longer safe with Mr. King's pack, the next obvious option is an SF safe house."

My stomach dropped, because if I shifted tonight under the full moon with Supernatural Forces members surrounding me that would mean . . .

Nausea churned through me. I couldn't possibly handle witnesses. To see their surprise, disgust, or possibly fear? I would be a total pariah, or worse, they'd want to study me like a lab rat.

I twisted my hands. "I don't know where . . ." I took another breath. "I mean—"

"She's staying with me." Kaillen's words were clipped.

The commander's nostrils flared, and she opened her mouth, but Kaillen abruptly stood and pulled me to my feet. "We're done here. You have what you need. We'll show ourselves out."

Before the vampire could utter a response, Kaillen blurred us to the front of the SF office and out the door. Cold autumn wind swirled around us, and the scent of snow lingered in the air.

Within a second, the hunter's whirling yellow portal waited before us just as the commander barreled through the SF's front door. "Mr. King!" she barked.

But the hunter already had his arm around me as he sucked me into his portal's winds. He did it all so quickly. So commandingly.

Fury burned in Commander Klebus's eyes. It was the last thing I saw as we disappeared, but the anxiety in my stomach lessened. That suffocating feeling of being exposed and judged receded.

My emerging wolf side was still hidden, and the only one who would be witnessing what was to come tonight would be the hunter at my side.

CHAPTER THREE

After Kaillen's portal dropped us into his living room, I let out a sigh of relief. I wasn't happy to be shacked up with the hunter in his home again, but I was grateful for the privacy. Right now, I needed it. No way in hell was I going to shift into a wolf for the first time with an audience, and here, I didn't have to hide. I could be me . . . whoever the new me was.

I gritted my teeth, then whispered the words to release my cloaking spell. My shoulders relaxed when its restrictive cage disappeared, but it didn't stop the inner tension rolling through me. Because despite being able to be myself here, that didn't stop what was coming tonight.

Kaillen's nostrils flared, and he took a step closer to me, his wolf shining in his eyes. "We'll find a way to keep you safe here, so you don't need to go to an SF safe house."

"Right. If you say so." That was totally wishful thinking, and we both knew it.

His amber eyes blazed. "I'll figure something out."

I placed my hands on my hips. "Have you ever thought that it's not for *you* to figure out? That maybe I need to?" His mouth opened, and he took a step forward, but I raised my hand. "I'm going to call Prish, if it's safe for me to do that here?"

"The wards will stop anyone from tracing your calls."

"In that case, just give me some space for a bit, okay?" I fled from the room as crimson fire rolled in his irises.

I flew up the stairs, irritation still biting me, but then my damned practical side kicked in. I knew that all of Kaillen's betrayals had been instigated by the mate bond— the need to protect me and keep me safe. But that didn't mean I was hunky-dory with what he'd chosen to do. Because of him, I was going to turn all furry tonight, which meant I was stuck here until that shit show ended.

If not for the damned full moon, I could have taken Commander Klebus up on her offer of an SF safe house— even though that didn't particularly appeal to me either— but at least I'd be left alone there. 'Cause right now I needed to figure out what the hell I was going to do. Jakub was still hunting me, and I was so freakin' tired of being prey.

"Fucking wolf mating bonds," I said under my breath as I opened the door to my room. I reminded myself that I had the right to be pissed at Kaillen, so I was going to hold on to that fact whether he liked it or not.

That incessant itching under my skin began again when I closed my bedroom door. I plugged my phone in to charge, then paced around my room as I waited for it to have enough juice to turn on. The entire time, the itching grew and burned as if my skin were heating and rippling.

I shuddered.

This was beyond weird and uncomfortable. Before I knew it, I would probably have hairs sprouting through my skin and claws elongating from my nails.

Eww, eww, eww.

When my phone's screen finally glowed to life, I punched my taps onto it so aggressively, I was worried I was going to crack the screen.

"Tala?" Prisha said in a surprised voice when she answered.

"Prish! Oh my gods, it's so good to hear your voice."

"Um, yeah, but what the hell? I thought you didn't have your phone?"

"I do now, at least temporarily, but who knows how long that'll be the case, since Jakub's still hunting me, and I'll have to leave here, and . . ." I carried on, rambling non-stop, but being the amazing friend that she was, Prisha let me fill her in, listening patiently as I vented, sobbed, raged, hiccupped, and generally acted like a complete mess. I told her everything, not holding anything back, and when I finally calmed down enough to take a deep breath, her stunned silence followed.

"Are you serious?" she said eventually. "You're going to shift into a *wolf* tonight while you're staying at the Fire Wolf's home in Montana?"

"So he tells me." I scratched at my chest again. It still felt as though ants were crawling under my skin.

"What the hell? How is that possible?"

"He thinks it's because he combined his blood with spells when I drank it, and the result is me becoming a female werewolf who can actually shift. I'm officially a freak of nature." I hung my head as Cameron's words came back to bite me.

An abomination.

I shoved that memory down. No way was I letting that vile loser get into my head.

"So what's going to happen? Can you feel anything now? Is your wolf, like, inside you or something?" Prisha asked, concern lacing her tone.

"Not that I know of, but I itch like a motherfucker, and I've eaten enough food today to feed a small country."

She let out an aggrieved sound. "This is just so *weird*. I can't even believe it."

"I know, right? I keep hoping it's all a bad dream."

Prisha and I talked for another hour as I lamented and she listened, and when I finally turned our conversation around and asked what was going on in her life, she filled me in about her last couple of weeks.

Thankfully, nothing quite as epic had happened to her, but she was having issues again with one of the offices she ran for her family's corporation, and she said Chicago was incredibly dull without me. But she was enjoying having our goldfish in her apartment. She'd picked them up for us when it became apparent we weren't returning anytime soon.

"So Agent Orange and DJ Finster are still swimming happily?"

"They are," she replied. "And I haven't killed them, so I'm obviously an amazing goldfish-sitting aunt."

I laughed, loving that we could joke around again. When I sobered, I said, "You know, it just hit me that we've never gone this long without speaking or seeing each other before." Prish and I had been best friends since we were eight and had met at a supernatural community event. Of course, I'd been one of the poor kids who'd been dragged along by a social worker, and she'd been one of the volunteers helping the poor kids. But our connection had been instantaneous despite our opposite walks of life. Prisha's mother was initially hesitant about welcoming me into her daughter's circle, but Prisha's begging had eventually won her over. And once Azad—Prisha's father—had gotten a hint of my magic, well, I'd officially become part of their family.

Prisha sighed. "I know. I was thinking the same thing. I hate it. Chicago isn't the same with you gone. I wish you could just come back here."

"Me too. I'd take sixteen-hour work days every day at Practically Perfect instead of this."

"Do you want me there with you?" she asked. "You know, when you shift or whatever?"

I glanced out the window. Afternoon had arrived, but the snow had stopped and it had warmed up enough that most of the flakes that had fallen this morning had melted. "I don't think Kaillen would allow it, since that would involve disclosing his home's location. He's kinda secretive like that."

"You could come to me and shift here at my home. It could be just you and me."

I frowned as I tried to imagine going through whatever was going to happen to me tonight with a non-werewolf at my side while staying in a city as big as Chicago. Something told me that could end in disaster.

"I better stay here, just in case things don't go well, and also 'cause Jakub's still out there. I don't need to be leading him to you."

"I could take him."

I laughed. "I know you could, but I would never do that to you."

She let out a long breath. "Fine, only 'cause I know I can't talk you out of it. But even though you and the Fire Wolf are in a difficult place at the moment, at least he can help or guide you, or whatever, when you shift tonight."

"Hopefully."

And I hoped he would, because I realized I would need it. Even though I'd dated Carlos—a werewolf—for years, had visited his pack on multiple occasions, and had generally considered myself somewhat educated in werewolf culture, I literally had no idea what to expect with a first shift. For one, they always happened when wolves were younger, around puberty. And since most wolves kept to their packs, it wasn't like I'd gone to school with dozens of werewolves when I was in middle school. So I couldn't even say I'd heard about the experience secondhand.

And two, shifting only happened to boys. Since it wasn't something females ever experienced, I didn't have any werewolf women friends I could call up to ask what they remembered of their first shift.

I was completely on my own here.

"How much longer will you have your phone?" Prisha asked.

"Probably not long. Klebus wants me to go to an SF safe house."

"Seriously?"

"Yep, as long as Jakub's still on the loose, I'm a sitting duck." Anger burned through me again. I was so over all of this.

"Gods, this is all so incredibly unfair and sucks so much."

"No shit," I replied quietly. "Everything about this sucks."

We talked for a few more minutes with promises to catch up again soon and talk as much as we could while I still had a phone.

After we hung up, for a moment I just sat there, staring forlornly at my mobile while feeling so incredibly isolated. I couldn't remember ever feeling anything as bad as this.

A knock came on my door. I startled, not having heard the hunter approach on his silent footsteps.

"Yeah?" I called.

Kaillen cracked the door. "Mind if I come in?"

I shrugged. "It's your house. I can't really tell you where you can and can't go."

A muscle ticked in his jaw, and then a flicker of gold appeared in his amber eyes. "I'll leave you alone if you want, but I wanted to discuss a few things with you, about what you can expect tonight."

My throat bobbed, and I hastily nodded. "Okay, sure. Come in."

He prowled into the room. Since his hair was clean, his face shaved, and he didn't look quite so horrible, I figured he'd showered and had taken a catnap.

"You look a bit better," I commented.

Instead of a sly jab or a preening swagger—a response he would have given when we'd first met—he merely sat down on the floor opposite me, his expression heavy and clouded in so many unsaid emotions that I hastily looked away.

I clutched my phone, then ran a finger over the smooth turquoise case.

The silence stretched around us, but then I became aware of his sounds—the steady *lub-dub* from Kaillen's heart and his soft breathing. It seemed true silence was a thing of the past.

"How do you deal with this?" I brought my hands to my ears. "It's all so much. The smells, the sounds. I'm okay with the sharper eyesight, but the other ones? No thanks. Klebus smelled like a damned corpse. It was nauseating."

I thought that last comment would get a lip tug from

him, or some kind of smile, but that aching pain was still etched on his face.

"I'm sorry. I'm sorry again that I did this to you." His scent shifted, and a new tang, almost like mandarins and honeysuckle, entered it. Some inner instinct told me that he was being genuine. He wasn't lying. He meant that statement to the depths of his soul.

"What does it smell like when someone's being truthful?"

He cocked his head. "It kinda smells like oranges, but it's a bit different."

Hence why I also thought of honeysuckle. My throat thickened. So Kaillen was sincere in his apology, and hearing him apologize again cracked something inside of me. Even though I wanted to stay mad at him and rage at him, that damned practical side of me knew that he never would have intentionally done this to me. I knew deep down that if he hadn't been so consumed with fear and the mate bond in the throes of my death, that he never would have spelled his blood, and then all of this never would have happened.

"I know," I finally replied. "I know you're sorry."

A long pause followed, his breathing and heartbeat the only sounds in the silence. "Does that mean you forgive me?" he finally asked.

I rolled my eyes. "I wouldn't go that far."

The first hint of a smile ghosted his lips.

I smirked. It was just too damned easy to fall back into our old bantering and sarcastic ways.

He shifted from where he sat. "Has the itching started?"

I nodded. "It feels like ants are crawling under my skin."

"And do you sense her yet?"

"Sense who?"

"Your wolf."

My eyes widened to saucers. "I'll *sense* her?"

He nodded. "That part's unavoidable. From tonight onward, she'll be within you. You'll always be able to sense her, feel her, and talk to her."

"Gods, that sounds so crazy. Like I'll have schizophrenia or something."

"Unfortunately, medication won't fix this."

I raised an eyebrow. "Was that your attempt at a joke?"

"It was, and it was a pretty bad one, eh?"

I shook my head. "Your Canadian's coming out."

The golden light in his eyes flared, his lips curving. "It is, eh?"

I bit back a smile as some of the panic in me eased. Maybe, just maybe, this wouldn't be super awful and painful. Perhaps Kaillen could distract me through the entire thing. "So you and your wolf talk, do you?"

"In a way. Our inner wolves don't speak English and are fully animal, but it's a symbiotic relationship. I help him. He helps me. Coming to learn who your wolf is and co-existing with them is vital to a happy and healthy relationship."

That twisting sensation started in my stomach again. So maybe this wouldn't be easy. "But what if I don't like her? Or she doesn't like me?"

"That rarely happens."

"But what if it does?"

"It most likely won't. Our wolves are a part of us. They blend into our beings and are an entirely natural entity within us."

"Maybe natural for you, 'cause you were born to be this, but natural for me? I don't think it's ever going to be."

Some of the sparkle that had appeared in the hunter's eyes dimmed again. "I know. I'm sorry."

"You don't have to keep apologizing." I scratched my arm again, then my legs. *Ugh.* It was like I had the chicken pox without the rash. "So does that mean I'll have to, I don't know, think about her or ask her permission about things?" That thought left a *very* sour taste in my mouth. In fact, all of this did. I already had a witch-twin bond with my sister. Having a second bond, or entity inside me, would just feel crowded.

Kaillen reached into his pocket and pulled out a small vial of cream. "Use this. It'll help the itching."

As I began to slather it on my limbs—*and oh my gods that felt so much better*—he added, "The human side is the ultimate ruler, but your wolf can have strong opinions about things and try to rule you. You just need to make sure you exert your dominance."

I stopped smearing whatever this magical lotion was. I'd pretty much used it all up anyway. "In what ways does one's wolf try to rule?"

"The mate bond for one." His eyes burned brighter, that gold hue flashing.

"Oh. Right." 'Cause the dude had been totally controlled by his wolf when it came to me. My shoulders slumped as I was once again reminded that his attraction to me was due solely to his wolf. And thinking of *that* only reminded me that we hadn't even broached that subject again.

The one time I'd brought it up and been honest with him about why I wasn't jumping into a relationship with him, he'd disappeared for a run and then I'd been abducted.

I figured at this point, Kaillen had either forgotten about my rejection, or he was feeling guilty about putting me in that position so hadn't brought it up again. I couldn't blame him. I was in no hurry to start that convo again either.

I cradled my face in my hands. "I don't want this. Any of this."

A low grumble came from him. "They don't rule us completely. My wolf didn't make me—" He cut himself off.

I lifted my eyes to his. "Make you what?"

His eyes burned brighter, but then he glanced down when I began scratching my arms again. "Never mind. We don't need to get into that now."

I bit my lip as that cryptic statement swirled through my thoughts. Had he also been thinking about our conversation the morning I'd been abducted?

I was tempted to ask him, but then my stomach let out a huge growl and the sudden need for *food, food, food* completely overtook me.

"Oh my gods, I could eat a horse." I clutched my stomach. "Or maybe I should eat a cow. Perhaps I should go that route since it's more socially acceptable."

"Not if you're in India."

"True, good thing we're in America."

He shook his head, amusement lighting his eyes before he rolled to his feet. "Come on. I'll make you lunch." He held out his hand, his expression guarded, almost as though he was waiting to see if I would take it.

I looked at his outstretched hand—the long fingers, the large palm—and warmth began tingling through me. The need to be with him, touch him, fuck him . . . my attraction to him hadn't abated in the slightest.

It never had. Despite all that had transpired, my soul still wanted him, my body still craved him. Bottom line? I still wanted him as much as his wolf wanted me.

Oh fuck it. I grasped Kaillen's hand and let him pull me up.

CHAPTER FOUR

The hunter did indeed make me lunch. In fact, he once again made enough food to feed a dozen linebackers, and I shamelessly devoured all of it.

As I finished the last mouthful, Kaillen opened the freezer to grab some ice, and I spotted a box of frozen desserts. "Is that chocolate cake?" I asked, my eyes lighting up.

He chuckled. "It is. They're lava cakes. Do you want one?"

"Or ten."

He grabbed the box, then turned the oven on, not commenting once that I'd just eaten the equivalent of twenty supersized McDonalds meals and was still hungry.

"How much do you spend a week on groceries?" I asked when I spotted how well stocked his cabinets were.

"Probably what a family of six spends."

"So I should start budgeting my grocery bills for a family of twenty?" *If I could even afford that . . .*

His amusement dimmed. "It won't always be this bad. The first few months are the hardest."

I tried not to let that comment rattle me, but it was now close to five in the evening. Night was fast approaching whether I wanted it to or not, and the only good thing about being here with the hunter was that I didn't have to worry about Jakub for a few days because of the hunter's strong and complex wards.

I watched the clock on his stove with apprehension as the lava cakes began to warm. The entire time I was wishing and hoping that I could make time stop, or at least slow it so that I could put off the inevitable for just a few minutes longer.

But fate would not be ruled, and I had a wolf that wanted to be born.

And when the sun at last set, and the moon began to rise, I felt it. The itching and burning sensation that had been plaguing me all day began to abate as a stranger and deeper sensation started to emerge. It almost felt as if something was expanding and rumbling inside me, as though my wolf was waking and groaning, readying for the shift to come.

"Do you feel her?" Kaillen asked quietly as twilight was upon us.

The scent of chocolate cake still lingered in the kitchen even though I'd polished off his entire box of desserts hours ago.

All I could do was nod in response. Now that the time had come, too many emotions were blazing through me to do anything else.

The hunter and I stood by the sliding glass doors that overlooked the pastures behind his house.

I stood in nothing but shorts and a T-shirt even though it was late autumn. Kaillen also wore easy to remove clothes, those damned loose pants again. Normally, I would have had a hard time keeping my eyes off his ridged abs and strong shoulders, but now, all I could do was watch that large ball of pale light glistening on the horizon as it began to rise.

That tug started in my chest again, stronger and more insistent than it had ever been before.

"I want to go outside," I whispered. "I need to."

He opened the door, his face completely blank, but the ashy scent that had plagued him on and off all day, again wafted from his skin. He'd done his best to prepare me and tell me what was to come, but given that I was the first female werewolf in the history of the world to shift, neither of us really knew what to expect.

If I truly did shift, according to Kaillen, my wolf would emerge when the moon was at its peak. She would rise and be born in an explosion of magic, and since it was the first shift, I wouldn't have complete control of her. She was bound to run and be wild. For all I knew, I'd spend the night as a passenger while she chased down deer or bunny rabbits. Who the hell knew.

"What was your wolf like on your first shift?" I asked

when the cold wet grass slid along the bottoms of my feet. I was barefoot, so was Kaillen, but the cold didn't bother me. If anything, I welcomed it. I was burning up inside.

"Boisterous," Kaillen answered with a faint smile. "He wanted to play with the other wolves in the Ontario pack."

"Did he?"

A pained look came into Kaillen's eyes. "He did. I actually spent that first night with Gavin. Our wolves, strangely, get along quite well. Or they did, until Cameron put a stop to it." His lips thinned, and he didn't convey any further details about his brothers or his first shift.

Hearing about his brothers reminded me of all of the problems he had back in Ontario, and for some reason— maybe it was my impending shift and the fact that I was turning into a wolf and wolves adored affection—I reached for him. I wanted to touch him. Needed to.

The second I made contact with his skin, his breath stopped. Golden light flared in his eyes, and he didn't hesitate. His warm palm engulfed mine, and that deep golden glow grew in his eyes. I hadn't seen many appearances from his demon today. Those eerie black flames from last night were gone. Mostly, I'd only seen his wolf. Whether that was because Kaillen was forcing his demon down or the full moon called to his wolf too, therefore, making him stronger, I didn't know.

But I did know that I didn't feel alone. Not at this moment. And right now, that was what I needed.

"I'm so hot," I said with a humorless laugh. I released his hand since that haunted look had left his eyes. I fanned my

T-shirt against my chest. "Which is so weird 'cause it can't be warmer than forty degrees out here."

"Did you want to leave your clothes on until you shift?" he asked.

I fanned my shirt again. Truth be told, I didn't. I wanted to strip bare and stand naked under the moon. Something inside me, an instinct or calling, pulled at me. The moon was controlling me again, owning me. So yeah, I was seriously going to be one of those people that lived at those hippy communes or whatever. 'Cause if it were up to me, I would be walking around naked as a jaybird and completely unabashed about it.

"This is pretty much as embarrassing as I thought it would be," I mumbled, gripping my shirt. "You can't tell anyone about this, 'cause if I start barking, or dancing naked under the moon, or eating squirrels, that shit *does not* leave this ranch."

Kaillen let out a laugh, his face splitting into a broad grin, and a tugging sensation began in me again, except this time it wasn't toward the moon but instead toward *him*.

Weird. I brushed that thought off, 'cause some strange crap was going down right now, and I wasn't gonna analyze it.

"Do you mind?" I asked, my hands on my shirt's hem.

His laughter died, his eyes immediately zeroing in on my hands. "Do I mind if you take your shirt off?"

I nodded.

His lips parted as a wild glow entered his eyes. "Uh, no,

I don't mind," he replied, practically tripping over his words. "By all means, take it off."

I swallowed a laugh. "Pervert."

He didn't respond as his eyes burned brighter.

I didn't even care, though, even if everything about this was totally fucked up. So I followed that deep-seated need inside me that told me to get naked and stay under the moon.

I lifted my shirt up and over my head, then slipped out of my shorts. When I stood naked and bare amidst the glittering stars and cold night sky, my breasts peeked and my skin pimpled into goosebumps. Strangely, though, I didn't feel cold.

A steady beating thrum came from Kaillen, his heart's *lub-dub* increasing with each second that passed. The sound of his ragged breaths came next, not loud, but subtle enough that I wouldn't have detected them before these new sensations began to take hold of me.

When I glanced at him, the hunter's jaw was locked, his throat bobbing in a swallow as his gaze drank me in.

"Are you okay?" I asked as that heated feeling began in my blood again. I shifted from foot to foot, a restlessness beginning to consume me.

He made a non-committal sound, but that wildness stayed in his eyes. His expression was so fierce, and filled with so much longing and heat, that I had a feeling he was having a hard time remembering language. Another groan came from him before he finally said in a deeply guttural voice, "Tala, you're so fucking beautiful."

I turned to face him, a part of me aware of how unabashedly ballsy I was being. I was naked. Outside. And I didn't give two shits about it.

I just wanted to be free. To run. To howl. To fuck.

Okay, where the hell did that *thought come from?*

But it was true. I felt alive, on fire, and that tug began in my chest again. Not toward the moon, but again directed toward the hunter.

I felt her then, something stirring inside me, waking, and stretching. I looked down, as if I could see into my body, which of course I couldn't, just as something deep and primal yawned inside me.

"I . . ." I brought a hand to my belly. "I can feel her."

Kaillen's ragged breaths increased, and with the deft flick of his hands, his loose pants fell to the ground. A rich, musky aroma surrounded the hunter, and one glance southward revealed evidence that the dude was *very* turned on.

A pulse began low in my belly, not related to my wolf or my magic, but to the hunter. I ached to touch him, caress him, kiss him. His large cock called to me, begging me to drop to my knees, to wrap my mouth around him, and suck his rigid length.

He groaned. "I can scent your sex. Your arousal—" He paused. "*Fuck,* Tala."

And since it was the night of following instincts, I didn't question it. I dropped to the ground and pulled him toward me. He came readily, his large erection spearing the night.

In a blurred move, I had my hand wrapped around the base of his shaft and the head of his dick in my mouth. Gods, I'd wanted to taste him and feel him for *so* long.

A guttural groan came from him as I began sucking his cock fast and hard. I needed this, needed *him*, and I had no idea why. So I sucked and licked, bit and fondled. I couldn't get enough of his taste, his scent, his feel.

"Fuck, Tala." He strained against me, his hands fisting my hair. "I can't stop it. Your mouth—"

A deep, primal roar tore from his throat. His knees bent as he came fast and hard. His bellow stretched across the meadows and up to the stars. His entire body shook as his orgasm pulsed through his thick erection and his hot cum flooded my mouth.

I drank down every drop as his orgasm went on and on. I loved it. Loved every second of it as his cock stayed buried deep in my mouth and my newly emerging wolf side relished the taste and scent of him.

And when he finally finished coming, when his claw-like hands at last released my hair, I stood as sweat glistened along my body and the pulsing ache in my core abated. I was still turned on, still aroused, but making the hunter climax had calmed some part deep inside me. Some part of me that was being born.

The hunter's eyes glowed a savage gold when I met his gaze. In a blurred movement, he had me in his arms and his mouth on mine.

He kissed me deeply, his arms like steel as he held me tenderly, yet with so much force that I knew he'd never let me go. There was a primal longing to his kiss, as though he were claiming me right then and there, and demanding that I be his.

When he finally pulled back, his harsh breaths clouded in a fog in the cold air around us. I smiled, then licked my lips as I savored his taste.

He cupped my cheek, his thumb trailing along my lower lip, as his chest rose and fell unsteadily. So many emotions were pouring off of him right now. So many emotional scents that I couldn't yet identify. "You have no idea how long I've dreamed of you doing that."

But I didn't reply, because the moon was calling to me again. I turned to face it, my chin tilting up as that heated feeling grew within me. Kaillen's hands stayed on my waist, his touch fierce and possessive. He stepped closer until his chest brushed against my back as his grip stayed firm on my hips. *Mine.* He didn't have to say the word aloud, but I knew that was what he was feeling.

Because, strangely, a similar feeling was growing in me.

"She's getting stronger," I murmured.

"Let it happen," he rasped. "Don't fight her."

I gulped as the itching began in my chest again, growing and heating as the moon rose steadily in the sky, higher and higher as my wolf began to circle and pace within me.

"I can *really* feel her," I whispered as my eyes flashed wide open.

Another consciousness came to life inside me, another mind caressing my own. Yet hers wasn't human. I didn't detect language. I didn't talk to her or introduce myself. All I sensed were emotions and the presence of something else.

Inside, I tentatively reached for her, as if I were extending a hand in her direction, toward that heated darkness, because I wanted to touch her and greet her. I was doing as Kaillen advised, letting my instincts guide the way and not trying to fight her.

She shifted forward in the darkness until I felt her draw near. I gasped, my consciousness still turned inward, and I could have sworn that I felt her soft fur meet my palm, like a caress and a tentative hello in return.

"Do you sense her?" Kaillen asked.

"Yes," I breathed. I'd had no idea that this moment would be so *magical*. "She's inside me. She senses me too."

"It's almost time then."

I knew he was right. The throbbing began in my chest again as the tingle and pulse of blazing, foreign-feeling magic spread through my veins. But it wasn't Kaillen's magic. I wasn't pulling on him with my awakening power. No, this was new magic, *her* magic. It was my werewolf powers coming to light.

The moon was so high now, nearly at its apex, and more than anything I wanted to run and howl at that beautiful glowing orb that shone as bright as snow.

"Tala?" The hunter shifted closer to me, his hand brushing down to caress my thigh.

My wolf whined softly inside me, the first sound she'd made. I startled. Inside, she nudged me, trying to get me to shift my attention to Kaillen. When I apparently wasn't moving fast enough, she whined again, her body straining, her entity wanting to be free. To be free with the hunter.

No, with the hunter's *wolf*.

"Kaillen, I think she's trying to—" She slammed against my insides. I cried out as an explosive burst of magic skated along my skin, scorched my nerves, and ignited my senses.

Heat consumed me as I fell through a void of time and space. The cataclysmic feeling of my body shifting and breaking and awakening into something else happened all at once.

I fell inward. Down, down, down. And then I was looking through eyes closer to the ground. As the cold wind ruffled the fur on my body, sharp scents rolled into my senses, and the urge to run and play, nearly overwhelmed me.

A flash of power came to my right, and then another wolf stood at my side. So much bigger and so powerful. His beautiful russet-colored fur intermixed with dark-gray, cream, and black. The bleed of colors shone in the moonlight.

I took a step toward him, for a moment feeling clumsy. I was on four legs, not two, and nearly fell over because of it, but then my wolf nudged me to the side, and commanded our limbs and senses again.

I was pushed down, almost feeling as though I were drowning within, as I became a passenger in my own body.

That tug in my chest ignited when my wolf beheld Kaillen's magnificent beast.

A deep rumble came from Kaillen's wolf, and he padded forward.

My wolf playfully yipped in response before she licked his snout, then splayed out on her front legs, her rump in the air.

Kaillen's wolf began to wag his tail, then his entire body vibrated in eagerness.

And then we were running, flying across the grass, our bodies streaks of fur and power as we blazed toward the distant mountains while the moon shone overhead.

My wolf ran and ran. She ran as fast as the wind while the moon shone down on us and the stars stretched to the horizon.

And the entire time, Kaillen ran at my side, his eyes glowing, his tongue lolling, and even though my wolf was mastering my body and commanding my senses, a part of me remained.

And the part that stayed, that knew, that was *aware*—that part of me knew that the throbbing in my chest was what the hunter had been feeling since he'd caught my true scent.

CHAPTER FIVE

I awoke to find soil in my nose, leaves crinkling underneath my cheeks, and the sound of the moaning wind as it rustled through the trees. My skin was bare and cool, yet I didn't feel overly cold. Just slightly chilled.

"Tala?" a deep, husky voice said beside me.

I pushed a mass of blond hair from my eyes and rolled onto my side to see the hunter laid out as naked as the day he was born. He was propped up on his elbow, a half-tilted curve to his lips, and a deep-seated glow lighting his eyes.

My heart jolted as I took in our surroundings. We were in a forest, on the ground, and both of us had apparently joined the naked hippy commune.

"What time is it?" I didn't bother covering my bare breasts which were smudged with dirt. My nipples were erect, standing on end in the chilled air, but at this point, I was beyond trying to maintain any dignity.

Kaillen's nostrils flared as the halo of gold brightened around his eyes. His gaze skated over my bare abdomen and my breasts' taut buds. "No idea, but my guess is mid-morning."

"So we spent the entire night out here?"

"We did."

I rolled my bottom lip between my teeth and tried to remember what had happened. I vaguely recalled giving the hunter a blow job. The need to do so before I'd shifted had been so overwhelming that I hadn't questioned it. My cheeks heated a bit at the thought of how brazen I'd been, but I also remembered that the hunter *really* enjoyed it.

But after I'd shifted, everything else got fuzzy. What I did recall told me that there'd been a lot of running, nipping each other's heels, howling, and chasing. Yep, I'd gone into full-blown doggy mode.

Gods . . .

I hesitantly felt inside myself for my wolf, and found her curled up and asleep. *Thank the mother of all the realms.* I didn't want to deal with whatever her demands were this morning, because knowing that I'd been naked since last night, had felt no hesitation whatsoever about giving fellatio in the great outdoors, *and* had run around yipping like a hyena all night? *Yep.* I needed a minute.

After plucking a few soggy leaves from my hair, I ran a hand through a snarled tendril. The icy breeze caressed my skin, and I finally crossed my arms, 'cause the hunter was obviously *really* enjoying the view if his throbbing erection was any indication.

My gaze snagged again to his cock, and a fuzzy memory surfaced of the feel of him in my mouth and the taste of his cum on my lips.

An ache curled low in my belly. It would be so easy to roll him onto his back, straddle his hips and sink down onto that glorious shaft. I could ride him until the pulsing need in my core exploded into another mind-blowing orgasm.

My mouth went dry when I envisioned how absolutely enthralling sex with the hunter would be. I'd experienced the oral side of it a couple of times, but he had yet to penetrate me. But twice I'd let him pleasure me to climax, and that alone had made me see stars. I couldn't even imagine what riding his dick would be like. It would probably transport me to a new realm.

I curled my fingers tightly into my palms, so I wouldn't cave in to this instinct.

His nostrils flared, and a low rumble vibrated in his chest as another throb made his cock bob. He opened his mouth, but I forced my gaze up and asked before he could say anything, "Do you know where your house is?"

He cleared his throat, his breathing fast, as the strong *lub-dub* of his erratic heartbeat reached my ears. "About two miles that way." He pointed through the trees and rolled languidly to his feet, his large body agile and sleek. He took a step closer to me, heat wafting from his skin. His cock bobbed again, and I was *so tempted* to reach for it.

A slight smile curved his lips, as that glow blazed in his eyes. "I enjoyed last night."

I pushed to a stand as that pulsating need inside me grew. "You did?"

His look turned entirely predatory. "Very much."

"Does that mean you remember it?"

"I do. I've had my wolf with me for years. It might be hazy for you since it was your first shift, but the more you get used to cohabiting with your wolf, the more you'll be in sync with her. Soon, when she's in control, you'll be there too."

"So yours isn't sleeping right now?"

"No, he's wide awake. He usually sleeps when I do."

"So he's always awake when you are?"

"Usually."

"Mine's not. She's still asleep."

"That's normal when you're newly shifted. Eventually, you'll be in sync with one another."

"So weird," I whispered. I tried to concentrate on what I'd just learned, which was a feat in itself because the hunter's citrusy cedar scent intermixed with a heady dose of musk told me that I wasn't the only one wanting to climb the other right now. Liquid heat pooled between my thighs at the thought.

Another low growl came from the hunter. "Your scent is mouthwatering, *colantha*."

I gulped, because more than anything I wanted to wrap my legs around him and fuck him till I no longer knew my name. I knew he would let me, that he'd welcome it. I could push him to the ground, climb on top of him, straddle him, and ride him until I was screaming his name.

Breathing hard, I forced my thoughts to shift to more practical matters and tried to dispel this overwhelming urge to *mate* with him.

I released one of my crossed arms and ran a hand through my hair, trying to work out the tangles as lust consumed me. My breasts jiggled with the movement, and the hunter's attention drifted south.

The musk in his scent grew so potent that it was the only scent I could detect from him. He took a step closer, his hand drifting to my waist. His fingers curled into my flesh, his touch as hot as a brand, and I knew he was holding himself back. That if things went his way, he'd be fucking me against a tree in my next breath.

"About last night. About what you did *before* you shifted . . ." he said in a low, husky tone.

"I don't remember most of it!" I slammed my hands to my eyes just as a stirring sensation began inside me.

My wolf roused, stretching and then yawning as she became aware of the hunter's presence. She whined, her nails scratching against my insides, her eagerness to run free making me take a huge step back.

"You don't remember what you did to me before you shifted?" His nostrils flared.

Knowing he could scent my deceit, I came clean. "No, I do remember it."

"Does that mean—"

"Fuck, this is *weird*." I scratched at my chest, wishing she would go back to sleep, because I had enough to deal with right now given my own reaction to the hunter's nudity.

Kaillen cocked his head, his attention coming back to my face, but that potent musky fragrance still clung to him. "Is it your wolf?"

I nodded, not able to meet his eye. The dude's boner was still commanding all of my attention.

My wolf whined again.

I nearly tripped when I heard that sound inside me, but I did my best to ignore my wolf's growing interest, because the reality was that Kaillen and I were *naked in the woods.* This was full-blown streaker activity on steroids. Not to mention, I'd just spent the night as an animal, and now all I wanted to do was climb all over the hunter right out in the open. What the hell? Had I completely lost all rational and sane decision-making abilities?

"Can we go back to your house?" I scratched at my skin again. "I want to shower and put clothes on, and you know, feel human again."

His expression didn't falter, but another scent rose from him that hinted at anise. "Are you okay?"

"Fine, totally fine," I said through clenched teeth. My wolf whined again, urging me toward the hunter.

Stop it! I snapped at her.

Her head jerked back, as if I'd just slapped her, but then she bared her teeth.

Are you fucking kidding me?

But I didn't direct that question at her, that one was entirely for myself at how absolutely insane this entire situation was.

I scrubbed my hands against my face, then stilled when

I sensed Kaillen's presence directly in front of me, only inches away. He touched my waist again.

"It'll get easier," he said quietly.

His hand began making soft, soothing motions. He felt so good, so warm and solid. But the hunter's gentle words and touch only fueled the rising flames of my *freaking-the-fuck-out.*

"It shouldn't have to get easier." I lunged back, breaking our contact. My wolf growled, but I ignored her. "I wasn't born a werewolf. I shouldn't be in this position."

Kaillen's jaw locked, some of his potent arousal dimming. "No, you shouldn't be, but it was either give you my blood or watch you die."

"But you didn't have to *spell* your blood," I reminded him, then crossed my arms. "You didn't need to bind me to you, and in the process, give me your werewolf mojo or whatever the hell happened. If you hadn't, I wouldn't be naked in the woods with a canine growling at me."

He frowned. "She's growling at you?"

"You're missing the point."

He took a deep breath. "Right. Sorry. I'll keep apologizing if it makes anything better." That mandarin and honeysuckle scent rose from him like before, and I knew he was being genuine. *Ugh.*

"Why are you being so nice right now?"

He quirked an eyebrow. "Why wouldn't I be nice to you?"

"Because you're also a demon?"

"Look, I know this is hard for you." He closed the distance between us again, and his fingers brushed mine.

My wolf whined eagerly.

I pulled my hand back. "You said your house was that way?" I jerked my thumb behind us.

He nodded, so I did a one-eighty and began walking in that direction. I felt his gaze rake over my frame with every step I took. His musky scent once again *saturated* the air.

"It's rude to be perving right now," I called over my shoulder.

He chuckled, then jogged to my side. "It's hard not to. You have the sexiest ass I've ever seen."

I snorted, even if another aching curl knotted my belly. "Did it ever occur to you that there might be other people out here watching us? What if there's a hunter in a tree stand right now videoing us and posting it on social media?"

"There's nobody out here but us."

"How can you be so sure?" I stepped over a rotting wood log, not entirely sure where I was going, but I figured Kaillen would steer me back on track if I headed the wrong way.

"This is my land."

"All of it?" When he nodded, I asked, "How many acres do you own?"

"Fifty thousand."

My eyes bugged out. "Seriously? That had to cost a fortune."

"Perhaps, but it also means I can run in my wolf form whenever I like and not worry about neighbors."

"What about trespassers?"

"There aren't any. My wards encircle the perimeter. Besides, you'd be able to scent them if they somehow managed to get through it."

"Oh." Of course, I could, because now I was also part-werewolf.

Tentatively, I sniffed, smelling the breeze. The hunter's natural fragrance mixed with his heady arousal hit me first, then the smell of trees and soil, along with other alien fragrances that I had no idea how to identify. They all rolled into such a tornado of scents that I couldn't decipher what was what. I grumbled.

"You'll learn how to use it better," he said. "I know it's confusing right now, but that's because you're mostly dependent on sight since that was your strongest sense before. But as a wolf, you'll learn to use your hearing and sense of smell more. They can become as reliable as your eyesight."

My gut twisted as my wolf once again brushed inside me. She was wide awake now and practically begging for Kaillen's wolf to take notice of her.

Kaillen grunted, then muttered something under his breath.

"What?"

He shook his head. "Nothing. It's just my wolf."

My gaze snapped to his. That flaring golden light encircled his irises again. "Is he being weird too?"

"That's one way of putting it. Now that you're awake, he's becoming a bit restless."

"What's he doing?"

He smirked. "You don't want to know."

"What if I do?"

Kaillen gave me a look, as if to say he'd warned me. "He wants me to rut with you. Right now. For as many times as you'll let me."

I tripped over my own feet, but Kaillen caught me before I fell. I hastily pulled my arm free as soon as I righted myself.

"He wants you to do *what?*" I squeaked.

Kaillen grinned, the expression transforming his face into a portrait of male sensuality. "I told you, you wouldn't want to know."

I hastily looked away as my heart hammered wildly while my wolf whined again. I absentmindedly scratched my chest. "Is he like that because I'm your . . . mate?"

"Yes, but also because he's even more eager to seal the bond now. He's absolutely infatuated with your wolf."

Seal the bond. As in, claim me. If we did that, Kaillen would bite my neck, infuse his magic with mine, which would render us forever connected. No, not connected. *Mated.*

My jaw dropped at his total honesty and willingness to share that information just as my wolf barked, then yipped again. I trembled in exertion, because the urge to join with Kaillen nearly overtook me. Gods, what the actual fuck? It was like I had even less control of my life now.

"I think my wolf feels the same," I finally mumbled.

"Really?" That pineapple and sunshine scent again rose from him.

I gave him a glower, then turned my expression inward. *Just go lay down or something,* I snapped at my wolf.

She bared her teeth at me, so I did it right back at her. Huffing, she gave me her rump, and I rolled my eyes.

Kaillen inhaled. "You're irritated."

I snorted. "You picked up on that?"

"I can scent it. Among other things."

Since my arousal had dimmed because my anxiety had grown, I figured that was what he was referring to. "This is just so weird. You want me because your wolf told you to, and now my wolf is urging me to be with you too."

"Would it be so hard to listen to them?"

I stopped to face him. He stood completely still, not one muscle moving in his body. His face was a total blank canvas, yet, I detected other things. His heart was beating fast, much faster than it had been a second prior, and that sunshine and pineapple fragrance hit me like a Mack truck.

With a slamming sense of awareness, I realized what emotion that fragrance was—hope.

"You want us to be together."

His throat bobbed. "And if I did?"

My breath hitched, and I glanced away. The cool wind still swirled around us, and the forest's edge was nowhere in sight. Nothing surrounded us except towering pines, gnarled oaks, and slender aspens. Crunchy leaves crumbled beneath my feet when I fidgeted, and a slushy patch of snow brushed the tips of my toes.

"Don't you want to make your own choices?" I finally said.

"I do make my own choices."

"Not in this matter, you don't. For you, it's not real. It's all from your wolf."

He took a step closer to me. "I've been meaning to talk to you about that."

My lips parted, and I searched his face. That hopeful fragrance still rose steadily from him, but something else did too, something I couldn't put my finger on. "What?"

"It's not just my wolf who wants you." My heart beat as hard as a drum when Kaillen took another step toward me. "I want you too."

I shook my head. "No, you don't. I remember how you were. You weren't attracted to me. You thought my arousal was *funny*."

His thumb and forefinger pressed against my chin, tilting my head up to meet his gaze. "I found *you* amusing, because you're actually quite entertaining, but I didn't find your arousal amusing. I found it . . . unsettling."

"You did?"

He nodded and his head dipped. He still held me captive between his fingers, and his lips brushed against mine so softly that I jerked back.

"I've found you attractive since the moment I laid eyes on you," he said quietly. "And that isn't something I'm used to feeling. In the past, I've been turned on by women, but I didn't feel any attraction or interest in who they were. They were just a body to fuck. But with you, even during that first night at the Underbelly, you intrigued me. You were fearless and stubborn. That in itself took me by surprise, but I also *felt* something in that moment. That's not something I've experienced before, which is why I turned down your job. Like I said, it unsettled me." His tongue darted out and stroked across my bottom lip. "But now I'm not fighting it. I want you. My wolf wants you. Your wolf wants me. The only one left to convince is you."

My breath shuddered, and then his lips sealed to mine, his kiss full of heat and fire. In a blink, he had me completely crushed to him, his hard body touching mine in a blaze of scorching limbs and flames.

I opened my mouth under his, my hand curling around his neck as his tongue swept in to dance with mine. Gods, he tasted good. *So good.* And I wanted this.

He groaned and deepened the kiss as my skin tingled, becoming alive with the feel of him. An aching pulse began low in my core, and my mind reeled as his boner brushed my abdomen.

My wolf yelped in excitement.

That sound was like a bucket of ice water being dumped over my head.

I lurched back, my hand going to my mouth in shock, as my wolf bunched and strained inside me. My heart pounded.

What just happened?

And then it hit me. It was our *wolves* driving our touches.

Panting, I gazed up at him, as longing filled me so deeply that I was drowning in it. "But don't you think it was still your wolf that made you intrigued by me?" Because it had to be. These feelings . . . they were so over-powering, but they weren't *ours*.

The glow in the hunter's eyes brightened. He prowled another step toward me, but I jumped back just as fast. "I don't know, but I don't think so."

"You don't know."

"Why are you focusing on that one sentence?"

"Because it sums up everything about us. You don't know. You think you might like me, but your wolf has been interested from the beginning, and even more so since he caught my true scent, so that probably influenced your decision too."

He took another step forward.

I took two back.

A sly grin lifted his lips. "Is it strange that I enjoy when I have to chase you?"

"Maybe. I mean, yes. You're getting off track again."

"But I'd much rather be chasing you than talking."

"I wouldn't." I lurched behind a tree, and his deep chuckle followed.

Blurring, I ran to the next tree, not able to believe that I'd just moved that fast. "You should put some distance between us, see if you still actually want me when your wolf isn't raging at you!" I called.

"Too late. I already know I want you!" he yelled from somewhere in the forest.

He blurred to my side, and I squeaked in surprise, then moved again just as fast, except this time farther, nearly a hundred yards away. My wolf yelped again, her tail now wagging since she obviously saw this as playing.

Oh shut up! I snapped at her.

She merely gave me a side-eye, her attention still focused on Kaillen.

"And you're wrong about one thing," he added, his voice close when he appeared directly in front of me, pinning my back to an oak tree. "It's true that my wolf didn't go insane with need for you until he'd caught your true scent, but *I*, the man as you say, had interest in you before then, before I think my wolf was even aware of you."

"You did?"

"I did."

My wolf leapt in joy, her barks and yelps so loud inside me that I was tempted to cover my ears. Hairs sprouted across the back of my hands and along my stomach and arms. I glanced down. My entire body was suddenly coated in fur.

Disgust rolled through me as I stared at myself. I looked like a freakin' sasquatch. "Oh my gods, oh my gods, oh my gods. What's happening to me?"

Kaillen's hands locked onto my hips, holding and steadying me despite my grotesque appearance. "It's okay. She's just trying to break through. She wants out, but you can control her."

My entire body began shaking. "I . . . don't know . . . how!" I managed through chattering teeth.

"Try to push her down. Make her submit. Show her that you're the more dominant one."

I closed my eyes and focused on her. *Back down!*

But all of her attention was on Kaillen, on the wolf inside him. She howled.

Claws emerged from my fingernails, the keratin elongating until sharp points graced all ten of my fingers.

"Kaillen!" I screeched in panic.

"It's okay," he said soothingly. "She really wants to shift. Maybe let her. She's as new to you, as you are to her. And she senses her mate in me. She's probably pushing as hard as my own wolf."

"But you don't look like Bigfoot!"

His lips tugged up, just a touch. "It's because I've had years to learn my wolf. He's pushing against me just as hard right now, but I'm fully dominant over him, and your wolf is obviously quite strong if she's pushing this hard on you. You'll need to gain the upper hand at some point, but right now, maybe just let her out. She wants to play, and all of this is new to her too. She might just need to work it out of her system."

"But I don't want to. I want to be like I used to be. I want to feel *human*."

That ashy scent wafted from him again. "I know, my love. I'm sorry."

Burning anger again flared inside me, so much so that I barely registered the endearment he'd just called me, because my wolf was now growling at me, snarling even. Her power was rising as she lunged toward Kaillen and his wolf. She wanted her mate, and I was standing in the way.

And that final leap of hers snapped any control I had. Before I knew what was happening, an explosion of magic overwhelmed me, and then I was a wolf on all fours, leaping onto Kaillen.

He caught my wolf just as she landed on his chest, and in another blink and swirl of power, Kaillen shifted too.

Since my consciousness was now *inside* my wolf, I railed and fought, as I tried to figure out how to shift back to a human. But I had no clue. All I could do was beg and plead with her, but my wolf snarled and pushed me back more, her wolfy mate completely bewitching her.

I sensed Kaillen's wolf's happiness. He was just as eager to be with my wolf as she was to be with him. For the two of them, it was very simple. He wanted her. She wanted him. End of story. Neither of them had the complex thought patterns that humans did. She didn't give a damn that their bond was decided by the gods and magic, and not by her own inner self.

I pushed more, trying desperately to break free, to be *me* again.

But she wouldn't back down.

Damn you! I wailed at her, because this wasn't fair. So much of my life was slipping out of my control, and now, I no longer even had control of my own body. It'd been bad enough to deal with my awakening power while trying to learn how to understand it, all while Jakub was hunting me, but now this? Now I had another *being inside me* who could override my wishes and shift as she chose. Not cool at all.

I curled up inside myself as my wolf and Kaillen's frolicked through the woods.

A sob shook my chest because none of this was okay. But I had no idea how to make it right.

CHAPTER SIX

Hours later, my wolf finally relented when I began pummeling her with my fists. She let me shift back, and I emerged in a shudder of sweaty limbs shaking with exertion. I fell to the forest floor like a newborn fawn. Rage made me tremble. My wolf had literally *taken over my body* for hours.

Kaillen shifted instantaneously, his large nakedness hovering above me. "Tala?" He gently lifted me up, but my breathing was still coming too fast.

"I *hate* her. I hate my damned wolf!"

His eyes dimmed as the late afternoon sun dipped toward the mountains. "She's strong. It might take a little longer than normal to gain control, but I have no doubt you're more dominant than her."

I huffed, not even wanting to remember the past few hours that were clearer this time, not nearly as fuzzy as my first shift. My wolf had been over the moon, running, hunting, and playing with Kaillen's wolf. She'd done it all while I'd fought her tooth and nail, but she didn't give a damn about my wishes because she was with her mate. She'd been happy, so ecstatically *happy*.

I wiped at my mouth and was surprised that no blood coated my fingertips, because an hour ago, our wolves had hunted a small deer and eaten it for lunch.

Gag. But at least my human senses hadn't been awake for that, so while I was mentally aware of my wolf happily munching away on deer organs, I couldn't actually taste it. Still, *so gross.*

"I hate this," I said again.

A groove appeared between Kaillen's eyes when his brow furrowed.

"How do you do it?" I asked him. "How do you shift so easily and at will?"

"It takes time to learn. You'll get there."

"Right." I shook my head. "Can we go back to your place before she takes over again?"

His frown grew. "It's not usually like this, Tala. Males' wolves are puppies when they emerge in us. They're easy to mold and shape, but your wolf is fully grown and very dominant. You've been born with a wolf as strong as you."

I dusted the leaves off myself. "Meaning what? That she's in control now? That I no longer have any say in who commands my body?" I shredded one of the leaves clinging to me, then shredded another just as furiously. Gods, how could I live like this? I couldn't work or drive or go to restaurants if I would suddenly shift just 'cause my wolf got the notion to howl at the moon.

Kaillen's throat bobbed. "I don't know. I didn't anticipate this, but I know you're just as strong as her. The gods don't give us wolves that we can't control."

"Except the gods didn't give me my wolf. *You* did."

Cold hurt slammed into his face, and I glanced away. I didn't want to hurt him. While I was still grappling with what he'd done to me, I knew he hadn't done it maliciously. But what I'd said was true. *He'd* done this to me. Not the gods. And now I was a freak. *An abomination.*

Cameron's taunting jeer came back to me in full force, and I gritted my teeth. "I'm sorry. I didn't mean it like that, but can we please go back to your house? All I want is a shower and normal food right now."

That ashy scent wafted from him again as black flames leapt into his eyes. I sighed. Perhaps it was for the best that his demon came out for a bit. Then maybe my wolf would shy away and leave me alone for a while.

A muscle in the corner of his jaw worked. "Do you want me to carry you? We're about five miles away from my house."

"Would it be faster than me running with you in my human form?"

He cocked his head. "I hadn't thought of that. You have her strength and speed now. Do you want to try?"

"Yes." I needed to because I was so freakin' angry at how my wolf had controlled me that if I didn't work off some steam I was going to be howling in rage. Probably a wolf's howl. *FML, seriously.*

"Follow me." Kaillen took off, breaking into an easy sprint.

I let my toes sink into the mud, still reeling from the fact that I'd been nude outside all day during November, and I still wasn't freezing my ass off. *So weird.*

I pushed off the forest floor and took off after him, catching up with him easily. The wind whipped through my hair as my arms pumped at my sides.

He smiled at me, hesitantly at first, but when my lips curved at how amazing it felt to move this fast, he grinned.

We dipped around trees, leaped over logs, and sailed clear over small streams. The entire time, I kept pace with Kaillen and stayed at his side. It couldn't have been more than ten minutes before we reached his house. He slowed at the outer pastures, and I jogged at his side.

"You're fast," he commented when we finally slowed to a walk.

Both of us were winded, but the strange thing was that I didn't need to stop. I felt like I could keep going.

I made a face. "I guess raw venison agrees with me."

He cast me a crooked smile, even more so when I scrunched my nose up. "You needed calories, and she knew that. Just 'cause your wolf has been ruling you, doesn't mean that your hunger fades."

I gave him a sideways look. "But raw deer? Yuck."

"You'll get used to it."

I tried to smile but all I managed was a grimace, 'cause would I?

When we reached his home, we slid in through the back patio door. According to the clock, it was nearly five in the evening. I ground to a halt, my jaw dropping. It was already the next *evening*.

Only twenty-four hours ago, I'd been shoving choco-latey lava cakes into my mouth while dreading the full moon. Now, I had a bitch of a wolf who felt entitled to rule my body.

"Will the moon force another shift on me tonight?" I asked when Kaillen closed the door behind us.

Our feet were caked in leaves and mud, and we left filth in our wakes as we padded across the floor. "No, only the true full moon can force a shift for newly born were-wolves. It'll be that way for the next year, and then it will get easier. Eventually, the moon won't control you at all. The urge will still be there to shift, but it's something you can stop if you choose to."

"But my wolf isn't normal."

"True. She may want out again tonight. It's hard to say how persistent she'll be." Kaillen grabbed two glasses from his cabinet, filled each with water, and handed me one.

I drained the entire glass in continuous swallows, then grumbled as I processed what could happen *again* when the moon rose. I made sure to keep a big mental distance from my wolf. I didn't want to shift again. Not tonight. Not ever. Losing control like that . . .

A sour taste filled my mouth. Luckily, my wolf seemed

content at the moment, but who knew how long that would last.

I set my glass on the kitchen island and wiped my mouth. "She's a pushy bitch, that's for sure."

Kaillen filled his glass for a second time. "She's as strong as you. You can't hold that against her."

"So you're siding with her now?" I placed my hands on my hips, and his gaze dipped, that glow forming in his eyes when he took in my naked body. Right, I was still in my birthday suit, but I was also dirty and sweaty. Although that apparently didn't matter 'cause the hunter's boner was growing at this very second. But even though that would have enticed me a few hours ago, now, all I felt was irritation. "My eyes are up here you know."

His head whipped up in time to see my nostrils flare.

That ashy scent around him grew. He raked a hand through his hair. "Sorry, you're just so damned beau—" He shook his head. "Sorry."

"I'm going to shower." I swirled away from him before his huge erection could draw me to him. Because even though we'd broached the subject of where we stood as a potential couple and how we felt, we still hadn't reached a resolution on what to do from here, and honestly, the last thing I wanted to do was have that conversation with leaves and twigs in my hair and smoldering fury churning in my gut. Especially when he'd just sided with my wolf.

"Damn demon wolf hunter," I mumbled as I jogged up the stairs.

I hurried to my room and into the bathroom. The

second the water was hot in the shower, I stepped under it and scrubbed every inch of my skin three times over. Muddy water riddled with leaves swirled down the drain. I would probably clog the stupid thing, but I figured that would serve the scourge of the Shadow Zone right for turning me into a damned werewolf.

When I emerged, I toweled off and dressed. The entire time, an ache pulsed in my chest and my wolf paced in my belly. The urge to leave my room and find Kaillen throbbed inside me.

"What the fuck," I whispered.

My wolf whined. I could feel her restlessness rising. She'd only been suppressed for an hour, yet already she wanted out.

"Not happening, lady," I muttered to her.

She bared her teeth.

I bared my teeth right back.

A growl slipped past her, and she swelled, pushing and moving inside me, wanting out again.

"Stop it!" I hissed at her. "What the hell is the matter with you? This is *my* body, not yours!"

An image formed in my mind. Amber-hued eyes gazed at me out of a strong, masculine face. Square jaw. Dark hair. An achingly beautiful mouth.

Kaillen's face hovered in my thoughts, begging and pulling at me.

I squeezed my eyes shut and tried to dispel the image, but it formed again, and then again. I jolted to a stop as I picked up my brush to untangle my damp hair, because it suddenly struck me that it was *my wolf* putting these images in my mind.

Was that what Kaillen's wolf constantly did to him? Flash images of me to him, not relenting until Kaillen did what he wanted?

I set my brush back down. "Are you trying to talk to me?"

She whined.

"What? What do you want from me?"

This time she placed a memory in the forefront of my thoughts. It was of Kaillen's strong broad shoulders brushing against mine when we trained in that room back in Ontario.

"You want Kaillen?"

Her whine grew.

And then it clicked. She wanted me to go to the hunter, to be with him and to stay near him.

"But we just got done running with him," I whispered, and for the first time, I realized I was talking out loud. *Not crazy at all, Tala . . .*

My wolf let out another soft yelp. Obviously, I was on the right track.

I picked up my brush again and began forcefully pulling it through my hair, wincing a few times when I brushed too aggressively through the snarls. "But *I* don't want to go down there. I want to take a freakin' minute to process what the hell is happening right now."

She let out a growl, a soft one, not a domineering one, but clearly a warning.

A freakin' warning. As if she had the right to boss me around.

"Not happening!" I snapped at her. I finished brushing my hair and threw the brush back into my bag. "You've had your way for the last eighteen hours. I'm taking a break from all things werewolf and mate driven, got it?"

Her power pulsed, and I nearly doubled over. I ground my teeth, fighting back. So my wolf wanted her mate. Well, too damned bad. Just 'cause I wanted the hunter too didn't mean I'd joined at the hip with him. We didn't need to be together every freakin' second of the day.

But apparently, my wolf thought that we did.

Fisting my hands, I fought and struggled internally against my wolf's rising power. She growled and snarled, then flashed another image. It was of Kaillen and me in bed, him over me, his eyes glowing as his canines elongated right before he bit into the tender flesh on my neck and sealed the mating bond.

"Quit trying to force me!" I squeezed my eyes shut and pushed her down with everything I had. "You just got here and have no idea what's going on. Kaillen wants me because his wolf told him to, and now that I see how annoyingly pushy one's wolf can be, I'm only becoming more convinced that his wolf is the only reason he's pursued me at all!"

When her only response was to sprout hairs through the backs of my hands, I knew she wasn't going to listen to reason.

"Fuck this." I snatched my phone up as sweat beaded along my brow.

My eyes widened when I saw the half dozen texts from Prisha wanting to know how my first shift went. I furiously tapped in a reply, letting her know that I'd survived, but I couldn't muster more than that.

My muscles were still burning from my attempts to avoid another shift as I began to ask her if I could stay with her, but then with an aching realization I knew that escaping to my best friend's home wasn't an option.

Jakub-Dipshit was still looking for me. I couldn't bring him to her doorstep.

Deleting that part, I hit send on my half-assed reply to let her know I'd indeed shifted and was still breathing. Following that, I made a call.

"Good evening, thank you for calling the Supernatural Forces, Chicago division. This is Shelley, how can I help you?"

Thank the gods, Jeff's not working tonight, so the phone's actually being answered.

"Shelley, it's Tala Davenport. I need your help."

CHAPTER SEVEN

The scent and sound of sizzling food drifted through the air when I hurried down the stairs with my bags in tow.

Kaillen stood by the stove, his back to me, as he sautéed something in a pan. He'd obviously showered too and must have used one of his fairy charms, because the muddy footprints and leaves we'd left along the floor were gone.

My nose twitched as heady aromas bombarded me. Onions, spinach, mushrooms, and hints of basil, olive oil, and spicy sausage wafted through the air. I could scent the difference between each ingredient. Not weird at all . . .

Inside, my wolf wagged her tail, her power rising again as her excitement grew at being in the same room as her mate.

This is bordering on codependency you know, I said to her, but she ignored me.

Sighing, I let my bags fall with a thump and curled my

fingers into fists. The urge to approach Kaillen and run my hand up his arm and around his waist nearly overtook me. *Want, want, want.* I *wanted* him. No, I *needed* him. That insatiable desire again nearly overwhelmed me.

Frowning, my chest rose as my breaths increased. Because was it *me* who wanted to touch him like that or my wolf?

Kaillen was still moving the veggies around in the pan with a spatula as he added a huge can of tomatoes to the mix.

"I hope you like Italian," he called over his shoulder. "I figured it was best to get you something to eat before the moon rises again, just in case we go for another run. Who knows, maybe they'll pick rabbit tonight. Not sure how you feel about bunnies, so I—" His hand stopped mid-air, the spatula hovering over the pan when he took in my appearance.

I was fully dressed with my coat on, and my bags sat at my feet.

Something in his eyes flickered, a brief flare of emotion burned in them so hot yet so lightning-fast that I couldn't decipher it before he turned back to the pan. "Going somewhere?" Despite his casual question, his movements turned stiff and aggressive as he stirred the sautéing mix.

"I'm going back to Chicago. I can't stay here."

Another scrape of the pan. "Can I ask why not?"

"Because my bitch of a wolf can't be around you without taking over. I need some space."

He didn't reply, but another scent filled the kitchen—that metallic iron scent. Anger.

Huh, imagine that. The fucker turns me into a wolf and then gets mad when I'm not enjoying it.

"Can you create a portal for me?" I crossed my arms, hating that I had to ask for his help. If I could get a cab or rideshare to the nearest airport, I would, but as I was still being hunted, venturing solo anywhere wasn't smart.

Thank you, Mr. Jakub-Dipshit.

"Where in Chicago are you going?" Kaillen lowered the heat on the stove as the sauce simmered. My stomach growled, that insatiable hunger clawing at my belly again.

"The SF Office. Commander Klebus said I could join Tessa in her safe house until they catch Jakub."

He stilled. The only movement was his chest moving faster and faster as his breathing sped up. The ever-increasing pounding of his heart reached my ears next.

"What about *us* catching Jakub?" he finally said.

My jaw snapped together, and I said through gritted teeth, "Kinda hard to do when this new animal inside me is constantly trying to take over."

He finally turned to face me, and his expression was so taut, that I was surprised his cheekbones hadn't cut through the skin. "Why are you running from me?"

"Because I can't handle this!"

He took a step forward, then said in a rough voice, "I can help you through it."

"No, you can't. Your presence only makes it worse. My

wolf wants out, all of the time, because she wants to be with *you*. I have *no* control."

In a blink, he stood before me, right in front of me, and his scent and strength flooded everything in my system. The urge to take that last step forward and mold my body to his swam through my veins in hot vicious rivers. My wolf wagged her tail, yet I held my ground and clenched my fists. I would *not* be ruled by her.

Kaillen's eyes flashed gold. "You feel the bond just like I do."

"So?"

"If you allow yourself to succumb to it, the strain will go away."

Hearing that was like a blow to my gut. Was *that* the reason why he pursued me so aggressively? So the *strain* would go away?

Somehow, I managed to say without choking, "Is that what you've done?"

His eyes softened. "No, because you won't let me."

"So is that what this is about? You're pursuing me so your damned wolf will stop trying to take control of you too?"

Fire rolled in his eyes. "I told you, I was attracted to you before my wolf knew what you were."

"Are you sure about that?" I said quietly.

Gold flared around his irises, the rings so bright they were mesmerizing. "You want me." He inched closer until our chests nearly brushed.

A quiver ran through my belly. *Damn* him.

His hand drifted around my waist, his touch feather-light. "I can scent it."

My entire body jolted as my wolf whined inside me again. Another image of Kaillen biting into my neck filled my mind.

Back the fuck down! I snapped at her.

"Why can't we just let this happen?" His face was at my neck, his lips fluttering against my skin.

I arched against him, my head lolling back as though I had no control of my movements.

A soft growl came from him, and then he was kissing me, his lips firm yet achingly soft as he pressed kiss after kiss to my throat. His strong fingers stroked my lower back as that musky scent rose from him and swirled through the room like a fog.

Before I knew what was happening, he had me sitting on the island, legs spread as he hooked my calves around his waist and began unzipping my jacket. I waited docilely before him in a drugged state. I was high on him, on *us*, on this aching need that pulsed between our souls.

"Stay," he pleaded.

The heady desire in my mind grew, as his hands were suddenly everywhere. Running up and down my sides, over my thighs, around my ass, to the sides of my breasts.

And his mouth . . . fuck, his *mouth*. He kissed along my neck, over the tops of my breasts, down the length of my collarbone. His mouth was heaven and evoked tingles of arousal down every path they traveled.

His tongue darted out, tasting that sensitive skin at the base of my neck, right where the mating mark would go.

Wait, what? Mating mark?

With a jolt back to reality, my breaths came in heavy pants. My jacket was on the floor. My legs were wrapped around the hunter. Half of my shirt was unbuttoned and off my shoulder as the tops of my breasts strained against the material. And the hunter's hands were locked onto my hips, his musky desire pulsing through the air and wrapping around my own heady scent, as his erection strained against his jeans.

We were two seconds away from fucking, from *both* of us giving into our wolves, when I realized that for the first time, my wolf had gone quiet.

Completely silent.

She was still present, still inside me, but she'd stopped pushing, stopped trying to assert her dominance.

Because she'd won.

I'd been about to let the hunter claim me.

I slammed my hands into Kaillen's chest with so much force that he went flying ten feet back.

Somehow, he managed to stay on his feet, a true miracle given how violently I'd shoved him. He ground to a skidding halt on the hardwood floor with a glazed look of arousal coating his eyes. His chest rose and fell unsteadily as he looked at me with unconcealed *hunger*.

"Tala," he said gruffly.

I shook my head frantically as a warning snarl came from my wolf. *Shut it!*

But she pushed and swelled, fighting me again since I hadn't given into her wishes.

I clamped a lid on her growing power just as hairs pierced the backs of my hands. I leaped off the island and frantically whipped my jacket back on.

"Make me a portal. Now!" I gulped in a breath of air and then another. The urge to go to Kaillen was so unbearably strong. "Now!" I yelled again when he just stood there.

He shook his head, that fogged expression still clouding his features, and a wave of crashing sadness nearly brought a sob to my lips because did he really want me? Actually want me? Despite what he'd said? Or were he and his wolf so entwined with one another that he didn't see his wolf's prodding and manipulations?

Because my wolf was a brand-new being inside me, and all of the pulls and urges to go to Kaillen were different than they had once been. Before it'd been a desperate longing and insurmountable attraction, but now . . .

I gripped the stone countertop behind me. My fingers dug into it, my knuckles turning white, and some of the stone pulverized beneath my fingertips, turning to fine dust.

Because now my desire to be with the hunter was a necessity. I *needed* to be with him. Needed to have him near me, with me. It was no longer an attraction or interest in getting to know him.

Now it was a requirement. Without him, I couldn't live, couldn't breathe, couldn't exist.

Mother of all the realms . . . This was so fucked up.

"Tala, please." Kaillen took a step toward me, the ache in his tone nearly my undoing. "Don't do this. Don't run from me."

"I have to." I gathered my things, my hands trembling with the amount of exertion it took to maintain control of my movements, because my wolf was still snarling and thrashing inside me. She was desperately trying to gain the upper hand and force me to stay.

But I gritted my teeth and called upon my witch powers, using all of the witch magic inside me to fight the werewolf strength battling against it.

Her power and mine collided in a flurry of fur and sparks. Yet it was all internal, all contained within my soul. To Kaillen, I probably looked strained and stressed, but it was such a false appearance. It didn't remotely capture the hell I was experiencing at this very second as I fought to maintain control of who I was.

I was careful to keep my distance from the hunter, because every step that took me closer to him had my wolf whining in anticipation and fighting me even more.

"Make the portal. *Now*." I gritted my teeth and prayed that he would obey. "Please," I added, my tone pleading when he continued to simply stand there.

His hand dipped with jerky movements into his pocket. The gold flaring around his eyes was so bright that I could only imagine what his inner wolf was doing to him too. With forced-looking movements, his arm swirled through the air, that flashing yellow light emitting from his crystal as his portal began to form.

The second the void appeared, my wolf lunged and strained against the cage my witch magic had tried to trap her in.

And even though she snarled and let out an achingly forlorn howl, I didn't hesitate, didn't even give it a second thought, as I jumped through the hunter's portal in a single leap, and time and space swallowed me whole, while my wolf's desperate cry filled my ears.

CHAPTER EIGHT

K aillen's portal deposited me at the Supernatural Forces' doorstep. Literally. I jumped through it so fast I came flying out and nearly smashed right into the front door.

Righting myself, I managed to stay on my feet as another howl came from my wolf. She was walking circles in my belly, crying and yelping.

But I ignored her and straightened just as a painful growl of hunger came from my stomach. I huffed in irritation and grabbed my bags, nearly storming inside the office until I remembered that I wasn't wearing my cloaking spell.

Grumbling, I whispered the words to activate it. The thick spell wove around me, clouding me in its familiar weight. My shoulders sagged, more from the feel of it than from any actual physical presence, because this time, I knew I couldn't release it anytime soon.

Welcome home, Tala.

With that depressing thought in place, I pushed through the front door.

"Tala, I'm glad you got here so fast!" Shelley zipped around the front desk to greet me. She stopped mid-stride when she took in my expression, and her smile wobbled as she added, "Commander Klebus has a squad ready who can take you to the safe house Tessa's staying at." She glanced over my shoulder, a frown puckering her brow. "Did you come *alone?*"

"Yes, I know, I know." I tried to smooth my expression, but it was damned hard when I had a crying wolf in my belly and a never-ending hunger eating my stomach. I was seriously giving hangry a whole new meaning. "I'm aware that it's not safe, and I know that I shouldn't travel by myself, but if it makes you feel better, the portal literally dropped me two feet from the front door, and I came right inside." Of course, the hunter would already know that, no doubt the blood bond clueing him into my whereabouts. It was probably the only reason he'd been okay with me traveling here alone.

Regardless, remembering that we were also bound by his blood had my teeth grinding together.

"I'll need your phone back for storing again." Shelley gave a sympathetic smile.

"Oh, right." I reluctantly fished it out of my bag. "I just need to send a quick text before I turn it off."

I hurriedly tapped in a text to Prisha, letting her know that I was moving to an SF safe house and had to hand my phone off to the Supernatural Forces once again. A frown pulled at my lips when I watched Shelley power it down and store it away.

So much for talking with Prish again anytime soon.

Guilt bit me hard. I should have called my best friend after my shower. That was where my priorities should have been, but instead, I'd nearly let the hunter bang me.

Gritting my teeth, I watched Shelley tuck my phone into her desk drawer just as my stomach let out another ferocious growl. Her eyes bugged out. "Are you hungry?"

Understatement of the year. "A bit."

"Follow me. I'll grab you a sandwich from the break-room that you can eat on the way."

"Do you think I could have a few sandwiches?"

She frowned. "Um, sure. I can grab a couple."

She took one of the bags from my hands, but I kept hold of the others. Even though I was carrying three bags, they felt light and easy to maneuver—thanks to my newly formed werewolf strength—but that didn't lighten my mood because my wolf was still prowling inside my belly, angry and snarling. At least, she was no longer pushing against my skin and trying to break free, so I didn't resemble Bigfoot. Silver lining.

My wolf let out another lonely howl, and a flash of guilt flooded me. For a second, she seemed like a pet canine who was sad, angry, and feeling alone. And why wouldn't she? Her mate wasn't here and even though she could run as fast as the wind, she couldn't run the thousand miles to Kaillen's home. Well, she probably could, but I wasn't going to let her. And even if I did, how would she know where to go? I had no idea where Kaillen lived. All I knew was that his home was in Montana.

My steps faltered when I realized that I had no way of returning to him unless he escorted me, but I quickly brushed that thought aside. I'd made the decision to leave his property so I could avoid any more mate-driven wolfy motivations.

And thankfully, it appeared to have worked.

Even though my wolf was mourning, she'd given up on her insistent urging to shift and be with the hunter.

As if sensing that I'd won, she bared her teeth at me before giving me her rump.

I scoffed. *It's my body, you know,* I countered. But for some reason another twinge of guilt twisted my gut. I'd just separated her from the only thing she wanted in this world.

My wolf glanced over her shoulder at me, gave me a flash of canine, and then ignored me completely.

I rolled my eyes and smothered my guilty feeling as best I could. So be it. If Mrs. Wolfy wanted to be mad at me, she could. 'Cause at least I wasn't looking like a sasquatch anymore and was once again firmly walking on two legs.

"You can wait here." Shelley escorted me to a waiting room with a window that overlooked a huge underground garage that appeared to double as a hanger.

Numerous SF vehicles were parked against one wall in the garage, but a large plane or jet, or whatever the hell it was, sat in the center of the massive chamber. Technicians scurried about the aircraft as a squad of SF members stood in the corner. They huddled in a circle, their squad commander issuing orders to them from the looks of it.

"I'll grab those sandwiches." Shelley disappeared out the door and I let my bags fall at my feet. She returned a minute later, and handed three sandwiches to me. "Will this be enough?"

No. I managed a smile. "Yes, thank you." My fingers were shaking when I took them, and my stomach let out another painful growl as I all but attacked the food.

I was halfway through my last sandwich, my gobbling bites making me feel more monkey than human, when Carlos walked into the room.

I swallowed my mouthful of ham and bread, embarrassment making my cheeks flush. Crumbs littered the floor around me, and a morsel of food was stuck in my hair. I resisted the urge to lick it off.

"Hi," I said sheepishly.

Carlos's lips curved, his eyes tender. "I heard you were back and looking for SF protection. Sounds like you've finally said goodbye to the Fire Wolf?"

"Oh, well," I replied lamely. Had I? "I guess I'm not sure."

My wolf snarled inside me, then turned that growl on my ex. Yep, Mrs. Wolf wasn't a fan of the newcomer.

Calm down, I'm not jumping him.

Her lip curled.

"I see." Carlos leaned against the wall, then shoved his hands into his pockets. His ebony hair shone in the lights as his dark-brown gaze traveled over me, drinking me in.

Since his nostrils didn't flare, and he didn't look at me any differently than he normally did, I knew my cloaking spell was also masking my new werewolf scent. *Thank the gods.*

But my wolf didn't seem to care. All she did was growl more since Carlos was checking me out. I rolled my eyes internally. No wonder mated werewolf males were so monogamous. These inner wolves were pushy as fuck.

"Thirsty?" Carlos produced a water bottle that he must have had stuffed into his back pocket. It was one of those fancy ones, claiming to be spring water from some far-off mountainous region that was untouched by humans and had been filtered for a thousand years or whatever. He'd probably nabbed it from a vending machine or the staff breakroom.

I gratefully took it. "Yes, thanks." I took a long swallow, then wiped my mouth. A few crumbs fell, but overall, I thought I was clean and didn't have mayonnaise spread across my cheek or anything mortifying like that. Still, for good measure, I threaded my fingers through my hair too, just to make sure more food particles weren't stuck in it.

Once somewhat assured that I didn't resemble a one-year-old who'd just dived face first into a birthday cake, I tentatively finished the last of my sandwich, but I did it at a slower pace even though my stomach was still cramping from hunger.

Because with Carlos in the room, I was painfully aware of my troll-like manners, and I didn't feel the comfort with him that I did with the hunter.

When I'd polished off two plates of food yesterday morning, Kaillen had merely watched me acceptingly, even approvingly since I was taking care of myself, and I knew that he genuinely thought nothing of me eating a mountain of nourishment.

Yet, even though Carlos was a werewolf, I felt self-conscious. My usual confidence had blown right out the window when my werewolf traits emerged. And even though my rational side told me that surely he would understand how I was feeling, especially if he knew that I was a brand-new shifter, the other part of me felt closed off. Like I didn't want him seeing that part of me.

As for why I was all of a sudden feeling so self-conscious around someone I'd never felt that way with before . . .

My wolf's lips peeled back as her hackles rose.

Ah . . . so that's why. My bitch of a wolf was needling her way into my very essence.

With a shudder, I sighed and finished the bottled water after I'd officially inhaled all three sandwiches.

"Are you feeling okay?" Carlos asked, his eyebrows rising.

"Yeah," I said a bit too quickly. "Why do you ask? Do I look like I'm not doing well?"

"No, it's not that. I just know that when a woman leaves a man that sometimes they're . . ." He shrugged.

"Oh! No, it's not like that, really it's not." I nibbled my lip because it *wasn't.* I hadn't left the hunter. How could I when we'd never officially been together? But I did need a break from what my wolf brought out in me. Although, no one here knew that. All they saw was a woman running from her mate, but I would see Kaillen again. Surely, I would.

My stomach bottomed out at the thought of *not* seeing him, and my wolf began to pace inside me, chuffing and letting out soft whines. But that dipping motion in my tummy was *my* feeling. It had to be.

Or was it?

I let out another heavy breath. Who knew. Seriously, who the fuck knew what was my desire versus my wolf's desire at this point.

That gnawing sadness scraped at me again. Because if this was even close to what the hunter had been feeling, then how could he possibly be convinced that he, the man, was interested in me, and that it wasn't entirely from his wolf?

"Did you get my letter?" Carlos asked.

My head snapped up, all thoughts about mating bonds and the dark hunter fleeing from my mind. Carlos's letter. *Right.*

Carlos had written to me when I'd been in Oak Trembler. He'd told me that he still loved me and wanted to be with me. He'd also said he was willing to wait for me if needed.

I'd never replied to him, not that I'd had the chance to, given that I'd been abducted the morning after reading it.

"I did," I replied tentatively.

His eyebrows rose.

Well, okay, then. It looked like we were having this conversation right now, but it was probably for the best. If there was one thing I was certain of, regardless of where the hunter and I stood, it was that my feelings for Carlos were in the past. I'd moved on, even if he was hoping to rekindle something.

"About that." I slipped a hand into my jacket's pocket. "I'm glad you brought it up, because I've been meaning to talk to you. I read your letter, and I really appreciate—"

"Tala Davenport?" An SF member poked his head into the room. He wore one of the gleaming obsidian suits and had military written all over him. "We're ready for you." He gave Carlos a curt nod. "Private Lopez."

Carlos saluted. "Corporal Braxton, sir."

"We're leaving now?" I glanced toward the garage. The flying spaceship, or whatever it was, was fired up and near the mouth of the hanger, obviously ready for takeoff.

"Yes, ma'am," the SF member replied. "I'm Corporal Braxton of Squad Twenty-eight. We'll be escorting you to your safe house."

"Thank you, sir," Carlos said, then ran an agitated hand through his hair. "Would it be okay if we spoke for another minute, sir?"

The corporal dipped his head. "Two minutes."

Once the SF member left and strode back to the team assembled near the flying contraption, Carlos took a step closer to me. A pineapple and sunshine fragrance rose from him. *Oh gods*, this was so awkward. I felt like I was about to break up with someone that I wasn't even with.

Carlos brushed my side, and a golden glow lit his eyes just as a slight scent of musk rose from him.

My wolf snarled and let out a rumble of rage.

I stepped back, breaking my contact with him.

"What were you saying before we were interrupted?" he said huskily and took another step forward, seemingly oblivious to the space I'd just put between us.

I twisted my hands, then fidgeted from foot to foot. "Um, I was about to say that I really appreciate what you wrote in your letter, and I—"

"Tala Davenport?" A robotic voice blared through the speaker in the room. "Please report to the garage immediately."

I halted, my body stiffening. Apparently, our two minutes were up.

Carlos's nostrils flared, but he reached for my bags, taking all of them. A muscle ticked in his jaw, but he gave me an understanding smile. "I'll walk you out."

"Oh, okay, thanks." I ran a hand through my hair, because I didn't know what else to say or do given that we'd nearly launched into a conversation about our non-existent relationship that one participant was hoping to rekindle and the other wasn't. Not awkward at all.

The rumble of the aircraft filled the large garage when we entered it.

"What is that?" I asked as we walked toward the plane.

"An infinity craft," Carlos replied. "It's how we often transport when portal keys aren't used."

Squad Twenty-eight stood at attention, several

members rushing forward to whisk my bags away, which left me standing by my ex as they all waited for me to climb aboard.

I ran a hand through my hair again as my stomach let out another growl. "I guess I'll see you later then."

Carlos nodded, his expression impossible to read, yet his eyes swam with veiled emotions.

I was about to open my mouth, to try to figure out a way to tell him before I left that things were over between us without coming across as insensitive, when he abruptly pulled me into a hug.

His large frame swallowed mine as his scent washed over me. My wolf let out a vicious snarl, but Carlos's affection caught me so much by surprise that I automatically hugged him back.

"Think about what I said in my letter," he whispered into my ear. "We can talk about it later."

Before I could respond or pull back, he pressed a soft kiss to my neck, just below my ear. A shiver ran through me since that was a sensitive area on me and my ex knew that.

His crooked grin was splitting his face when he pulled back, 'cause he no doubt sensed my physical reaction, even though internally my wolf's hackles were entirely raised. Yep, Mrs. Wolfy was *not* happy about that sexy gesture.

Another rush of that sunshine and pineapple fragrance burst from Carlos. Even amidst the scent of gasoline from the infinity craft, I detected it.

Shit. I really needed to learn how to filter these scents

so I wasn't being constantly bombarded, and I really needed to set things straight with Carlos. He was honestly hoping we would get back together, and that wasn't happening.

I squeezed Carlos's hand in an awkward goodbye. "We'll talk soon."

He nodded, that hopeful scent still there, and I hated that I couldn't tell him right here and now that things were over between us. But with Squad Twenty-eight members surrounding us, I didn't want an audience for that conversation. When I rejected Carlos once and for all, it would be in private so he didn't have to deal with the embarrassment of his co-workers watching the entire ordeal. Carlos deserved better than that.

I gave my ex one last smile then climbed aboard the craft. It rumbled beneath me as a squad member directed me to my seat, then buckled me up.

The entire time, Carlos stood in the garage, hands stuffed into his pockets as he watched me leave.

My stomach dipped when the infinity craft lifted, as if hovering in mid-air, then a wash of magic prickled my senses as the exterior shimmered from an invisibility cloaking spell layering it.

Following that, the craft shot out of the garage and into the night. My jaw dropped and my stomach bottomed-out from the force of it, but then my attention snagged to the bright moon hovering in the sky.

My wolf perked up, her attention gluing to it too.

Oh crap.

But even though she grew aware, all of her attention focusing on that glowing orb, I didn't feel that restlessness from her, that need to shift. But I could have shifted, if I'd wanted to. Already, I could feel her magic shimmering under my skin, the call of that lunar body pulling at both of us.

It wasn't like last night, though. It wasn't inevitable and completely out of my control.

So I pulled up my witch magic, much like I had earlier tonight when I'd shoved my wolf down.

She gave a low growl, but that was it, and then she curled up and stuffed her nose under her tail.

Phew. Crisis avoided.

I sank my head back against my seat and closed my eyes. More than ever, I knew I'd made the right choice to leave the hunter just so I could avoid my wolf's incessant pushing to be free and with her mate.

Settling more in my chair, I tried to relax into the flight, but what I'd left behind still lingered at the forefront of my thoughts. Because it wasn't just the *two* werewolf males who I still had unresolved issues with. Nope. It was so much more than that. I still had a psycho sorcerer hunting me, I had a magic shop that I hadn't even checked in with in nearly three days, and I hadn't spoken with my best friend yet to even lament my first shift. Prisha had no idea that my wolf was a pushy bitch.

I sighed. What a freakin' month.

CHAPTER NINE

We flew for two hours to wherever the SF was taking me. Since I had no idea where they'd hidden Tessa, or how fast this craft flew, I couldn't gauge the distance or direction.

All I knew was that it was late, and I was nodding off by the time we landed.

When we disembarked, a warm breeze caressed my skin, and sandy terrain surrounded the runway. Cactuses and dry shrubs sprouted from the land.

The moon still shone, but its heavenly body was lower in the sky, and that throbbing in my chest had eased. The pull from the moon was abating, and if that was the worst it would be on non-full moon nights over the coming year, then I could learn to live with it.

My wolf had stayed relatively quiet during the flight. The few times she'd risen from her slumber, as soon as she realized our mate wasn't present, she'd given me another rumble of discontentment, just to make sure I knew she didn't approve of my choices, and then she went back to sleep.

Phew.

I figured as long as I didn't let other males get close to me—as I had with Carlos—and I kept my distance from the hunter, it was possible that I could learn to cohabit with her, since at this point, my new werewolf traits seemed to be permanent.

But that thought still didn't sit well with me. Essentially, I was either with the hunter or I was alone. With a mated wolf inside me, I had a feeling it would be near impossible to ever date anyone else again. My wolf would no doubt make my life a living nightmare if I tried.

I scowled. In other words, free will was now a thing of the past.

I ran a hand through my hair as I began following the SF members across the tarmac, grumbling to myself. Was this how Kaillen felt? Perhaps he'd been more accepting of it, since male werewolves were raised to know that once they found their mate, their fate was sealed. But me? I'd been an independent witch up until now. Granted I had some other weird powers inside me that I still couldn't make sense of, but I'd been my own decision-maker for as long as I could remember.

So was that life officially over now? Was I no longer the ruler of my own destiny?

I was walking in such a fog that I didn't even look up until I heard a squeal and someone say, "Tala!" from the distance.

I snapped my head up to see my sister sprinting toward me at full throttle across the runway. Despite the late hour, a grin streaked across her face.

She barreled right into me, hugging me with a flourish, and I laughed despite myself.

"You're here! You're here! I'm so glad you're here!" she shrieked.

"Hey!" I replied with a laugh and wrapped my arms around her.

Tessa squeezed me harder. "Oh my gods, I couldn't believe it when I was told you were coming! I'm so happy you came. I have so much to tell you. You're going to die when you hear about these two guys that work here, and how we're—" She stopped her prattling when she caught my expression. "What's wrong? Why are you crying?"

I shook my head as tears streamed down my face. She wiped at them, her sapphire gaze searching mine.

"It's nothing." I sniffed. "I'm fine. I'm just so happy to see you." And I was. The Tessa before me was the sister that I loved. She was happy, bubbly, and so full of cheer. Her positive optimism and love of life was enough to make even the darkest soul see the sunshine.

I hadn't realized how much I needed that, needed *her*. A bit of normalcy in my life right now was a much needed tranquilizer, and the tears streaming down my face were more from relief and joy at seeing her than anything else.

"Did something happen with your delicious hunter?" Tessa quirked an eyebrow.

"How about we don't talk about him?"

Her lips parted. "Oh, Tala Bala." She pulled me back into a hug, wrapping me in her warmth and radiance. "If you two are arguing right now, don't give it a second thought. It's you and me here, just like it's supposed to be, so I'll do my best to keep you distracted."

When I finally stopped gripping her, she released me, then eyed the SF members standing a few yards behind us who were awkwardly avoiding our gazes since we weren't exactly keeping our conversation discreet.

"Can you grab her bags?" Tessa asked one of them sweetly, her eyelashes fluttering.

"Of course, ma'am," he replied, dipping his head and taking my bags from me.

Even though my sister had basically just asked him to be our bellman, he seemed relieved for the task. It probably beat watching two young women cry and fawn over each other.

Tessa flashed him a coy smile, then linked her arm through mine. "Come on. I'll show you where I'm staying."

"Do you have any idea where we are?" I glanced at the surrounding dry terrain again.

"Nope." From her tone, she didn't seem overly concerned about our geographical location as she tugged me along.

"We must be in a desert." Anyone with eyes could see that.

"Yep, definitely in a desert, but I have no idea which one." She gave a tinkling laugh.

"So no other notions where then?" I asked as curiosity got the better of me. "Perhaps the southwest, or Mexico, or maybe northern Africa?"

She gave me a little squeeze. "We're not supposed to know, nosey. We're just supposed to enjoy it."

I rolled my eyes but laughed. My chest felt lighter, my wolf was asleep and not bothering me, and for the first time since Tessa had been abducted, I actually felt like myself.

"Gods, I needed this," I mumbled to no one in particular.

"Oh yay, so you *are* going to enjoy it here!" she squealed. "I thought you might get restless or insist on talking to our employees all day, or working to craft more spells and potions for Practically Perfect, or grumbling about that hunter of yours."

"Ugh, don't remind me about Kaillen or the store. 'Cause I should be doing all of those things. Speaking of which, you and I will need to sit down at some point and talk about Practically Perfect's future."

"Oh?" She cocked her head. "What do you mean?"

"I mean that with everything that's happened, I don't know if things will return to how they once were. I'm worried that my true witch magic could become common knowledge," I said under my breath so the SF members strolling behind us wouldn't hear. "Which means the locals might start to question our business. We haven't exactly been honest with them. There might be a backlash because of that."

A groove appeared between Tessa's eyes. "I hadn't thought of that."

I elbowed her good-naturedly. "You never do. That's the problem."

"Well, there's an easy solution to that one."

"There is?"

"Of course," she said nonchalantly. "We get ahead of the story before it truly gets out and we weave it to our advantage. We could say something about how you hate the limelight and prefer privacy and that you were terrified at the thought of people knowing it was *you* behind our spells, and then I could swoop in to save the day and claim I'd done it all for you. We could spin it so that it came across as two sisters lovingly working together and supporting each other in the best way possible."

A laugh escaped me. "That's not that far from the truth."

"Exactly, which means it'll be easy to pull off."

I laughed again, because I had to admit that she had a point. When it came to charming people and deceiving them in a way that didn't make them feel manipulated, my sister truly had a knack for it. "Have you thought that marketing or PR could be your true calling?"

She scrunched her nose up. "Does that job involve getting up every day at eight o'clock and sitting behind a desk?"

"Not necessarily."

She inclined her head. "Well, I don't know then. Perhaps it is what I'm destined for. As long as it's exciting." She gave me a sly side-eye, then grinned. "You have to admit that our lives right now are *very* exciting. Life is much more interesting now than it was last month."

"Perhaps, but I don't know if it's exciting in a good way."

"But don't you enjoy it? Just a little?"

I groaned. Even though I loved my sister to death, she was so trying at times. "I'm not really sure that all of this"—I gestured to the SF base around us—"is something to be excited about. Your choices are affecting many people's lives. Have you thought about that?"

She shrugged. "Well, if nothing else, it gives all of them something to do. After all, this is what they're paid for, are they not?"

"Tessa, seriously, don't you feel guilty? At least a little bit?"

She frowned, and a contemplative look came into her eyes as she seemed to mull it over. "I do regret what it's done to you. I am truly sorry for that."

I squeezed her arm. It wasn't the admission I'd hoped for, since she hadn't taken full responsibility for her actions, but it was a start. I could live with that.

"How long do you think you'll be here?" she asked.

"Not sure. I suppose as long as I need a break from him." When she gave me a quizzical glance, I switched subjects. "Have you talked to Nicole lately? To ask how the store's doing?"

"I did actually. I called her yesterday." Tessa beamed, obviously quite impressed with herself that she'd taken the initiative.

"What did she say?"

Tessa shrugged. "She gave me the weekly financials and told me how sales have been since we've been gone."

"How's she holding up?"

"Fine, as far as I can tell. She actually seemed to be enjoying it. I think she likes being the boss."

A breath of relief escaped me. Since I'd been so caught up in everything that'd happened in the past few days, I'd completely neglected Nicole—the employee we'd put in charge of Practically Perfect while we were gone. "I'm so relieved to hear that."

Tessa bumped elbows with me. "You should take a break from the store while you're here, you know. You never take any time off, and after everything you've been through, you deserve a little vaca."

It was the same words Prisha had uttered to me, but while I was used to my best friend thinking of my well-being, I was less used to hearing that from my sister. Usually, Tessa thought about Tessa and nobody else.

I squeezed her hand. "Maybe you're right."

We'd nearly reached the end of the runway, and in the dark sky, I could make out tall shapes that rose in the distance. A backdrop of endless stars loomed over them.

"Are those mountains?" I asked, pointing toward the black shapes.

"Yep, I think we're in a valley between two mountain ranges."

A small, well-lit hanger loomed ahead of us, but unlike the SF hanger in Chicago, this one wasn't hidden or underground, suggesting that wherever we were was remote since the SF wasn't worried about humans seeing us. That, or they had some serious illusion spells around this base's entire perimeter.

About twenty small houses and a large concrete building rose behind the hanger, but I didn't see any other buildings, which told me this base was fairly small. "Are there other families or other supernaturals needing protection who live here too?" I asked, nodding toward the other houses.

"Nope, just me," Tessa replied. "Those other houses are where the SF members live. From what I've been able to figure out, the safe house I'm in is the only one used for that purpose. I think this base is mostly used for military training." She nodded toward the hanger.

With my newly enhanced werewolf eyesight, I was easily able to make out six aircraft in the hanger. "A training facility?"

"I think so, but honestly, I haven't spent much time worrying about it."

"Of course, you haven't." I laughed.

She laughed with me, then steered me toward a walkway off the runway. Several SF members stood at attention near the hanger when we passed. The one closest to us nodded as the members carrying my bags trailed behind us.

"Where are we going?" I asked.

"To my little home. It's only a few minutes' walk up this way, and it's absolutely fantastic. There are two bedrooms, a stocked fridge, a TV with all of the channels you could ever imagine, and there's even a *pool* in the backyard! Can you believe it? I've been sunbathing and swimming every day. It's absolutely amazing."

My sister's ecstatic expression only made me shake my head and smile more. "You're making it sound like you're on a trip."

She laughed, that tinkling sound like a soothing balm to my nerves. "It feels like one in a way, although most vacas don't come with hot guards holding particle guns." She waggled her eyebrows and side-eyed the guards we'd just passed.

I muffled a snort. "I don't think I packed a bathing suit."

She patted my hand. "Don't worry. I packed a dozen."

"Why am I not surprised?"

She grinned, her eyes sparkling in the starlight. "Isn't it nice to be out of Chicago with winter looming? I asked Commander Klebus to send me somewhere sunny and hot."

I frowned, the first time I'd done so since arriving. I'd just spent the past twenty-four hours running around naked outside with slushy snow on the ground and hadn't felt cold at all. So while my sister may be enjoying the dry, hot climate, I didn't know if I would.

"Why the sad face again?" she asked, her lips out in a pout.

I immediately forced a smile. "No sad faces. Only happy ones from here on out."

CHAPTER TEN

I didn't tell Tessa about my new werewolf side until the next day. By the time we arrived at her home, I'd been so tired and hungry that I didn't have the energy for anything else. But Tess obviously knew something was up when I polished off two frozen pizzas, all by myself, before going to bed.

So the next morning when we sat around the breakfast table, as that itching began in my chest again—yep, Mrs. Wolf was *not* happy that it appeared I was settling in here—I finally spilled the beans.

I told Tessa everything. About the mate bond Kaillen felt toward me. How he'd bound me to him with his blood. How that binding had also born some serious werewolf mojo in me and I now had a wolf of my own. And then there was my awakening power, that I'd sadly neglected in the past few days as I tried to get used to the latest hurdle thrown at me.

When I finished, Tessa sat in stunned silence, but I also caught the envy in her gaze. My sister had barely recognizable magic. She could cast a few spells and had enough magic to use portals, but that was about it, and now I'd just unloaded on her that on top of my incredibly strong witch magic and my forbidden power, I also had my new awakening power *and* all of the magic that came with being a werewolf.

"Please don't look at me like that," I finally said and dropped my eyes down to my coffee cup. "I can't help how I was born, and I can't help that Kaillen turned me into this."

She bit her lip, then a forced smile streaked across her face. "Well, I guess that would explain the pizzas last night and your, uh, large breakfast this morning."

I'd eaten an entire box of cereal that had been covered with a gallon of milk. I gave a meager smile. "Maybe I should start using mixing bowls as my place setting. Then I can honestly say I only had one bowl of cereal."

She laughed, the sound genuine, but I still caught that envious gleam in her eyes.

"Don't hold this against me too," I said, returning my attention to my cup. "I didn't steal anything from you in utero, Tess, and none of what I have now was stolen from you either. This is just how we were made, how we were born—minus the werewolf part—and it's really awful if you keep begrudging me for it."

I didn't look up at her, not right away, because I'd never said that so plainly to her before. Well, not without a lot of anger behind it 'cause she usually brought up her theory of me stealing her powers in utero when we were in the middle of a fight. But now, we weren't fighting, and I needed my sister to be on my side.

Her eyes softened when I finally looked up. "I don't hold it against you, Tala Bala. Am I jealous?" Her smile trembled. "I would be lying if I said I wasn't. Of course, I am. I've always been jealous of your power, but at the same time, I know it's not your fault that I don't have any of it."

She reached across the table and squeezed my hand, and a rush of such gratitude filled me that I squeezed her right back.

But I obviously didn't realize how hard I'd squeezed until she yelped and pulled her hand back, flapping it in the air. "Ouch, girl! Watch those new werewolf powers of yours!"

She fanned her hand again, and I gave a sheepish smile. "Sorry, I'm still getting used to it." I let my head fall into my hands before sighing heavily. "It's just so much, you know? First the new awakening power and now this. It's a lot."

"I'm sure it is."

And for some strange reason, my sister actually sounded genuine.

My shoulders relaxed more as some of the stress I was feeling lifted.

"So where do you think your new power comes from?" she asked. "The one that sucks others' magic from them?"

I took another sip of coffee. "No idea, but I can't help but think about something Mom told us. Remember when we were kids and she told us how important it was that we keep my forbidden power a secret?"

Tessa's lips pressed together as her cheeks flushed, but she nodded as an ashy scent rose from her.

"You don't need to feel guilty. I've forgiven you for telling Star Tattoo Dude." I reached across the table to her.

"His name was Preston," she said primly.

I rolled my eyes. "Whatever. Any guy who works for Jakub doesn't deserve a name if you ask me."

She tapped her chin. "True."

"Anyway, do you remember what Mom said?"

Tessa leaned back in her chair and propped a knee up. She was already in her neon-orange string bikini with the straps bowed-tied at her hips and around her neck. A kimono-styled sarong covered it. The sheer material reminded me of tropical cruises, but the material's flimsiness did little to hide the body her bikini had on full display.

"She was always talking about how we couldn't tell anyone because of the Bone Eaters." Tessa scrunched her nose up. "Is that right?"

"Yeah, that's what I remember too. She said to never tell anyone and to keep it a secret at all costs or the Bone Eaters could be summoned. That's what I remember most of all, the word *summon*."

Tessa leaned forward, dropping her chin into her palm as her excited expression grew. "Do you think since the word is now out about your powers that they will be summoned?"

I made a sour face. "You don't have to look so happy about that."

"But it could be exciting."

"Or I could end up dead."

"Oh pooh." She waved a hand at me. "You're too strong for that. Look at how you rescued me in New York."

"With the help of Kaillen. I couldn't have done that on my own." Thinking about the hunter brought a sharp pang of longing to my chest. My wolf stirred, beginning to pace again in my belly as she had done on and off all morning. I quickly shoved that feeling down.

Tessa cocked her head. "Couldn't you have saved me by yourself, though? With all of your power now, I bet you could have."

Hearing that reminded me of what Kaillen had started calling me. *Colantha.* He equated me to a fae animal that was queen of her jungle, and apparently, my sister had taken a similar mindset.

My wolf began to wag her tail since my thoughts had shifted to her mate again.

That's not important! I told her. I called upon my witch magic, doing my best to maintain a barrier between me and my wolf. My wolf's lips curled and her hackles rose, but I just piled more magic into my invisible barrier. So far, I hadn't shifted or lost control, and I wanted it to stay that way.

"Anyway," I said, shaking my head once I felt any urges from my wolf receding. "We're getting off track. I want to learn more about the Bone Eaters and who they are. I mean, if they even exist, because I can't help but think that my awakening power is tied to my forbidden one, which means this new power could also be related to the Bone Eaters."

"Okay," my sister replied with a shrug, then began to inspect her nails.

I bit my lip as I thought back to what Prisha had said the morning after the first abduction attempt on me. My bestie had brought up a very good point, saying that Jakub-Dipshit may somehow be in cahoots with the Bone Eaters. Or . . .

I sat up straighter. What if Jakub *was* a Bone Eater? Perhaps that was why he was after me.

My heart pounded more. I nudged my sister when she continued inspecting her latest coat of nail polish. "I'm serious, Tess. We need to figure out who they are. What if Jakub's one of them?"

She dropped her hand, her eyes widening. "Do you think he could be?"

"I don't know, but I know he's after me. *Really* after me."

"But who summoned him?"

"You and your big mouth?"

She blanched.

I quickly put an arm around her. "I'm sorry. I'm not blaming you. Honestly, I'm not. At this point, we can't change the past, but now that my secret's out, we need to figure out what exactly is going on."

"Okay, you're right." She nodded, her dangling earrings swaying with the movement. "And since I . . . told someone about your forbidden power, I suppose that means I'm obligated to help."

My jaw dropped. Had my sister just taken responsibility for her actions? I snapped my mouth closed and squeezed her again. "You'll help me?"

Tess gave me a small smile. "I can look into it for you, if you'd like."

"How would you do that?" I waved at the small airy home and desolate surroundings out the window. "There's not much going on around here, and since they don't let you use the internet or your phone, how would you find anything?"

Her smile turned coy. "Well, one thing I've learned in the past week is that the SF has access to these *huge* libraries that contain information on pretty much everything. One of the members on this base, Archie, is obsessed with them. I could ask him to do some research for me, maybe even join him."

I laughed, then nudged her playfully. "Pretty sure Commander Klebus won't let you leave the base to do library research about a potentially mythical group."

"But if she didn't know that I left the base, then it would be fine."

I scowled. "Tess, you can't do that. Jakub is actively hunting me, and he could pursue you to get to me if the opportunity arose. Besides, you *promised* me you wouldn't do anything like that."

She sighed and flopped back on her chair. "Fine. Okay, I

won't leave, but I could still ask Archie to take a look and see what he finds."

I pulled my bottom lip into my mouth as I thought about it. "Don't you think Archie will want to know why we're curious about a group called the Bone Eaters? You can't tell anyone else about my forbidden power or my new one."

She gave me a sly look. "You underestimate me, Tala. Leave Archie to me. I'll have him like putty in my hands within the week, and I won't have to tell him anything you don't want him knowing. Promise."

I laughed, 'cause Tessa was right. My sister may not have a lot of magic, and she might be flighty as hell, but when it came to charming people—especially those of the opposite sex—she was truly a master.

"So who is this guy?"

"One of the new members that works in the command center here. He's involved in the intelligence side, not the fighting units. Kinda like Carlos is." She dropped the hair she was twirling. "How is Carlos anyway? He didn't look happy about you and the Fire Wolf sitting so closely after you—" She swallowed, and a slight uptick in her heart rate followed, the sound like a steady thud to my enhanced hearing. "After you fell out of your window."

I placed my hand over hers. "I never got to thank you for saving me."

She scoffed. "I didn't save you. Your hunter did."

"But you called him. If you hadn't, I'd be dead."

She swallowed again, and tears formed in her eyes. "Let's not talk about things like that."

My own eyes moistened, and once again, I felt so damned grateful that we were both still okay and safe. "Fair enough. But as for Carlos . . ." I sighed and told her about his letter, then how he'd acted in Chicago before I'd flown here.

"You're kidding. He wants to get back together even though Kaillen's in your life now?"

I gave her a perplexed look.

She rolled her eyes. "Tala, come on. Anyone can see that you and that hunter are meant for each other."

I shifted on my seat, my wolf perking up again inside me. "That's not true. His wolf is interested in me, and now my wolf is interested in him. That's kinda different than *him* wanting me."

"Oh, please." She gave a dismissive wave. "So what if your wolves are the driving factor. There are a lot of very happy mated werewolf couples who gave in to the mating bond. Just let it happen."

"But it's not *real*."

"It's real to all of them."

Her words made me pause, and for the first time since Kaillen had walked into my life, I wondered if I'd been looking at this all wrong, 'cause my sister had a point. A *lot* of mated couples were very happy together, even if the bond had forced the arrangement.

I sighed. "Okay, this conversation is getting too heavy for nine in the morning." I yawned, still feeling sleep-deprived since I'd arrived here so late. "So what are we doing today?" I was guessing her agenda included sunbathing and swimming, given what she was wearing, but a knock came on the door before she could answer.

Tessa sprang out of her chair, her sarong flowing behind her as she pranced to the door.

"Good morning, ma'am," I heard a masculine voice call from the entryway. A pause came next. "Are you Tessa or Tala?"

I angled my head to get a better view of them.

"I'm Tessa!" My sister beamed.

The newcomer, a freshly scrubbed new recruit from the looks of it since he didn't look much older than eighteen, stood at the threshold.

When he caught me peeking in his direction, he dipped his head. "Ma'am, Commander Klebus just arrived, and she's requesting to see you."

CHAPTER ELEVEN

I joined my sister at the front door. "Commander Klebus is here? I thought she was still in Chicago?"

"She's here now," the young SF member replied, "and it's important that she speak with you."

A frown tugged at my lips, as Tessa held the door open for me with a wink. I pinched her arm 'cause all my sister heard was that an SF Commander had flown all the way here to see me, which in my sister's mind meant *exciting things were on the horizon.* Never mind that those exciting things could be bad news for all.

"Stay here and stay out of trouble," I said to her in a stern voice.

Her only response was a cheeky grin as I closed the door behind me.

Outside, the air was hot and dry, reminding me of an oven baking brick stones until they were crisp and dusty. Fanning myself, I longed for a hat.

"You'll get used to the heat," the young private said, obviously noticing that I was melting.

"If you say so."

He chuckled.

I fanned myself again and asked, "Did the commander say what she wanted me for?"

"She didn't, ma'am."

He rounded a bend in the walkway, and with a start, I realized neither of our footsteps made a sound. Given the private's build, I guessed he was a werewolf, since he moved with the smooth grace that was so common among that species. *My* new species.

My nose twitched, and I subtly inhaled, remembering what Kaillen had said about needing to learn how to use my newly enhanced senses better. A slight scent drifted from the young SF member, hinting at earth and pine. The same subtle fragrance had clung to Kaillen, Carlos, and Cameron. A werewolf's aroma.

Holy shit, I just identified his species through his scent. That realization made me strangely giddy.

"Right this way." The private steered me toward the large concrete building that I'd gotten a glimpse of last night but hadn't seen yet in broad daylight. It rose two stories and took up roughly a city block of space. While it wasn't overly large, it looked intimidating, and I figured it was the command center Tessa had spoken of.

We marched toward it as the sun shone brightly overhead. The entire landscape was awash with light so piercing that I wished again for a hat or sunglasses. Dusty hills rose around the base as arid mountains filled the distance. We were definitely in some remote desert.

When we reached the command center, the SF member scanned his hand, then a robotic voice greeted him before the door clicked open.

"Ma'am?" the private said politely. He held the door open for me.

"Ladies first?" I gave him a small smile.

The corner of his mouth tugged up. "Yes, ma'am. It's how my mama raised me."

I detected a slight southern accent in his words and wondered what pack he heralded from. There were only three werewolf packs in the United States but they all originated in the western states: Montana, Idaho, and Wyoming. Yet, sub-branches of those packs existed in other states as well, although they were still ruled by an alpha in the western region. I figured this private hailed from a sub-branch down south.

"Thank you," I said and stepped inside.

The door closed behind us as cool air conditioning washed over my skin. I inhaled the sterile odor of cleaning solution and the tangy wards surrounding the building. There were no frills or unnecessary artwork on the walls. Everything was orderly, precise, and stark. Magic swam in the air letting me know the entire perimeter had solid wards and probably illusion spells too. This command center reminded me a bit of Chicago's SF division.

"This way." The private led me down a long hall to

another door, and after scanning us in, I stepped into a small conference room.

Commander Klebus sat at a table, another SF member beside her, but when I saw what was on the table, all of my attention was focused there.

"Where did you get those?" My eyes turned to saucers.

"I see you recognize them." The vampire commander waved to the blue cuffs on the table, the same blue cuffs that Jakub's thugs had shackled me and the Fire Wolf with, which had contained our magic.

"Yeah, you could say that."

The young private who escorted me saluted Commander Klebus before leaving the room. My eyes darted to the SF member that sat at the commander's side. I didn't recognize him. He appeared to be tall, although it was hard to say for sure since he was sitting. His bright orange hair flashed in the light, and his face was angular, his ears slightly pointed, and a heavy pulse of magic swam around him.

A fairy, who I guessed was a high-ranking SF member since he seemed so casual around Klebus. When he saw me assessing him, he gave a polite nod.

The vampire commander inclined her head toward him. "Tala, this is Major Bavar Fieldstone from our Idaho headquarters."

Idaho? The SF's headquarters sat just outside of Boise, hidden amidst the hills from humans. Yet within that vacant area the sprawling Supernatural Forces lay. It held a bustling command center, a huge training facility, and barracks for hundreds of SF members. It was where all new recruits went to train once they'd joined the SF ranks. I'd never been there so had no idea what it actually entailed, but that was what Carlos had told me.

"Major Fieldstone has joined this investigation due to a few setbacks we've had." Commander Klebus waved toward the seat across from them. "Please sit."

"Setbacks?" I asked curiously as I pulled my chair out.

She gestured toward the cuffs, ignoring my question. "I'd like you to formally identify these for me if you will. Do you recognize them?"

I settled in my seat. "Yeah, those are what Jakub placed on me and Mr. King when we were captured. Where did you get them?"

"Mr. King gave them to us."

My jaw dropped. *"What?"*

She cocked her head. "He didn't tell you?"

I somehow managed to pick my jaw up off the floor as annoyance swirled through me. "No, he failed to mention that." *Just another secret he kept from me.* "But where did he get them?"

"He said that the man who tried to abduct you in Philadelphia dropped them when he fled. Mr. King retrieved them before contacting us."

So he'd not only gone to his man cave to get his ax as I'd sat bloody and helpless in his living room in Montana, but he'd also gone back to Philadelphia to get the cuffs he'd obviously seen left behind. I didn't remember Jakub dropping them, but I had suffered a concussion, so who knew what else I'd missed.

Bottom line? Kaillen was still keeping secrets from me. My stomach roiled, hurt and anger swirling through me simultaneously.

Commander Klebus studied me, as if deciphering an organism under a microscope.

I forced a sweet smile, and hoped I didn't look like an open book right now, because I was freakin' pissed.

Her nostrils flared slightly, her intrigued look growing.

Crap. I did a quick self-assessment of my cloaking spell. It was still as sturdy and strong as ever, yet I knew if the commander got a whiff of my new werewolf fragrance that her assessing gaze would turn as sharp as a razor until she pried everything from me.

Shit on a brick.

But all she said was, "Interesting."

I forced a bright smile. "Was that all you needed from me? To verify that those cuffs were used by Jakub?"

"Not exactly." Major Bavar Fieldstone leaned forward, his words crisp and slightly lilting in their accent. "What we've discovered is that these cuffs were specifically designed for you and Mr. King. From the report I've read, it seems the cuffs they placed on Mr. King in New York didn't fully contain his power. Is that correct?"

My heart began to hammer. "Correct."

Of course, I neglected to mention that the only reason those cuffs hadn't held him was because my extreme magic had managed to thin them after I'd combined some spells, and then my forbidden power had multiplied Kaillen's strength beyond measure, and the hunter had been able to shatter them. Without my witch spells and forbidden power, the cuffs would have held.

"And then it sounds like the cuffs were altered, so they were stronger when they captured you in Oak Trembler. Am I correct thus far?"

I managed to meet Bavar's gaze straight on. "Yes, that's right."

He settled back in his chair, the picture of nonchalance. "Very interesting indeed. Consequently, we've been investigating these lovely contraptions, because they are a very dangerous item for someone to possess. Luckily, we believe we've come up with a solution for their nasty side effects, but we can't be certain until we test them."

I arched an eyebrow. "Let me guess, the testing somehow involves me?"

"Yes." Commander Klebus waved toward the cuffs. "The reason I asked you here is because we need you specifically for the test. Our witches and sorcerers have developed a spell that we believe will counteract the debilitating magic of these cuffs. If the spell is successful, you should be able to break out of these shackles as Kaillen did in New York. However, without you or Mr. King to test the spell on, we've been unable to verify its viability."

"You asked Kaillen here too?" My wolf perked right up at that comment, her tail thumping madly.

"Not here, specifically. We invited him to our Chicago

division to have the spell placed on him." Her lips pursed. "He's still considering it."

Of course he was.

"But we are delighted to have you with us today," Major Fieldstone said with a flourish.

I eyed those hateful blue cuffs again. They weren't glowing. They simply appeared to be metallic cuffs with a robin's-egg-blue sheen. So deceiving. "And if the spell works, those cuffs won't contain my magic anymore?"

"Correct." Bavar smiled, a flash of his sharp teeth making an appearance.

I nodded. "Okay, that's fine. One question, though. How long will the spell last?"

"That is a very excellent question, indeed," Bavar replied. "If the spell works as predicted, you will have immunity from these cuffs indefinitely."

My spine snapped into a straight line. "Seriously? Then sign me up." 'Cause if Jakub did get his hands on me again, I knew his beloved blue cuffs would be part of my capture, yet if I could break out of them . . .

Major Fieldstone stood, his uniform crisp and his orange hair glowing in the overhead lights. He bowed slightly. "If you would be so kind as to follow me." He gestured toward the corner door.

I rounded the table, passing Commander Klebus on the way. Her nostrils flared, her gaze narrowing. Something in her face flickered, as though . . .

I quickly checked my cloaking spell again, but it was still in place. My witch magic, otherworldly powers, and werewolf capabilities were all hidden. Still, that look on her face remained.

I made a beeline for the corner.

Major Fieldstone pushed through the door, and it opened to a large training room. "We're ready for you, Eleni," he called to someone across the room.

Commander Klebus followed behind us and cast me another shrewd glance as her nostrils flared a second time.

It took everything in me not to fidget. Instead, I did my best to appear unaffected by her calculating assessment while remaining the portrait of innocence. But if there was one thing I knew about Commander Klebus it was that she wasn't easily deceived. I'd have to make sure to keep my distance from her after this, just in case she could detect changes in me through my cloaking spell.

Thankfully, everyone's attention shifted to the woman gliding across the room toward us. She wore a hijab of glistening purple silk, and her ochre complexion was clear and bright, hinting at her youth. Midnight-black hair peeked out of the top of her hijab.

"Eleni is one of our most talented up-and-coming witches," Major Fieldstone said with a smile. "She was instrumental in producing this exciting new spell."

I gave the young witch a hello. She returned it, then bobbed her head at the major. "May I, sir?"

Bavar swirled his hands elegantly in my direction. "By all means, please begin. Ms. Davenport has given her consent."

Eleni approached me on graceful steps. Her rosebud

mouth lifted in a small smile, and I was struck by how calm and composed she looked. It was unusual to see that kind of demeanor in someone so young.

"You might feel some tingling, but it shouldn't hurt." She lifted her hands and began to weave her fingers languidly through the air while whispering a spell. It was a long one, and what I caught of it told me that it was a mixture of complicated maximizer and cloaking spells.

When she finished, a subtle feeling washed over me that was there one moment and then gone in the next. It didn't have the same heavy feeling that my daily cloaking spell gave me, but it tingled and sparked my nerves, letting me know that it was strong.

"Did you invent that?" I asked her.

She bobbed her head. "With the help of my mentor."

"Shall we?" Major Fieldstone held out the cuffs.

I gave him my wrists. "And if this spell doesn't work? Do you have a plan to get those off me?"

"Of course." Commander Klebus crossed her arms. "Your mate has told us he possesses an ax that is capable of breaking them. If needed, we will call upon him."

My stomach fluttered at the mention of Kaillen again. My wolf wasn't any better. Once again, she was yelping and whining inside me, eager to be reunited with Mr. Swoony Wolf Hunter.

"Let's hope that the spell works," I muttered under my breath.

"What was that?" Bavar asked.

I flashed a smile. "Nothing. Go ahead and put them on."

He snapped the cuffs around my wrists, and that buzzing feeling washed over my skin when their power activated, but even though that draining feeling didn't begin, a fearful tremor ran through me as a memory flashed to the front of my mind. It was of Cameron betraying me, when he'd clamped identical cuffs around my wrists and had taken me from Kaillen's cabin. He'd laughed at my terror. Actually *laughed*.

Rage began to burn inside me, and I used that emotion to channel my witch magic while letting it hum through my body.

"It might be best if we all take a step back." Bavar waved Eleni and Commander Klebus to the corner. "Try your best, Tala."

The cuffs' magic buzzed along my skin, and a moment of trepidation washed through me as I dipped my concentration inward and tugged at my witch magic. My witch powers swelled and rose as I called upon a maximizer spell. They responded normally, but I wouldn't know if the immunity spell had worked until that power reached my fingertips.

I closed my eyes. *Here goes nothing.* With an explosion of power, I jolted a maximizer spell down my arms into my hands. When my magic reached my fingertips, I held my breath, but my spell flowed right out of me and engulfed me in momentary power. I wrenched my arms apart as hard as I could and felt my new werewolf strength inadvertently rise.

The cuffs snapped, easily breaking in two.

My jaw dropped when I beheld my free hands.

"It worked!" Grinning, I lifted my arms and stared at the separated metallic bands. The glow emitting from them flickered and then vanished, their metallic blue sheen turning dull and lifeless. All of the cuffs' magic that had been buzzing along my skin disappeared with it.

Eleni clapped in delight.

Commander Klebus eyed me, then inhaled again. "Very impressive . . . for a witch."

My face paled as a knowing look grew in her eye.

"Do you care to share with us how you broke them?" the commander added.

"I used a maximizer spell, and, um . . ."

We stared at one another, and with a sickening sense of dread, I realized she knew that witch magic alone couldn't have broken those cuffs. Even without the cuffs' magic containing my witch power, I'd just broken through *a metal chain*. A stronger species of supernatural—a vampire, werewolf, or fairy—could have done that as easily as I had. But a witch? Probably not. Even with a strong maximizer spell, that kind of strength would be incredibly rare, yet I'd just ripped through the cuffs' thick metal chains like tissue paper. I hadn't even struggled thanks to my wolf.

And Commander Klebus had seen that.

I ground my teeth together. Smart, wily, Commander Klebus. She'd tricked me after all.

I realized that was part of the reason she'd flown all of the way here. The SF could have used any supernatural to test Eleni's spell but they'd chosen me.

Because Commander Klebus wanted to know what I was capable of. I'd seen hints of her knowing looks before —her suspicion that I was hiding who I really was—and I'd just given her a front-row seat to it, proving beyond any doubt that her guesses had been correct. I wasn't a weak witch, and I wasn't just a witch.

Such an idiot, Tala!

Because the growing look in the commander's eye—the look she'd often reserved for Kaillen—told me that the Supernatural Forces would be knocking on my door in the near future in order to recruit me, just like they had done with Kaillen.

So much for anonymity. That was officially a life I no longer led.

I sighed in defeat, but then tried to cheer myself up. At least with Eleni's spell, I was immune to Jakub cuffing me in the future. But I'd just sacrificed my hidden identity to get that immunity.

Perhaps that had been Commander Klebus's endgame all along.

The vamp gave me a pleasant smile, her smugness disappearing. "Tala, would you be open to letting us test you—"

"No." I held up a hand, cutting her off. "I'm not open to any further testing, but I would like the SF to do one thing. Will you tell Kaillen that Eleni's spell works? If Jakub gets a hold of him again, he won't be able to break through those cuffs without Eleni's spell since they'll contain his were-wolf power and . . . other things," I added vaguely, since I had no idea if the SF knew the extent of his sorcerer magic. But the thought of Jakub getting his hands on the hunter twisted my stomach into waves of nausea. "He needs to be able to break them too."

"Of course." Bavar gave a graceful bow as the smug expression returned to Commander Klebus's face.

Yep, bitch. You won.

"We'll contact him again," Bavar added. "And we'll make sure he's offered the same immunity you now have."

"Thank you," I replied.

Something buzzed on Commander Klebus's wrist, and her communication device flashed. The smugness vanished from her features when she read whatever message she'd just been sent. She showed it to Major Fieldstone, and they shared a concerned look. After placing an earbud in their ears, both hurried to the corner to accept the call in private.

Eleni glided to my side to inspect what was left of the cuffs, but my ears pricked toward the commanders' conversation.

"Dammit," Commander Klebus said under her breath as she spoke through her device to whoever had contacted her. "If red tape is the reason that we're unable to capture him, I'm going to be furious!"

Silence followed while the speaker on the end of the line said something.

"Yes, right away," she replied. "Yes, he's with me now. We'll discuss further."

After they finished their call, Bavar sighed. "He's quite

evasive, is he not? Since the Supernatural Forces' jurisdiction ends with earth, what better place for him to escape to than my realm?"

"Hopefully you can help with that." Commander Klebus's lips thinned. "Have you spoken with the king and queen?"

"I have. My uncle and aunt are currently discussing whether or not they will allow SF squads into the fae lands to conduct the arrest."

Bavar's uncle and aunt are the king and queen of the fae lands? That would mean that Bavar was a royal fae. I frowned as I continued listening.

"Have they said how long their discussions will take?" Commander Klebus asked.

The bite in her tone had me wincing.

"No, but I'm hoping not long," Bavar replied.

Her nostrils flared. "Our new intel says Jakub was last seen headed toward Culasberee, north of the capital. We'll lose his location if we don't act soon."

I sucked in a breath. *Holy shit, they have a locate on Jakub!*

Even though my heart began pounding two hundred times a minute, I pretended to be preoccupied with what Eleni was doing. I kept my attention on the cuffs as the young witch worked through them with a metal cutter that she'd extracted from her pocket. Now that the cuffs were no longer magical, they'd lost their inherent strength. The metal cutter groaned as it cut through the thick bands, but the cutter was spelled, so it was able to do so somewhat easily.

I kept my eyes downcast, but my attention stayed on the commanders' conversation. Since they had no idea that I was now also part werewolf—even though Klebus knew I possessed strange powers that rivaled Kaillen's—they wouldn't know that I could hear everything they were saying.

Thank you, Mrs. Wolf.

My wolf straightened, her head cocking. For the first time since she'd been born inside me, I felt thankful for her presence. If it wasn't for her, I would have no clue that Jakub had escaped to the fae lands and that—from the sounds of it—the Supernatural Forces had run into bureaucratic issues given the governance of that land. The bastard was currently getting away.

"There you are. Do your wrists feel okay?" Eleni set the metal cutter aside and gave me a tentative smile.

I jolted my attention back to her and rubbed my wrists, just to make her think I was considering her question. "I feel fine. Thank you."

She bobbed her head.

"Please ask your uncle and aunt to grant access to our forces *now*," Commander Klebus said to Bavar. "If we don't catch him, I fear we'll have lost our opportunity to stop him once and for all, because if he's headed toward Culasberee, he might be headed for the sea. If that happens, it'll be harder to track him."

Bavar dipped his head. "I shall send them another message, although I can't guarantee if they'll feel the need to address it. They have meetings with the Solis fairies all week."

"They need to." Commander Klebus's lips pursed. "And while we're waiting, we need to ensure all of the activated squads are administered Eleni's immunity spell. We need all of them immune before we act."

Bavar inclined his head. "Right you are. I shall speak with my aunt and uncle promptly while you administer the spell to the squads."

"Yes, good plan." Icy rage was still etched into Commander Klebus's face, but when she saw that Eleni was done working with me, she strode my way.

Some of her ire melted away, from practiced force no doubt, as she held out her card to me. "We should meet soon, to discuss a few things."

I took her card automatically and gave a weak smile.

"I'm glad to see that new spell works," she added. "If nothing else, you now have the added protection of no longer being susceptible to those cuffs." She gestured me toward the door I'd used to enter the training room. "Private Wilson will escort you back to your residence. I look forward to seeing you soon."

With that, she turned on her heel.

A sick feeling churned in my stomach as I watched her depart. No way in hell would I be able to hide who I was from the locals in Chicago anymore. Tess and I were going to have to have some serious discussions about the future of Practically Perfect.

Sighing, I joined the young private again as he led me out of the room and down the halls.

But despite all that I'd unwittingly revealed to the vampire commander, that wasn't where my thoughts turned.

My mind was reeling because Jakub had fled to the fae lands and was on his way to Culasberee. The Supernatural Forces were currently unable to pursue him due to jurisdiction issues, and unless the fae lands' king and queen granted permission for the SF to enter shortly, Jakub could escape *again*. And from the sounds of it, Commander Klebus was worried he was going to do that via the sea, in which they would have a harder time tracking him.

I barely noticed the hot sun beating down on me when we stepped back outside.

My brow furrowed as the private escorted me back to Tessa's bungalow. The entire time, I contemplated what I could do to stop Jakub once and for all.

My wolf yelped in excitement as my plan began to take hold.

CHAPTER TWELVE

Tessa was the epitome of a relaxed sunbathing goddess when I found her lounging by the pool. Her blond hair was splayed out around her as sunglasses perched on her nose, while her tanned skin glistened in the sunlight.

"Tess!" I hurried to her side as my wolf continued to yelp in excitement inside me.

My twin slid her glasses down and eyed me over the rims. "Grab a suit from my room. You can't sunbathe in *that*."

"I can't stay here. I have to go."

She bolted upright. "Go? What are you talking about? You just got here."

"I know, and I'm sorry, but I need to contact Kaillen. Is there anywhere on this base that I can use a phone?"

Her forehead crinkled when she frowned. "No, they don't let us use phones. The one time I did was to contact

Nicole, and it was in the command center under supervision on a scrambled line."

"So there *are* phones here."

"Yes, but only in the command center, but we can't go in there." She swung her legs over the side of her lounge chair. "Why do you need to call Kaillen?"

"I have to tell him something, but I can't let Klebus know that I overheard her. She already knows enough about me," I added in a mumble under my breath.

Tessa pulled her sunglasses fully off, and an excited sparkle entered her sapphire eyes. "What did you overhear?"

"I can't tell you either. Only in case Klebus questions you," I added when she pouted. "Where else would there be a phone outside of the command center?" 'Cause even though I had a lot of talents, even my magic couldn't break into a secured SF building.

Tessa tapped her chin, her manicured pink fingernail shining from a recently applied polish. "There might be a phone in the hanger. We could try there."

"We?"

She gave me a devious smile. "You don't think I'm going to let you have all the fun while I stay here, do you?"

I rolled my eyes, but then a small smile parted my lips. "Do you think you could wield some of your charm on the guards while I search the hanger?"

Tessa jumped to her feet, her breasts bobbing with the movement. "Well, if I go like this . . ." She struck a pose, showcasing her tanned curves that her bikini did little to conceal. "I imagine I can distract the entire battalion."

I snorted but couldn't stop my grin. "I do love you, you know that, right?"

She winked. "Just like I love you. Now, let's go find you a phone!"

INSIDE THE BUNGALOW, Tessa dropped her Kimono-style sarong on the floor and picked up a sheer scarf. She wrapped it around her waist until it resembled a see-through mini-skirt. Following that, she donned a large T-shirt that she tied into a knot just below her breastbone, which exposed her abdomen.

"I'm ready!" she said excitedly. When I raised a questioning eyebrow at her attire, she merely added, "Trust me."

Nerves fluttered anew in my belly when Tessa and I left her bungalow. We followed the same walkway that the young private had led me on. Cactuses and creosote bushes lined the path, along with other desert plants I couldn't identify. Their scents hung heavy in the air as I tried to differentiate what was what and failed miserably. I sighed. Kaillen did say it would take time to learn individual scents.

"They let you go wherever you want around here?" I asked incredulously when she veered onto another side-walk that led to the hanger.

She shrugged. "There's nowhere for me to get lost, so they said as long as I stay on the base, I'm free to roam."

"Lucky for us."

"We should go this way." Tessa waved toward the hanger's south side. "That's where only men are stationed. Around the opposite side and the far end, there are women too."

I chuckled. "And my guess is that whatever you have planned needs a male audience only?"

"Well, heterosexual males." She winked.

My cheeks reddened at just the thought of what my sister had planned. While I wasn't a prude, I was somewhat modest and didn't flaunt myself or show off my curves even though they matched Tessa's. But my sister? She would happily prance around in a string bikini in Times Square if it meant enrapturing others.

When we neared the hanger, sweat beaded on my forehead and it wasn't from the sun. What we were about to pull off would land us in a world of shit if we failed.

"Hi there, Private Osmond!" Tessa called coyly to a young SF member stationed near the hanger's large open door. Inside, the aircrafts I'd seen last night sat silently.

"Ms. Davenport." Private Osmond's lips curved when his gaze shifted between the two of us. He glanced at my sister's exposed midriff and sheer skirt before snapping his attention up. "This must be your sister?" he added, although he seemed loathed to drag his gaze from Tessa's display.

"Yeah, this is Tala." Tessa waved flippantly in my direction, then coiled her finger around a long curl of blond hair. "I'm showing her around since she's new. Do you mind if I show her the airplanes?"

He made an apologetic face. "I'm afraid I can't allow you inside."

Tessa pouted prettily. "Even if you joined us?" She glanced toward the taller, dark-haired SF member stationed on the opposite side of the massive hanger door. "Do you think maybe you and Private Fitchberg could give us a tour? If it's not too much to ask," she added in a hurry with just the right amount of pleading and consideration.

Private Osmond looked toward the other SF member who'd begun striding toward us from across the eighty-foot expanse.

"These two want a tour!" Private Osmond called to him. "Do you think it'd be okay?"

Private Fitchberg reached us and eyed Tessa first, his gaze also lingering on my sister's considerable display of flesh before eyeing me.

My nose twitched as a subtle scent rose from him. It was musky yet not outright arousal, but it was similar. Interest, maybe? Or something that meant she'd caught his attention? I wasn't sure.

"I suppose that would be okay." Private Fitchberg shrugged. "But you'll have to stay with us. This isn't a civilian area."

Tessa ran her finger idly up his arm. That scent off him rose, but then she pretended to pick a speck of lint from his shoulder, before giving him a suggestive smile. "We'll stay right by your side. Promise."

Private Fitchberg grinned cockily. Okay, the dude was definitely interested.

"This way." Private Osmond gestured toward the aircraft.

"Wow, they're so big!" Tessa's eyes widened when we approached the first craft. "Do you two know how to fly them?"

I pretended to also show interest while scoping the far walls for a phone.

"We're in training," Private Fitchberg responded, pride in his tone. "That's part of the reason we're here."

"Do you fly them often?" I asked, just so I wouldn't come off as a complete nincompoop who was incapable of language.

Private Osmond gave me a crooked smile. "Five days a week."

They let us circle each plane, and while they gave us a few details about what each craft was and how they maneuvered, it was pretty obvious that they were intentionally keeping their answers vague. While Tessa may have sparked their interest, neither SF member was stupid enough to reveal classified information.

The entire time, I nodded and smiled while also scanning every wall and cranny for a phone.

When we reached the fourth aircraft, I finally spotted one near the corner door, which was sixty feet away . . .

I pinched Tessa and subtly gestured toward it while

Private Fitchberg explained the aerodynamics of the fourth airplane. She gave me a barely perceptible nod before moving toward the aircraft's nose.

She began fanning herself, pulling her T-shirt away from her breasts before it plastered back onto her. "All of this talk about flying makes me so . . ." She lifted her arm gracefully, then fanned her shirt again. The knot came loose, and she shimmied the shirt over her head, letting it drape down her back in a flourish as her hair flowed around her in loose curls. When Tessa finished, she stood with her shirt in one hand and only wore her string bikini and see-through mini-skirt.

The billowy skirt's material caught the light streaming in through the large door, which gave a perfect outline of her hourglass figure.

Both Privates stopped talking.

"Do you mind? It's just so warm." She smiled teasingly. "I'm sure you're both used to it, since you've been living in this desert for so long, but I come from Chicago where it's so cold, and this heat—" She shrugged and raised the hem of her mini-skirt, giving a flash of her bare upper thighs. She toyed with the hem again, lifting and teasing.

Both privates were outright gaping now. I choked on a laugh, but also knew this was my cue to make a beeline for that phone *now*.

On silent werewolf feet, I blurred to the phone, knowing that all it would take was one glance in my direction from Privates Osmond or Fitchberg to land me in a world of shit.

But Tessa continued her titillating show by bending over to examine parts of the craft or playing with the string on her bikini, nearly "accidentally" untying it at one point and almost revealing her breast.

Needless to say, the young men were entirely transfixed.

The entire time, she kept up a steady stream of conversation, acting so nonchalantly about the whole thing that one would never guess she was knowingly toying with them.

Honestly, my sister would have made an excellent spy. She was that good at manipulating people.

Heart hammering, I thanked the gods that I remembered Kaillen's phone number just as I dialed it.

It rang, then rang again, and I worried he wouldn't answer, but then a deep male voice said, "Hello?"

My insides twisted in juvenile excitement at the sound of his voice, just as my wolf let out an excited whine.

Since I didn't know if the SF recorded all calls, I simply said, "It's me. Can you come here?" I prayed he would recognize my voice and not ask questions. He'd said with the blood bond that he could track me anywhere in the world, and I guessed this would be the true test.

A heartbeat of silence passed before he said, "On my way."

I hung up. At least thirty seconds had passed since I'd blurred to the wall. Tessa now had her mini-skirt off, her string bikini the only thing covering her. She was near the plane's wing, standing on her tiptoes and hopping up and down, pretending to try to see something higher on the plane.

Both privates were staring at her bouncing breasts every time she hopped.

Swallowing a laugh, I blurred back to behind them on silent feet.

Tessa gave me a sly smile when I reappeared right behind the men. I flashed her a thumbs-up, so she yawned, arching her back and drawing even more attention to her mostly naked upper half. "Well, gentlemen, this has truly been a fascinating tour. My sister and I both thank you."

Private Osmond finally dragged his gaze away from my sister's bare body. He cleared his throat. "Of course, ma'am. It was"—he cleared his throat again—"our pleasure."

He did a double take of the area, as if realizing I was no longer at Tessa's side, but then relaxed when he saw me standing just behind Private Fitchberg.

"Thanks for the tour!" I said a little too cheerily.

"Do you two want to join us later by the pool in my backyard?" Tessa asked, while toying with the strap on her top. She slid it to her shoulder, letting it fall just enough that, for a moment, it looked as if her breast would pop out.

Private Osmond's eyes glued to the small triangle of fabric that barely concealed what was beneath. The stench of musk rose so strongly from both squad members, that I had a feeling my sister would be starring in their fantasies for the foreseeable future.

"Um, yeah." Private Fitchberg cleared his throat. "We could do that. Is seventeen hundred okay?"

"Seventeen hundred?" Tess cocked her head.

I almost snorted but managed to swallow down my laughter, because while my sister played the bimbo well, she was anything but stupid. She knew exactly when seventeen hundred was.

"It's five o'clock tonight." Private Osmond's voice dipped. "Seventeen hundred is military time."

"Oh!" she batted her eyelashes. "That sounds perfect! We'll see you two then." She waved playfully, then grabbed my hand.

Her hips swayed the entire time we sauntered out, and I knew, from the aroused scent we left in our wakes, that each private was still watching my sister until we rounded the corner.

Once we were out of eyesight, I couldn't stop my grin. "You're a shameless hussy."

She laughed, then said proudly, "I know."

We both fell into a fit of laughter, and I was about to ask her if she really intended to have both men over tonight, when a siren blared from the command center and electric sparks from the wards flared near the runway.

A dozen SF members ran from around the hanger, particle guns in hand, just as Private Osmond yelled to my sister and me, "Get back to your bungalow *now*!"

My heart jumped into my throat when the wards activated again, a skittering of green sparks shooting across the entire dome. My nostrils flared just as a shape took form outside of the wards.

A large male figure stood only a hundred yards away, testing the wards at this very second. And as the SF mobilized, obviously not knowing if he was friend or foe, a fluttery feeling began in my stomach as I took in the lethal grace with which he prowled along its perimeter, testing and provoking the magical barrier.

"Is that who I think it is?" Tessa whispered in amazement as a flurry of squad members flew past us.

My wolf whined in happiness, and my stomach became a twisting motion of nerves. I fought the excited smile that wanted to curve my lips and managed to reply, "It is."

The Fire Wolf had arrived.

CHAPTER THIRTEEN

"Well, if that's not a completely unnecessary entrance, I don't know what is." Commander Klebus fumed as she stormed by me. "And how the hell did he find this place?"

She began barking orders as the siren finally died from its never-ending wail. The mobilizing squads stopped racing toward where the hunter paced outside of the ward, and the heavy machinery that had appeared from an underground garage—that I hadn't even known existed— retracted back to its subterranean cavern.

"How did he get here so fast?" Tessa asked me under her breath. She hadn't bothered to put her T-shirt back on, and she kept getting double takes from a large majority of squad members.

"Long story." Inside me, my wolf yelped and whined. At least she wasn't pushing against me, so my hands stayed smooth—no wolfy hairs in sight. "Let's see if they'll let him in."

Tessa and I hurried to the edge of the base in time to hear the vamp commander admonish my hunter.

"Mr. King?" Commander Klebus planted her hands on her hips, her short black hair swaying against her shoulders. "Do you realize what kind of commotion you've caused?"

"You have my sincerest apologies," he replied in a mocking purr.

She bristled. "How did you find this place?"

"Not important." He tapped the ward again, since he still stood on the other side of it. Every time he tested it, his contact caused a flare of green sparks to skitter across the entire dome. "Drop this shield, Commander. I would hate to break it because I'm only here to collect my mate, not to cause problems."

Commander Klebus glanced over her shoulder at me, before addressing the hunter again. "You couldn't break this shield if you tried." She seethed, but then a look of worry passed over her face when Kaillen's next tap caused a bolt of electricity to flare on the shield. A tiny crack appeared in it before the ward healed itself.

The commander blanched. Yep, even Commander Klebus had no idea about the power my mate wielded.

Composing herself, she added, "And actually, it *is* important to understand how you found this facility. This is a top-secret location, which has never been breached before. I will need to ask you and your mate to accompany me to a conference room in order to determine how this information was shared."

"I'm afraid that's not possible," he replied smoothly.

My entire body hummed at the sound of his voice, and even though I was making myself stay rooted to the spot, what I truly wanted was to run right through the ward and throw my arms around him. *My mate, my mate, my mate. Mine. Mine. Mine.*

The words echoed in my chest over and over, like an incessant toddler that craved a shiny new toy.

Gods . . . The *pull* this man had on me. The absolute craving that sang in my blood was nearly overwhelming and made me want to act like a complete idiot.

But even knowing that and being aware of how entirely fucked up this was, the need didn't stop. That constant and incessant *want him, need him, must be with him* zinged along my nerves again and again.

I grumbled as the instinctual mate bond nearly over-took me, but I held myself firm, not moving a muscle while feeling truly sorry for every mated werewolf male that had ever lived and hadn't been able to claim their mate. 'Cause if this was what they felt every time their coveted female was in the same room as them, *ugh*, it seriously blowed.

"I'm afraid I can't let you walk out with Ms. Davenport." Commander Klebus crossed her arms, an icy expression on her face.

Kaillen stilled, his expressionless mask falling into

place. "Oh? And why's that?" he asked, his tone deadly calm yet promising violence.

"She's under SF protection."

"Not if she doesn't choose to be."

Commander Klebus advanced on him, stopping just short of the ward so they were nearly standing toe to toe. "She requested my help. I would consider that a choice."

"Actually," I said, stepping forward, "I would prefer to go with Mr. King."

Commander Klebus rounded on me. "Come again?"

"I'm sorry, but I don't want to stay here anymore." Might as well not beat around the bush. "I want to leave with him."

Ire flashed in her blue eyes, and her lips thinned. "Did you tell him about this location?"

"Of course not. I don't even know where we are."

"Then how did he find this place?"

"I'm a hunter. It's what I do," he replied from behind her.

She whipped back to face him, an incredulous expression forming on her face that was quickly replaced with wary excitement. "You could track her *here*? To a place clouded in illusion spells?"

He smirked, the portrait of male arrogance. Such a deceiving ass, but I couldn't stop my smile. "I could indeed."

"Fascinating," she whispered, so quietly, that only my enhanced werewolf hearing allowed me to hear her.

"Despite how enamored you are with me, Commander,

I'm afraid I can't stay to chat. If you would release Ms. Davenport, we'll be on our way."

Her eyes narrowed. "I'll need to complete the necessary paperwork first. This is highly irregular."

"So you say." His expression stayed disinterested, but when he locked gazes with me, a pulse of attraction sparked between us, so magnetic and hot that I swore it created an actual energy field.

My wolf whined in excitement again, and it took everything in me not to make a complete fool of myself and throw myself at him. Of course, that would only result in me slamming into the invisible wards and probably being electrocuted or something equally horrific in the process. Still, the *need*, the pull . . .

His lips curved, his nostrils flaring, as if he'd caught my excited scent even though that wasn't possible through the ward.

Commander Klebus snapped her fingers toward a young SF member. "Let Mr. King in."

"Yes, ma'am." The private hurried forward, then directed the hunter to an area ten yards away that allowed transfers in and out of the ward.

The entire time the young private explained the process, the hunter's gaze stayed on me. Fire flashed in those irises, hinting at the questions lurking within, but I couldn't very well tell him about Jakub yet. It would have to wait until we left and were far out of hearing range before I told the hunter that we had one shot to catch that bastard before he escaped via the sea.

Once inside the base, Kaillen's expression didn't change. He remained the portrait of insolence and boredom, yet I detected his emotional scents. They were subtle enough that I didn't know if Klebus was aware of them, but beneath his calm exterior I knew he was quaking with impatience and felt the calling that sang through my blood too. *My mate. Mine.*

"This way," Commander Klebus said stiffly.

Kaillen crossed his arms. "I'm not going anywhere. I'm here to take Tala and leave."

She cocked her head. "I merely want to discover how you found this place. Surely, you have time to answer a few questions?"

"Actually, I don't. And how I find things isn't your concern."

Her eyes flashed blue fire. "On the contrary, it's entirely my concern. I'm the commanding officer here."

"Regardless of your rank, it's within my rights to travel anywhere on this planet without disclosing why I choose to go where I do to the SF."

She advanced on him, but I stepped into her path. "Commander Klebus, I'm truly sorry for the commotion we've caused, but can we please be on our way now?" I gave her an apologetic smile as I tried to diffuse the situation, because knowing these two, it was either continued verbal sparring or an all-out war.

Her lips pursed, but some of the metaphorical steam wafting from her ears vanished. Straightening, she gave a curt nod. "You'll still be on the SF's watch list since you both now know about this place."

"We both understand. Don't worry. We won't tell anyone."

She gave me a shrewd glare, obviously not happy with how this situation had turned out.

"Thank you for letting me stay here," I added, hoping to pacify her more.

She crossed her arms. "This excursion cost the Supernatural Forces valuable time and resources. I transferred you here with the understanding that you would be staying under SF protection."

I nodded contritely. "I'm sorry. I didn't mean to waste anyone's time or money. Truly, I didn't."

Her tone softened, and that familiar gleam returned to her eye. "It was quite informative, though, I will say that. Do you still have my card?"

I gave a curt nod as Kaillen's eyes narrowed.

Her nostrils flared as she assessed me and the hunter again. Kaillen stood silently, his jaw working while he watched us. I had no idea what he was thinking, but I had a feeling I would hear all about it once we left.

"Private, please collect Ms. Davenport's things," Commander Klebus said to one of the soldiers, before she crossed her arms and faced the hunter again. "Where do you intend on taking Ms. Davenport?"

"She'll be safe."

The commander gave him a withering glare. "That's not what I asked."

"I know." He smirked.

I nearly pinched the bridge of my nose, but then Tessa abruptly lurched forward from the back of the group.

"Tala!" She rushed to my side and pulled me into a hug. "Stay safe," she whispered into my ear.

I squeezed her back. "I will."

Her bottom lip trembled when she released me, her eyes awash with unshed tears. I pinched her. "Have a little more faith in me."

But her worried expression didn't abate. Whether that was because her theatrics were drawing attention to her or because she was genuinely fearful for me, I didn't know.

Oh wait . . . I *could* know. I inhaled her fragrance, and a sour scent tingled my nose.

She was actually scared for me.

I hugged her again. "I'll be okay."

She squeezed me just as hard. Probably because she'd seen the horrors of Jakub's captivity. She knew what was in store for me if Kaillen and I didn't catch him and ended up being caught instead.

Harsh breaths reached my ears as the private whom Commander Klebus had sent to collect my things returned. He dumped all of my bags at my feet, then saluted the commander.

"Thank you, Private," she said, still fuming at my mate.

Kaillen ignored her and stepped forward before I could. He picked up all of my bags, no doubt that whole *must-take-care-of-my-mate-at-all-times* instinct kicking in.

I gave a final departing squeeze to my sister before following the hunter back through the ward's opening.

My sister and the remaining squad members all watched us leave. I waved a farewell to Tessa one last time before the hunter and I stepped into his portal and disappeared.

CHAPTER FOURTEEN

We arrived in Portland, just outside of his base. Kaillen didn't say a word before throwing my bags through his man cave's ward, threading his fingers through mine, and then tugging me through the perimeter.

It was only after we were safely encased inside his studio apartment, that I sputtered, "Why are we here and not in Montana?"

"Klebus may try to track me. I don't want her to know where I live." His brow furrowed as he stepped closer to me. "What's going on?"

"I know where Jakub is."

His eyes widened for the briefest second before his mouth set into a hard line. "Where?"

"The fae lands. As of thirty minutes ago, he was on his way to Culasberee. The Supernatural Forces can't pursue him because of fae lands and earthly politics. That may change, but if it doesn't, he's going to get away. The SF is worried that if he gets to the sea, they won't be able to effectively track him. But you could still find him, couldn't you? Since you know his scent?"

"I could," he replied, the groove between his eyes deepening.

"There's more." I explained in a rush that Klebus now knew the extent of my powers. That she'd seen it when I'd broken the cuffs. "She now knows that I'm as powerful and as rare as you. She wants to recruit me to the SF." I showed him the business card she gave me.

His nostrils flared. "Fuck, she's clever."

"No shit. The only good thing that came out of it, is that I'm now immune to those cuffs." I crossed my arms as I peered up at him, some of my ire returning despite my excitement at seeing him again. "She had a pair of Jakub's blue cuffs, courtesy of you apparently."

A veiled look descended over his face.

Even though my wolf was begging me to touch the hunter, to join with and be with him, the human side of me pulled back. "Why didn't you tell me you had them?"

He broke eye contact. "I don't know. It slipped my mind, I guess."

"Slipped your mind?" I repeated, my voice rising.

"Yes. No. I don't know." He tore a hand through his hair. "A lot's been going on the past few days."

"But you gave those cuffs to Klebus. When?"

"After I retrieved them. I went to Philadelphia first because I knew Jakub had dropped them. I got them before

I retrieved the ax and came back to you in Montana. I knew we needed those cuffs if we were ever going to learn what they were and how to break them. That's the one thing the SF is good for, so I gave them to Klebus."

I scoffed. "Well, you certainly got a lot done in a short amount of time."

He gave me a cocky smile. "I'm efficient."

Despite his teasing comment, I saw the worry in his eyes, even more so when he inhaled and no doubt caught the hurt in my scent.

My brow furrowed. "Why do you hide so much from me? Why don't you let me in?"

He studied me for a moment, that pineapple and sunshine fragrance beginning to waft up from him. "Do you want me to let you in? All you do is fight me."

"But that's because—" I let out a frustrated sigh. "*Ugh.* Why is nothing normal between us?"

"Because it's not, and it never will be, but if you want me to let you in, I'm willing to do that. I'll do whatever it takes."

"But you haven't so far," I countered. "If you had, you would have told me about the cuffs and how you suspected that I could be a werewolf." That icy hurt slid through me again.

An aggrieved expression overtook his face.

And in his scent, I knew that he was sorry. He was truly remorseful. I stared up at him as my tone turned pleading. "Why aren't you more honest with me? More open?"

He shook his head, then frowned, as though really

considering my words. After a moment, he said, "I think it's because I've spent my entire life on my own. Until you, I—" He let out a harsh sigh. "This is new to me, okay? I'm not used to sharing information with people. I work alone. I function alone. I've always been alone. Until you, I didn't want it any other way."

My heart tripped. *Until me.* And I knew that he meant that, because his entire childhood and working career, Kaillen had functioned solo. He'd learned from an early age to be self-reliant. He'd had to or he wouldn't have survived.

I brushed my hands next to his. "But I'm your mate." A lump formed in my throat, because as much as this were-wolf crap was messed up, I *was* his mate, and Tessa's comment back in her bungalow had hit a nerve in me. She'd been right. A lot of mated werewolf couples were very happy. Who was I to judge those relationships and say they weren't real? They were *very* real for all of those supernaturals. Even though they were different to anything I'd ever experienced, it didn't mean they weren't genuine, which meant it didn't mean that Kaillen and I weren't genuine.

Kaillen stilled, as though he'd sensed the shift in me just as I was coming to grips with it myself. "Yes. You are my mate. *Mine.*"

A tingle ran through my belly at that possessive claim, but I shoved it down, so I wouldn't get distracted. "Which means that you shouldn't hide things from me. Nothing should be hidden between us." And with a hard swallow, I realized that I meant that and *wanted* that. I couldn't fight this bond any more than he could. Now, more than ever, I realized that. So if we were going to jump into this head first, then I needed to know that I could trust him. Because true trust meant no secrets. "Knowing you're not going to hide things from me anymore is the only way this will ever work for me."

His hand drifted to my waist, as a low possessive rumble came from his chest.

My wolf yelped excitedly.

A predatory smile lifted his lips. "You're willing to be my mate now?"

"If you promise to work on that."

His face transformed into an all-out grin. "I'll work on it. But this whole sharing thing? It's new to me. Can you forgive me if I fuck up a few more times?"

I gave a small smile as the glow in his eyes grew. "Maybe. It depends how many times."

A chuckle escaped him at my teasing tone, then his chest rose when he took a deep breath. A musky fragrance wove into his scent as he drank me in. "You just admitted to being my mate."

"I did."

"And that we're going to be together."

"Yes, that too."

His nostrils flared as heat smoldered in his eyes and the musk in his scent grew so potent I was swimming in it.

It took everything in me to back up and put distance between us. "But right now, Jakub is getting away, and there's something I need to tell you too. In the spirit of not having any more secrets, there's one thing I've never told you, and I think it's important." I proceeded to tell him about the Bone Eaters, and what my mother had warned me of. It was the only thing I'd always kept from him. The one secret I'd kept as *mine*. But not anymore.

When I finished, he cocked his head. "The Bone Eaters?"

"Have you ever heard of them?"

"No."

"Me either, but I can't help but think that they're somehow connected to what's happening. Maybe Jakub's one of them. I don't know, but we need to find out."

He let out an agitated sigh, then raked a hand through his hair. "Right. Jakub."

He strode to his closet and whipped it open, as if wanting to catch Jakub as quickly as possible so we could get onto more *interesting* things. The familiar array of weapons and potions lay before him. He pulled out one of his chest harnesses and began layering himself with so many weapons and lethal potions that he became literal death on feet.

"Take what you want," he called to me. "Don't touch the ax."

I joined him and grabbed another chest harness. It swallowed me since it was so huge, but he cinched the straps down until it fit snugly, his fingers lingering on my skin.

My nostrils flared, detecting the thick aromas lifting

from him. Anticipation had joined his arousal, and I had a feeling his demon was looking forward to coming out to play.

"Has she been behaving?" he asked.

As if knowing that he was talking about her, my wolf thumped her tail inside me.

"For the most part. Without you around, she ignored me a lot. She wasn't happy that I left."

"That makes two of us." He finished with the straps, then began securing the weapons I'd chosen to the various cinches. "Did she try to shift last night?"

"No. It went okay."

"And now?"

I frowned, tentatively feeling inward for her, but she was so damned happy to be in the hunter's presence again that she seemed to be minding her manners. "She's happy and not trying to take over again."

"Good. Maybe it was for the best that you left. It helped you establish dominance. She learned that if she pushes too far, you'll take away the one thing she wants most."

"Her mate?"

A smile curved his lips. "Yes."

I cocked my head at him. "Does it bother you at all that we have no choice in this?"

"What makes you think we have no choice?"

"Because of these feelings. This *pull*. This need to be with you. It all comes from them, not us."

He gazed down at me. "That's what being a werewolf

entails. When you find your mate, that's it. They're the only one you'll ever want."

"You're saying that I'm the only one you'll want now?" My heart skipped, but then Carlos's warning came back to me—the warning he'd told me weeks ago. *Can't be a normal mate instinct.* But I had a feeling that Carlos was wrong about the hunter. I was beginning to think that Kaillen *did* feel a normal werewolf mating instinct.

Kaillen's brow furrowed as he gazed down at me, as though perplexed that I could even question him. "Of course it will only be you."

My heart tripped again, and any past worry I'd had about him being unable to be monogamous faded away. And that urge to weld myself to him, to wrap my legs around him, to claim him as *mine* . . . it was growing again.

"How do you wolves live like this?" I had the strongest urge to rub my thighs together. Fuck, I wanted him.

"It'll get easier." He took a step closer to me. "If you let me claim you, our wolves will calm down."

Claim you.

An image of the hunter and me in his bed formed in my mind. Naked. Writhing. Climaxing together as he bit into my neck and sealed our magic.

I peered up at him. "Could I claim you too? Since I can shift?" Because the bond was sealed by elongating one's canines, it was always the male who did the claiming bite, as female werewolves couldn't shift. But since I was the first that could . . .

An intrigued smile lifted his lips, and the musky aroma

in his scent increased. "I don't know. I suppose there's only one way to find out."

My nostrils flared, and I quickly grabbed a handful of potions. The urge to rip his clothes off was growing by the second. "What did you get up to while I was with Tess?" I said in a hurry, anything to distract myself from how much I wanted to ride the hunter's cock.

"I went to take care of Cameron."

My frantic movements stopped. "Take care of him? What does that mean?"

A deadly gleam entered his eyes. "While you were gone, I went back to Ontario. The entire pack knows that Cameron betrayed your location and handed you over to Jakub. Even for an upcoming alpha, a betrayal like that is heinous. The entire pack was up in arms about it, and I intended to make matters right."

I swallowed audibly. An image of the hunter's black-flamed eyes on the night he'd learned of his brother's betrayal rose in my mind. He'd said that he'd kill his brother for giving me to Jakub. But that had been in the heat of the moment. Still . . .

I twisted my hands and asked hesitantly, "Does that mean you . . . killed him?"

"No, only because he wasn't there. He fled as soon as he got wind that I'd come back."

"But you would have killed him if he'd been there?"

"Of course. I'm coming for him, and he knows it."

Gaping, I stared at him. Because he'd just admitted that he still planned to murder his brother so casually. He didn't even pause. And his expression hadn't faltered other than a lick of fire forming in his irises.

I drifted backward, away from the closet, more from shock than horror until the backs of my knees hit his bed, and I sank onto the mattress. "You're seriously going to kill your own brother? Even now, after you've had a chance to cool off about what he did?"

He prowled toward me, his expression giving away nothing, yet a new scent rose from him—metallic iron— *anger*. "He handed you over to *them*. There's no fucking way I'm letting him get away with that."

"But to kill him?"

"It's the werewolf way. You're my *mate*. Don't you know what losing you would do to me?"

"I know . . . I mean—" I shook my head, because I didn't actually know. I hadn't grown up in a pack. I didn't fully understand its traditions. And I never would know what losing a mate would be like unless I lost Kaillen, and *oh gods*, just the thought made me want to howl in agony.

Yet Kaillen was right. Cameron hadn't cared if I'd died. He'd ripped me away from his brother, and the absolute hatred I'd seen in Cameron's eyes had been disturbing, but to just *kill him*?

"I'm not going to apologize for what I plan to do." Kaillen's nostrils flared. "Cameron handed you over to Jakub, knowing Jakub would inevitably murder you, or if he didn't kill you, it would be something far, far worse. Cameron *purposefully* took you from me." A deadly gleam formed in Kaillen's eyes, that black fire making an appearance again, and I knew that his demon would relish the killing.

I licked my dry lips. "Wouldn't somebody try to stop you?"

"No. It's the werewolf way." Those black flames in his eyes grew.

"Not even Ocean or Paxton?"

"No. I'm owed my revenge, so not even my father or sister will try to stop me. Pack law and supernatural law warrant the killing." His lip curled up. It was as if just the thought of his brother made rage fill his soul.

An image of Cameron's body alight in the hunter's black flames filled my mind. And then came the knowledge that Paxton would have to stand by and let it happen, as gut-wrenching as that would probably be for him. I couldn't imagine a father standing by while one of his sons killed the other, but as Kaillen had said, such was the werewolf way. Because to knowingly kill another's mate—or attempt to—was punishable by death, and all males knew that, yet Cameron had still risked it. He'd hated me and Kaillen that much.

But I knew Cameron had done it because he hadn't expected to get caught. He thought I never would have been able to escape from those two sorcerers he'd handed me to, not when I'd been bound and gagged. And he had no idea about the blood bond that Kaillen and I shared, so he hadn't anticipated the hunter finding me. Cameron had thought it would all look like an unfortunate accident.

I licked my lips again. "Don't you think you'll feel guilty

after you do it, though? Even if Cameron is the king of douchebags?"

His eyes hardened, and he leaned down, placing his hands on the mattress, one on each side of me, before pushing me back.

I fell onto the bed, bouncing on the mattress before I lay beneath him, the soft covers shifting around me. My breaths came faster as his eyes shone with raging fire. Despite the horrific intentions he'd just shared, heated desire flooded my veins. *Want. Want. Want.*

His nostrils flared. "I will kill *anyone* who hurts you or tries to take you from me."

His statement was said with such lethal quiet, and filled with so much malice, that I knew he meant it. He would kill for me over and over if that was what it took to keep me safe. Violence swam in his eyes, but something else did too. Something fiercer and more primal.

My mate.

My wolf whined, urging me to join with him. To *be* with him. *Want him. Need him.* I balled my hands into fists.

Kaillen's breaths turned harsher as his heartbeat picked up, a thundering pounding in my ears. He sank lower, his body molding to mine when he said in a raspy voice, "So no, I don't feel guilty. Cameron's a sadistic prick. He'll get what's coming to him."

I thought about what Kaillen had told me of his childhood, how Cameron had bullied him mercilessly his entire life.

I shuddered from the absolute violence that could

accompany packs, but also from the predatory gleam which had entered Kaillen's eyes. It wasn't a gleam of violence though, it was a gleam of desire.

His gaze dipped to my mouth, the heat in his eyes growing.

Want. Want. Want.

The mating bond hummed in my chest, begging me to curl my hand around his neck and pull him flush against me. Gods, the *pull* . . . The incessant ache to mold myself to him. It was nearly overpowering in its strength.

Kaillen's nostrils flared more, and the musk in his scent increased, just as I knew my scent was growing too.

"Fucking hell," he growled, so low and throaty that my entire body clenched in need. "Jakub can wait. I want you, Tala, so fucking much." And then he was on me.

His lips found mine, sealing our mouths in a bruising kiss. My hands lifted of their own accord, threading through the hair at the nape of his neck as my blood boiled with lust.

Mine.

He hauled me up the bed in a blurred movement, never once breaking the kiss as his hands ripped and tore at the clothes covering my skin, mine doing the same to his.

Too many layers. Too many obstacles.

I needed him. Wanted him. Now. It had to be *now*.

My hands turned into claws, until I'd shredded every bit of fabric that barred my way. Thumps sounded and sparks flew when the weapons and potions we'd strapped to ourselves hit the floor in a flurry of torn leather and flying metal.

And then we were skin to skin. Only his hot smooth body greeted my fingertips.

"Tala," he growled against my lips, before he ripped his mouth from mine and pressed urgent kisses down my neck, to my breasts, across my stomach. He was everywhere at once, his body owning and possessing me as the energy crackled and grew between us.

But I wanted to touch him. *Needed* to.

In a blur of power, I flipped him onto his back, calling upon my wolf's strength. His eyes flashed in surprise before I draped myself over him, my legs parting until I straddled him and my tits hung in his face.

A rumbling sound of pleasure came from his throat as his eyes darkened, lust fogging them as crimson fire and golden light flared in his irises.

He nipped at my peaks, and I moaned when he rolled a taut nipple between his teeth. He locked his hands onto my waist, trying to dominate me again, but I brushed him off and leaned back until his firm erection grazed my entrance.

His entire body seized, turning into a stiff plank as his breathing grew ragged.

Despite his strained expression, I didn't slide back onto him or sheathe him inside me, even though my body was begging me to do it.

"I want to taste you again when I'm present enough to fully remember it," I whispered.

His breaths turned shallow, his eyes glowing like twin rubies rimmed by the sun as I traveled downward, rubbing my body on his while kissing every inch that I passed. His muscles bunched and coiled, his entire body like smooth rock and as hot as a volcano.

My eyes widened when I reached his impressive length. He was hard and throbbing, his dick so thick my fingers itched to encircle him. I marveled at his girth and the slight curve at the tip that I knew would scrape exactly where my pleasure lay. When I finally wrapped my hand around him, he let out a guttural moan and bucked beneath my palm.

I bent down and flicked my tongue over his tip. His hands curled into my hair, his eyes glowing so brightly when he gazed down at me, that the fire and gold swirled into one. "Tala?" he rasped.

Closing my eyes, I wrapped my mouth around his length and took him in, letting my movements answer him in a dance as old as time.

He let out a strangled sound as I moaned from the taste and feel of him. Smooth, hot velvet, brimming with fire and desire, filled my mouth. The urge to devour him flowed through my veins, and I began sucking and pumping my mouth on him in earnest.

His buttocks clenched, lifting his hips as his hands gripped my hair so tightly, pain flared on my scalp. But it only added to my need to be with him, taste him, and *claim* him.

"Tala!" he rasped again when I began to pump my hand

at the base of his cock as my mouth sucked him like a lollipop.

I only moaned as I let myself become lost in his taste and scent. The musk around him grew even more potent.

My movements turned frantic, enraptured even, as I savored every stroke and slide of his cock filling my mouth. Each taste and rub of him entering and exiting me wrought a new groan from him and heightened the desire flooding my veins.

I didn't think. Didn't question. Didn't analyze anything that was happening.

I just wanted. Needed. *Craved.* He was mine. My mate. My wolf. My demon. *Mine.* So I devoured him as his hands turned into talons in my hair, and a deep shuddering breath filled his chest. I knew he was near to coming, so I sucked harder, licked faster, and the coiling energy wrapping around him unleashed.

His hips jolted, and the roar of his release filled the room as his hot seed shot into my mouth. But the taste of him only heightened my lust. I drank down every drop, savoring the power I wielded over the indomitable hunter as his cock throbbed and pumped his climax relentlessly into my mouth.

It was only when his body finally softened from the rock-hard slab that lay beneath me, that I released him from my lips and lifted my gaze to his.

He was peering down at me, a look of disbelief and unfiltered lust clouding his eyes. His chest still rose and fell unsteadily as his harsh breaths filled the room.

"Fucking hell, woman," he finally breathed, then he hauled me up his chest.

In a blink, he had me beneath him. He breathed in my scent and then nuzzled my neck, his inhales still coming so fast. Somewhere in the last twenty minutes, I'd released my cloaking spell as instinct took over and I lay myself bare for him.

He kissed below my ear, then along my jaw, and finally my mouth. His lips molded to mine, but the urgency had abated, and he drew his kiss out, making it long and tender. Aching need flared in my core, and I curled my hands around the nape of his neck, savoring his taste and feel. So long. I'd wanted this for *so* long.

"Nobody, and I mean nobody, has ever made me come like that," he said softly, then nipped at my bottom lip. "Well, other than the first blowjob you gave me."

I chuckled, then wound my hands around his back, trapping him in my embrace as a flare of jealousy pummeled me at the thought of any woman ever touching or seeing him.

My wolf growled in agreement, but I shoved her down. This moment was between Kaillen and me.

"Is that jealousy I detect in your scent, my love?" His lips lifted in a wry smile.

I leaned up and bit his shoulder.

He grimaced, then laughed darkly. "So fierce. What has you jealous, *colantha*?"

My toes curled at that endearment. "You were talking about what other women have done to you."

A wicked smile curved his lips. "My mistake. It won't happen again."

My fingernails lengthened, my body automatically calling upon my wolf's powers as they turned into claws. They bit into his back, breaking through the skin until beads of blood were drawn so he would know how much I disliked that.

He hissed, the sound deep and low. "You're beginning to act as possessive as me." His wicked smile grew. "I like it."

I raked my claws over his back, but the slashes sealed instantly from his power. "Carlos told me you're a womanizer."

He stiffened. "Why are you talking about Carlos?" he growled.

"I'm talking about what he said. Are you?"

"Am I what?"

"A womanizer?" I held my breath, waiting for the answer.

"The community thinks I am."

I pinched him. Hard. "That's not an answer."

His lips twitched as he brushed my fingers away. "No, I'm not a womanizer."

"Then why do people think you are?"

"Because I want them to, so I've built that into my reputation."

"Why would you want people thinking that?"

He traced a finger along the curve of my breast. "Maintaining a certain appearance is imperative to my line of work. I need to come off as ruthless and someone who doesn't give a shit about who I hurt. Killing easily and being perceived as a womanizer are two ways to do that. The less people know about my true character, the better."

"Meaning that you actually *do* care about people? Is that why you also hide your man cave and what you've done here in Portland with the homeless kids? It's all part of your image?"

His lips curved. "That's exactly it, *colantha*."

"Do you like hanging out at the Black Underbelly?"

"Not particularly." He bent down to suck my tit, and I gasped. "But it's where half my jobs come from, so it's a necessity."

"You seemed to enjoy it when I first met you." The lust inside me grew when his hand traveled down between my thighs and his fingers parted my slick folds.

He rumbled in pleasure when he found how ready I was. "Good. Then I was doing my job well."

My nostrils flared, but I scented no deception in him. Only the scent of mandarins, honeysuckle, and heady musk. He was being honest, about all of it.

Satisfied and happier than I wanted to admit that he hadn't fucked every female in the Shadow Zone—and didn't actually enjoy random women offering him blowjobs—my claws disappeared until my human nails dug into his shoulders.

"That's better," he murmured. He leaned down again and gave me another long, sensual kiss as his fingers continued to tease and stroke. "I've dreamed of you doing that to me since the moment we met."

"Shredding your skin?"

He laughed darkly. "I was referring to the blowjob, but if you're into kink, we can do that too."

I gave a throaty chuckle. "Not really. Drawing blood doesn't do it for me."

He nipped at my mouth again, and my breath sucked in as his fingers continued to play me like a fiddle. "Good, 'cause I don't think I could stomach drawing your blood, but if you really wanted it, I'd do it."

"No blood," I said breathlessly when he nipped my ear. "Just fucking."

His eyes darkened, and he kissed me again as his hand wandered up, until he found my full breasts, aching with need for him. He squeezed, eliciting a rasped cry from me. "My mate. *My* woman."

Yes. And then he was kissing me again as his length hardened against my thigh.

His hands and mouth were everywhere again, sucking, licking, and biting. But instead of his mouth settling between my thighs as I had done to him, he shifted until he hovered over me, his eyes burning and questioning.

With a deft movement, he positioned himself between my legs, his stiff erection brushing my entrance, and I knew what he was asking.

"Yes," was all I said to his silent question.

He groaned when I parted my thighs more, and a deep growl of satisfaction and possession tore from him. In one swift move, he locked his hand onto my hip and tilted his erection.

His tip entered me first, the thick girth teasing me. I cried out, my fingernails raking down his skin again as the need to have him fill me made me pant.

He thrust more, entering me inch by inch, and his entire body began to tremble, the strain of what he was doing etching itself onto his face as his jaw locked and fire burned in his eyes.

"So tight," he whispered. "And *mine.*" His growl came out low and throaty, and then he slammed the remaining distance into me until he was fully sheathed.

I cried out at how huge he was seated inside me, but the way he was already rubbing me, scraping in me . . . my breaths turned harsh and desperate as I gripped his ass and begged him for more.

He began to move, long hot strokes of pent-up need and aching desire.

I tilted my hips, joining him and matching each pump and stroke. "More, more," I demanded.

He picked up his pace, his breathing turning as ragged as mine as his eyes glowed with unfiltered desire. I leaned up, kissing him and biting him as he rammed into me again and again.

Groaning, he kissed me back, then began fucking me in earnest, slapping against me as he rode me rough and hard. I cried out as the waves began to build, his huge cock demanding that I respond, and I was helpless to resist.

More. More. More. Mine. Mine. Mine.

Our bodies moved in sync, our breaths ragged and shallow. The fierce strain on his face grew, as the peak for me grew higher, then higher. I chased that mountain, the need to shatter all around him fighting me in its battle for this to never end.

But Kaillen wouldn't abate. His groans turned guttural, his pounding relentless, and his cock stretched and filled me so completely that I couldn't stop the inevitable.

"I'm going to come," I whispered.

His eyes flashed, and his canines lengthened as he kept up a vicious tempo.

And seeing that triggered something in me. My wolf whined, her power pulsing through my core. My canines shifted, tips appearing and elongating in my mouth.

I didn't think. Didn't question. I followed the instinct that had led me to this moment, to this day when I accepted that I was his and he was mine. So I leaned up just as he bent down.

Our sharp teeth pierced each other's flesh simultaneously. His magic flowed into me, and mine into him. It wrapped around us in hot waves of desire and power that molded our bodies as one just as the mountainous peek was reached.

I cried out as an orgasm ripped through my defenses at the same time he roared his release. My mouth clamped harder onto his neck, as his did to mine.

Our mouths stayed locked onto one another as the claiming bond took root. Magic poured through my veins, the hunter's essence coating my inside in crimson fire and black flames, just as mine wound around him in golden light and an explosion of sparks. Our souls fused, our bodies joined, and somewhere in the pure ecstasy of all that was happening, I knew that I had found where I belonged.

Home. The hunter was my home. He always had been, and he always would be.

Somewhere in the fog, I was aware that my legs and arms had entwined around his broad frame, and that his hands were clenching my ass, keeping his length firmly buried inside me as his seed poured into me in throbbing waves and our magic rippled with pulsing power through us.

It was heaven and rapture. Domination and submission. Magic and flames.

He was mine.

I was his.

And now, there was no going back.

CHAPTER FIFTEEN

My eyelids opened in a hazy flutter of languid bliss. I felt wrecked. Totally and completely spent.

The hunter was still on top of me and inside me.

Vaguely, I was aware that we were in his man cave. Our clothes were in ribbons on the floor. Our chest harnesses were shredded as weapons, blades, and potions were scattered about.

And Jakub was still out there, still on the run.

Yet, I couldn't move.

Kaillen shifted slightly, then his scent clouded around me when he buried his face into my neck. His tongue darted out, right where he'd bitten me.

My body jolted at the erotic sensation that intimate caress provoked, like someone had run a feather over my clit, demanding my attention.

My eyes flashed open as a tug came from my abdomen.

"Do you feel it?" Kaillen said huskily, his face still pressed flush against my neck. The tug came again, then an . . . *emotion* . . . strummed along it. Pure male satisfaction.

The hunter was preening.

I gasped, then brought a hand to my stomach, to where that feeling lay. "Is that . . . *you* I'm feeling?"

He lifted his head. Wicked delight shone in his eyes. "It is. We're bonded now. I claimed you, and you claimed me." He seemed immensely satisfied about that last part, as if I'd directly stroked his ego by making the choice to join with him.

He lifted himself onto his elbow, an arrogant smirk tilting the corner of his mouth. "Do I have a mark too?" My eyes widened when I beheld the crescent moon-shaped mark just above his collarbone.

My hand flew to my skin, to the same area. "You do. Do I?"

His lips curved in a possessive grin. "Indeed. I just licked it. And not only that, but you carry a hint of my scent too. Every male werewolf will know that you're mated now. You are officially *mine*."

Yet, instead of that remark terrifying me or filling me with despair, I felt nothing but elation. I may be his, but he also belonged to me. I tentatively sniffed, to see if he also carried my scent, and I caught a hint of freesia intermixed with his natural citrusy cedar.

"I can smell myself on you too. It's subtle but there. So I guess we're officially a couple now?" I said lightly and toyed with the hair at the nape of his neck.

He chuckled, then made a purring sound, falling into the movement as I caressed his skin. "Yes. You're officially off the market, so you better tell Carlos that." He growled after uttering my ex's name. "And if he ever sends you another fucking letter telling you he loves you and asks you to be his, I'm going to rip his throat out."

My eyes widened as I laughed, but then I sobered, because Kaillen probably would do something that violent if he felt Carlos was trying to take me from him. 'Cause if I thought the hunter had been possessive before the claiming, I had a feeling I hadn't seen anything yet.

I trailed my finger across his chest and said teasingly, "You know, you really shouldn't read my private letters."

"Then you shouldn't leave them laying around."

My finger stopped. "Are you kidding me? Is that how it's going to be between us?"

He shrugged. "No more secrets, remember? If I'm not going to hide anything from you, why should you hide anything from me?"

"Does that mean you're now an open book?"

"Probably not."

I whacked him on the shoulder, which got a dark grin from him.

Sobering, he added, "I am going to do my best not to hide anything, but you still might have to ask me a question or two to get all the information."

I rolled my eyes but still grinned, then stretched languidly. My body felt spent, loved, and thoroughly fucked.

"We should go," I said when I glanced at the clock in his kitchen. It was crazy that we'd only been here for forty-five minutes. It felt as if hours, or even days, had passed. I'd been that wrapped up in him, but the reality was that Jakub was still out there, and time was ticking.

"You do know what you're asking of me, right?" he said lazily.

"If you're referring to how I've asked you to join me in the fae lands so we can hunt down a psycho intent on abducting me, then yes, I am aware of what I'm asking."

"I'm not talking about Jakub. I'm talking about the fact that I've just claimed you, and all of my instincts are now begging me to fuck you continuously until I've planted my pup in your belly."

My eyes widened. "Please tell me that you're kidding."

An amused expression overtook his face before he said with mocking offense, "You're going to hurt my ego. If you're already ready to run from my bed, then I didn't pleasure you as I should have."

"Oh, you did. That's not the part I'm referring to. It was the pup part. I'm not ready for that."

He leaned down and nipped my nose. "I know, but we can certainly keep practicing even if pups aren't on the agenda yet."

His length began to harden in me, and my eyes widened. "You're ready, again?"

"You're my mate. All it takes is breathing in your scent, and my cock's hard."

"But what about Jakub? We've already spent—"

"This one will be quick. Promise." He began to move, and any thoughts about fleeing to the fae lands disappeared when he pulled out, and then thrust back inside me.

IF I'D THOUGHT that claiming one another would dispel this constant need to straddle the hunter and ride him till the cows came home, I was sorely mistaken.

But while a part of me felt more satisfied and more reassured that the hunter truly did want me on some level, the insatiable need to have him fuck me fifty shades from Sunday didn't let up.

The second time was quick. The hunter kept true to his promise, and even though I had another earth-shattering orgasm, the pull to be with him began again as soon as we came down from the high.

I marveled when his length grew for a third time, then a fourth time, and before either of us knew it, we'd spent two hours in his bed fucking like bunny rabbits.

"We need to go," I panted as my body lay limp beneath his. "We can't keep doing this."

"Oh, I think we could." He grazed his teeth along my skin. "Were you not warned about what newly mated couples are like? The need to constantly mate won't abate for several weeks."

"Weeks?" I screeched. "I don't know if my vagina can take it. I'm already sore."

He nipped at my neck. "Should I kiss the hurt away? Perhaps lick it?"

I laughed, unable to help it. The man was a sex god, and I had no doubt he'd make good on his promise, but I also knew that Jakub was on the run, and as much as I wanted to spend the next week in bed with the hunter pleasuring me over and over, I also knew that reality waited outside of these warded walls.

"We need to go," I said again, then pushed up before he could convince me otherwise. I dipped out of the bed even though his arm tried to snake around me.

"Have I ever told you that you have the most beautiful body I've ever seen?" he asked, his gaze firmly glued to me as his eyes raked up and down my frame.

My breasts were rosy and chafed from Kaillen's constant need to lick and suck them, but as I glanced down, my werewolf powers were already healing them. "Really? Looks like a normal body to me."

"I disagree. You are absolute perfection, especially your sexy—" His arm swiped out again, but I jumped back, my newly enhanced speed coming in handy for that.

"Missed me," I said teasingly. "Now get your nice ass outta bed. We're leaving."

"I have a nice ass?" He cocked an eyebrow.

I snorted, and rolled my eyes as I picked up my clothes, but was dismayed to see that they were shredded beyond repair. "You know you have a nice ass."

"You're right. I do," he agreed when he stood.

I couldn't stop my smile at his absolute cockiness, but

all amusement fled when he towered over me. He was naked, *completely* naked, and that predatory look had crept into his eyes again.

It took everything in me not to drink up the sight of him and say to hell with Jakub and the fae lands. My mate was pure masculine perfection. His body was so cut and hard, perfectly sculpted and tantalizingly broad. Already, my fingers itched to skate over those muscular ridges and smooth planes.

His nostrils flared. "If that motherfucker wasn't out to abduct you, I'd have you bent over this bed right now and be pumping into you."

"Don't tempt me," I breathed, my voice coming out raspy and low. I took a step back and held up my ruined clothes. "Looks like these will need to go in the garbage."

He nodded toward my bag, the one I hadn't opened since Oak Trembler. "There are more clothes in there. I'm particularly fond of the number on top."

Frowning, I went to my bag and opened it. My hand flew to my mouth when I saw the black lacy nightie that Tessa had packed for me. Kaillen must have seen it when he collected my things from Ontario and brought them to Montana. I'd completely forgotten about that garment. I held it up. "Do you think I should wear this to the fae lands?"

His eyes darkened. "No, if any other man sees you in that, I'll kill him."

I held the silky number up and over my skin, desire pooling between my thighs when I saw the reaction it elicited in him. Already, his pupils were dilating, his rod thickening.

He stalked toward me, but I grabbed a handful of clothes and ducked into the bathroom before either of us could succumb to our mutual lust. And it was only as I stood before the mirror, my hair mussed and my lips plump from so much kissing, that I saw the full extent of what our mating meant.

A faint crescent moon mark now shadowed the base of my neck. My breath sucked in as I angled my head. *Oh gods.* I'd done it. Really done it. I'd fully and completely given myself over to my wolf side.

Yet . . . my sister's words came back to me. *It's real to all of them.*

Some of my panic eased, even though our wolves had overrun our senses. Kaillen wanted me, perhaps would one day even grow to love me, and even though it would always be because of the bond and would never be because it was truly real, I was willing to accept that.

My wolf's tail thumped and wagged inside me at light speed. I shook my head but couldn't stop my smile. *Yes, yes, I know. You won.*

Her only response was to whine in happiness.

At least Kaillen had been right about the claiming calming her. Now that we'd given into our wolf sides, she felt even more subdued and content. I no longer felt her trying to control and dominate me. Instead, a languid feeling now ruffled through her. She was with her mate, bonded to him, and all was right in the world.

They truly were creatures that ran purely on instinct.

I sighed and finished in the bathroom, then pulled on sensible clothing—stretchy skinny jeans that were easy to move in, boots I could run in, and a black long-sleeved crop top that didn't restrict my arms. If we were going to the fae lands to hunt Jakub, I wanted to be ready for anything.

Once done, I joined the hunter.

Kaillen was also dressed in his combat gear and decked out in a new harness with his weapons and potions strapped to him again. My mouth grew dry at the sight, and that telltale arousal again licked my insides.

I knew the same had been born in him, not only from the heat growing in his gaze, but from the bond that was threaded between us. I scented his arousal but also felt it too. Fucking hell, the man gave *hornball* a whole new meaning.

His nostrils flared, and he winked. "You should eat before we go."

I eyed the high-calorie food that he'd put out on the kitchen table, not even realizing till that moment that I was starving. So, I did as he suggested and pretty much ate everything, but such was my new metabolism.

The entire time I was stuffing my face, he watched me, his gaze constantly dipping when my shirt clung to my chest or my pants snagged at my waist.

"If we don't leave now, I'm going to have you against that wall in about two seconds flat." Tenseness lined his shoulders, and his length was clearly evident through his pants.

Despite not wanting to, I sprang into action, knowing this was going to be a constant battle to fight our mutual lust, but we had a job to do at the moment, so going on a mating honeymoon wasn't in the cards just yet.

"Let's go."

His gaze ran up and down my frame when he assessed me in a new harness that was strapped with weapons. "Damn, woman. Just *damn.*"

I smirked. "Like what you see?"

He took a deep breath. "Fuck yes."

With that, we gripped one another's hand and jumped through his wards.

CHAPTER SIXTEEN

"I can't conjure portals to the fae lands, so we'll have to use a natural one," he said once we were in the alleyway, the brick wall of his man cave behind us. "Where's the nearest portal?"

"On the other side of town." He strapped his pack, then whipped out his yellow crystal and created a portal to transport us there. I also secured my backpack since we'd each carried a small bag with a few changes of clothes. I had no idea how long it would take to find Jakub, but we both agreed that traveling light was the best option.

Once we arrived across town, I took in the billowing green portal that would whisk us to the fae lands.

"Do you know where Culasberee is?" I asked.

"North of the capital, but before we go there, I want to make a stop. I have a feeling we'll need more than the two of us if we're going to take on Jakub."

"So you don't always work alone?"

He smirked at my teasing tone. "Usually, yes, but on the rare occasion, no."

"So where are we going?"

"To a bar in the fae lands. My friends are there."

My eyes widened with interest. "You have friends?"

"Don't look so shocked."

I snorted. "Does this mean I'm going to meet them?"

He glowered. "Unfortunately, yes."

"What's that supposed to mean? Are you worried I'll embarrass you?"

"Not at all. I'm more worried what they'll do to you, particularly Barnabas."

"Meaning what?"

"Meaning that as soon as he knows I'm mated to you, he's going to do everything he can to rile me."

I gave him a perplexed look. "What would rile you?"

"Let's just say that you have my full permission to dismember him if he gets a bit too friendly."

My jaw dropped, which got a grin from him.

"He won't actually do anything too unsavory," he added, "but he will enjoy provoking my mating instincts."

"Ah, so he'll flirt with me and whatnot?"

"Yes. I just hope it stops there. With how I'm feeling right now, I'm not sure whether I'll be able to control my reactions even if all he does is flirt."

I made a noncommittal noise, not entirely sure how to decipher that. I'd gotten the impression on multiple occasions that the hunter was possessive, but I had a feeling I hadn't seen the half of it yet.

THE PORTAL DROPPED us just outside of the fae lands' capital. We landed in a field, and a warm breeze brushed across my skin. I inhaled, my nose tingling. The wind carried pleasant scents that I didn't recognize, and a pale-green sky stretched across the horizon.

Ahead, the capital sat on a large hilly mound which swelled and stretched upward like a mountain. Houses and shops lined the rising landscape, thousands of stone-walled and thatched-roof buildings stretching along zigzagging streets, and at the top of that large hill perched a castle where the king and queen lived.

The castle shot up from the ground, its spires like thin rockets ready to launch. The combination of the beautiful golden walls and imposing structure was an architectural marvel.

And seeing that reminded me of Major Bavar Fieldstone. I wondered how his request to his aunt and uncle was coming along. The one in which he was hoping to allow entry for the Supernatural Forces to catch Jakub. Perhaps if we failed, the SF would succeed.

"Can you conjure your portals now that we're here?" I asked. It was at least a quarter mile to the capital's gates. The entire city was surrounded by a tall wall, sentries guarding each entrance point.

"No, not here. My portal-conjuring ability is limited to earth."

"Bummer. Should we run to the gates since we can't

portal transfer? Seems like such a short distance that it would be a waste of a portal key."

He gave me a crooked smile. "Race ya."

I let out a squeal of surprise, then annoyance, since of course he didn't wait for a fair start. But I quickly called upon my wolf's strength and speed and flew after him.

Her magic pulsed through me as the fragrant wind whipped through my hair, and in a second I was on Kaillen's tail, but since we were moving so fast, it only took a few seconds to reach the capital's gates.

Kaillen ground to a halt near to the sentries that guarded the gate, then grinned when I slugged him in the shoulder. "That wasn't a fair start."

He gave a mock pout. "Don't be a sore loser, *colantha*."

"I wouldn't be if you didn't cheat."

His eyes flashed in amusement, his demon rolling in that fire. "Since when do I fight fair?"

I rolled my eyes. "Noted, your half-demon-highness. I'll remember that for next time."

He chuckled. "I'll make it up to you tonight in bed."

Despite willing myself not to respond, my toes curled.

Threading his fingers through mine, he tugged me forward.

In front of us, the gate's large golden bars rose from the paved walkway. Two imposing sentries guarded the entrance, the sharp points of their long spears glimmering in the bright sun.

Their dark eyes stared down at us from their commanding height—a height that surpassed my mate's.

The sentries' golden skin was on show in their miniscule clothing. Both had heavily muscled chests which were exposed through their leather strap-like attire that only covered their groin area and part of their shoulders. Gold helmets, which matched their skin, adorned both of their heads.

When we stood only a few yards away, the sentries widened their stances and extended their spears toward the center of the gates, creating an X.

A loud *clang* reverberated through my body, and then a push of strong magic barreled into me. It felt as if we'd hit an invisible wall.

"State your reason for visiting the capital," the sentry on the right said.

"We're here to find a few of my friends," the hunter replied.

Something changed in the sentry's eyes as he studied my mate and the weapons strapped to him. The sentry's dark irises whirled, turning to shimmery silver. A rush of magic stole over my senses as they assessed Kaillen and me for treachery.

The magic dispersed, the sentry's eyes returning to their original inky-black color. With a swift movement, the two sentries simultaneously pulled their spears back to their sides.

"Proceed."

KAILLEN LED ME TO A *SALOPAS*—THE fairy version of a bar—in the Huntsmen Quarter. We ducked into the front entryway as rancorous laughter came from within.

I followed him into the dim interior. My werewolf senses adjusted immediately, sharpening the shadows into contrasting lines until the entire establishment appeared flooded in bright sunlight.

A long purple-hued bar ran the length of the room with a few supernatural patrons seated on the stools, and against the opposite wall, two full booths were filled with a large group of fae well into their drinks. The fairies were all howling with laughter, but other than that, the bar was vacant. It was obviously too early, and the capital's citizens were probably still at work.

A lone bartender stood behind the long bar, but there were no other staff. As was typical in *salopas*, magically enchanted trays floated throughout the room, serving the dozen customers seated. Waitresses weren't a thing in the fae lands.

Kaillen strode toward the back corner, not even pausing. In a discreet booth, two supernatural men sat at a horseshoe-shaped table drinking *leminai*. I hadn't spotted them when we'd come in.

The green drink was half gone in both of their glasses. I'd had the fairy alcoholic beverage on occasion but knew better than to indulge in more than half a glass. The stuff was potent enough to drop an elephant. Although, now that I had a werewolf's metabolism . . .

Hmm, perhaps I would have to retry that beverage, but obviously on a different occasion.

As we approached the table, I studied the two men. One was tall and lean with dark auburn hair cut close to his head. Chiseled cheekbones sat high on his face. His skin was pale, and he had eyes that nearly glowed indigo.

When we reached them, a subtle scent of decay rose from him, making my nose crinkle. So Auburn Hair was a vampire.

The vampire grinned. "Old friend! To what do we owe this great occasion?"

"Are you two free for a job?" Kaillen leaned casually against the wall by their booth.

The second guy was a hulking yellow-haired fairy with hazel eyes and pointed ears. "Always." He raised his glass in salute to Kaillen, then eyed me curiously.

I gave a small sniff in his direction. The subtle fragrance of spicy magic clung to him—the scent of a fairy apparently since Bavar had smelled similar.

Auburn Hair picked up his glass and drained it in one gulp. A glistening drop of the bright green liquid sat on his lip. His tongue darted out as he licked the single droplet. As soon as he finished, his eyes cut to mine, and the corner of his mouth tilted up. "Does this job have anything to do with this lovely lady accompanying you?"

A slight throb began in my core, the vampire's magic swimming toward me. Auburn Hair, who I was guessing was Barnabas, wasn't compelling me, but his sexual energy was on full power.

A low growl came from Kaillen as I called up my witch magic, letting it swim through my veins and blanket my senses. The vampire's pull diminished, and the pulsing desire in my clit faded.

I smirked. Despite my mate's concern over what Barnabas would do, this wasn't my first rodeo.

The vamp's eyebrows rose.

I smiled sweetly.

The low growl that had been filling my mate's chest disappeared, and Kaillen slid into the booth beside his friends as he dragged me in with him. It wasn't lost on me that he kept me close, a possessive arm slung low around my hips. "To answer your question, yes, this job has to do with my lovely lady. Barnabas, this is Tala."

The vampire's indigo eyes swam with interest as he assessed me with predatory ease. "Nice to meet you, Tala. Barnabas Galvenstein, at your service." He perused my body, his gaze skating up and down my frame as his smile grew.

Kaillen's nostrils flared. "Keep your perving to yourself." Before Barnabas could respond, Kaillen nodded toward the blond. "Tala, that's Fallon."

Fallon raised his glass toward me in a silent salute as Barnabas smiled, a flash of fang coming into view.

"Quite testy today," Barnabas commented as his gaze flicked down to the mating mark on Kaillen's neck. The vampire's eyes widened briefly, and a rainwater scent—a scent which I guessed meant he was surprised—rose from him before he assessed me too, noting the same mark on my skin. "Ah, now this is an interesting development. Last time I saw you, there were half a dozen sirens begging you to—"

A loud thump came from under the table, and Barnabas gave an aggrieved moan. "No need to kick me. If that's not a story you want me telling your new mate, all you need to do is say so." He flashed Kaillen an innocent grin.

Kaillen gave me an apologetic smile. "My mate doesn't need to hear about something that happened three months ago in the Shadow Zone."

I figured that was Kaillen's way of telling me he'd been upholding his reputation in whatever scenario Barnabas was referring to. I clung to the fact that whatever had happened with those six sirens, it'd meant nothing to him.

"Well, that's no fun." Barnabas grinned, as Fallon's expression didn't waver. "Now, tell me, how did you end up mated? Last time I saw you, you were as single as a horny new vamp."

"I hired him to find my sister," I cut in. "And apparently, his wolf took a liking to me."

Barnabas raised his eyebrows. "And why would you need my dear friend to find your sister?"

"She was abducted. I needed somebody to hunt her down."

Barnabas's indigo eyes turned awash with curiosity. "Is your sister as beautiful as you?"

I arched an eyebrow. "Would it matter?"

He inclined his head thoughtfully. "No, but it would

give me some good fantasy material for my next lonely Friday evening." He waggled his eyebrows.

Kaillen grumbled, then bared his teeth at his friend, but I snorted a laugh at the vamp's blatant flirting. I had been warned, after all, and since I'd been hit on by more vamps than I could count, I dismissed his comments for exactly what they were—a vampire succumbing to his carnal lust and never-ending desire for sex and flesh, even if I was his friend's mate.

I cupped my chin. "Considering Tessa and I are identical twins, you could say she looks a bit like me."

Barnabas's eyebrows rose. "So there are *two* of you? How fascinating. Tell me, have you ever—"

Another muffled thump came from below the table, and Barnabas let out an exaggerated wail. Kaillen turned fiery eyes on him. "Don't even go there."

I muffled a laugh as Fallon snorted and took another drink.

"Let me guess." I tapped my chin, and said in a mockingly flirtatious tone, "You were about to ask me if my sister and I have ever been in a threesome with a vamp dude?"

Kaillen gave me an incredulous look as if to say *don't encourage him,* but Barnabas merely laughed.

"Oh, I like her." The vamp nudged Kaillen, then said to me, "And yes, you read my mind. That was exactly what I was going to ask."

I swallowed a chuckle. "For a vampire, you're not very

original. I think I get that question about a dozen times a year."

Fallon snickered, the first slip to his stoic mask, as Barnabas threw back his head and howled in laughter, before he clapped Kaillen on the shoulder. "I *really* like her."

"Just don't get any ideas," Kaillen replied in a throaty growl, but a smile still tugged at his lips. "I'd have to stake you."

Fallon continued to sip his drink. I got the impression that of the three of them, he was definitely the quietest one.

"So are you two going to tell me what you're here for?" Barnabas picked up his drink again, eyeing me suggestively. "I'm guessing you're not on a mating honeymoon if you're here for our help."

Kaillen opened his mouth to reply, but an explosion of magic flared from a few yards away. I ducked on instinct just as Barnabas hissed and Fallon whipped a dagger from his belt.

The next thing I knew, a whistling sound of something flying through the air passed me.

I opened my mouth to call out a warning, but the flying object careening toward Kaillen came to an abrupt stop mid-air. A razor-sharp knife hung suspended in front of Kaillen's face, the hunter's hand gripped tightly around its handle

My heart hammered. Kaillen had literally caught the

knife in mid-flight. If he hadn't, it would have gone through his eye.

A low growl came from my hunter, and I whipped my head toward where the magical explosion had occurred.

A tall supernatural stood at the long purple bar, his lip curled back in disgust. Fallon let out a sigh while Barnabas gave a delighted laugh.

"Oh my, someone wants to play. Looks like things are about to get more fun." Barnabas's tongue darted out as he licked his upper lip. Another wave of pulsing hot desire shot through me, and I realized I'd let my guard down for a split second.

Cheeky bugger. When I glared at Barnabas, he winked.

I quickly called upon my magic again as the vamp's hot sexual energy pounded through me, my body clenching in sudden need. Considering the energy coming off the vampire had increased ten-fold, potential danger obviously increased his sex drive.

Kaillen's nostrils flared. "Hands to yourself while I'm gone. I mean it." He gave Barnabas a look full of retaliation, then picked me up and slid out of the booth. In a blink, he'd placed me back on my seat before launching himself toward the supernatural who'd apparently just tried to kill him.

I blinked. "What just happened?"

"Occupational hazard," Fallon said in a bored tone. "No need to worry."

Sure enough, Kaillen was already upon the tall man.

Grunts and snarls came from Kaillen's direction, and I

looked at Barnabas and Fallon, wondering if they were going to help their friend, or if I should, but Barnabas merely watched with a languid expression as Fallon continued sipping his drink.

"Doesn't he need help?" I said, my voice rising.

Fallon didn't even glance up. "No."

A groan came from the tall supernatural as my mate gave him an uppercut to the jaw.

"Ooh, that had to hurt." Barnabas's pupils dilated as blood went flying from the supernatural's lip. When it splattered across the wall, the vampire clucked his tongue. "What a waste."

"Who is that?" I asked as my heartbeat calmed since Kaillen did seem to have the matter under control.

Fallon set his drink down. "That's Olaf Hoffsteder. He's had a bone to pick with Kaillen since his wife hired your mate to track him down."

"And why did she hire Kaillen to find her husband?"

Fallon picked up his drink again. "She was convinced he was meeting a mistress every weekend instead of going on business trips."

So the hunter also did domestic jobs. Interesting . . . I would have bet that was easy money.

"Let me guess," I said when Kaillen landed another punch, and the tall supernatural doubled over. "She was right about her hunch?"

Barnabas angled his head. "Indeed she was. Olaf has had it out for Kaillen ever since his ex-wife got most of their money in the divorce. This isn't the first time Olaf's tried to kill him."

Fallon nodded in agreement, then took another sip from his drink before he pulled out his phone and began scrolling through his email.

"Why hasn't Olaf been arrested?" I asked as their fighting continued.

Barnabas gave me an affronted look. "And tell the world we're not capable of handling our own scuffles by running to the authorities?" He *tsked*. "I'm guessing you're new to our kind of business."

Hearing that reminded me that I hadn't even known Kaillen for a full month, yet we were now mated. For the first time since we'd claimed one another, a sense of unease slid through me that my wolf immediately let me know her displeasure about.

Oh, can it. I might be a werewolf now, thanks to you, but that doesn't mean I've completely lost all sense.

She settled after realizing that my practical personality was simply who I was, but still . . .

How many other surprises was I going to learn about my new mate?

When Olaf again attempted to slash Kaillen's stomach open with a new knife from his belt, while promising to never stop trying to kill him, Barnabas called loudly, "Would you like some assistance?"

The hunter sighed, seeming more annoyed by Olaf's attempts than anything.

In a flash of speed, Kaillen had Olaf pinned to the wall

as Olaf's knife clattered to the floor. He held the supernatural by his neck, so it wasn't surprising that Olaf's face began to turn blue, his eyes bugging out, as he unsuccessfully tried to get Kaillen to drop him.

The other patrons in the bar, and the bartender, all continued watching the fight with detached interest. I had a feeling this kind of behavior happened somewhat regularly here.

"I would be delighted to drink from him and compel him at the same time," Barnabas called again. "Perhaps then he would finally leave you alone."

"Compel him?" My jaw dropped. "That's illegal."

Barnabas gave me an amused smirk. *Oh. Right.* Something told me he didn't see anything wrong with partaking in illegal activity.

Kaillen gave him a side-eye. "Might be useful. I'm getting tired of his attempts."

"If you would excuse me, dear Tala." Barnabas slid my way so I stood from the booth. The vampire glided past me, his hand brushing my waist in the process.

"Just had to cop a feel, didn't you?" I called.

Barnabas gave me a wicked grin. "You do smell quite delicious. You can't blame me for trying."

"Keep your hands off my woman, Barnabas," Kaillen called through clenched teeth.

Barnabas winked. "He can be quite testy, can't he?"

I swallowed a laugh as the vampire waltzed toward my hunter.

As Kaillen held the disgruntled ex-husband to the wall,

Barnabas compelled him to leave my mate alone once and for all. Since nobody even glanced in their direction, I guessed that meant the Fae Guard wouldn't be called to intervene, so I slid back into the booth and eyed Fallon curiously.

"How is it that the three of you know each other?"

Fallon looked up from his phone. "Business."

"Shadow Zone kind of business?"

He inclined his head, then replied to a text.

"Are you and Barnabas also hunters?"

"No." Fallon finished with his phone and slid it into his pocket. He picked up his drink and took another sip.

A strangled sound came from Olaf as Barnabas bit into his neck and began drinking. Kaillen was no longer holding him, merely standing back with his arms crossed. I figured Barnabas's compulsion was holding the disgruntled ex-husband in place and that the vamp was now drinking from the man since he was an easy meal.

Wow. Definitely against the law.

Kaillen's gaze dragged my way, and I caught the question in his eyes. I gave a small smile, my insides churning a bit as I got a glimpse into what his life was normally like. Even though we were mated now, it struck me that there was still so much I didn't know about him. Like what he and his friends got up to in their spare time . . . Apparently, illegal activities.

An image of six sirens straddling, kissing, and fucking Kaillen entered my mind. My wolf snarled, and I quickly shoved that picture away. Vampires who compelled supernaturals who were trying to murder my mate, I supposed I could live with, but sirens intent on riding his cock? Not so much.

Clearing my throat, I returned my attention to Fallon. "So if you're not hunters, then what are you?"

Fallon stroked his chin, and I inhaled but didn't detect any emotional scents from him. He was either wearing an incredibly complex cloaking spell that hid his emotional reactions, or he truly wasn't feeling anything at all right now. "He didn't tell you anything about us, did he?"

"Other than Barnabas being a horny pervert? No." I shook my head.

Fallon snorted, then lifted his jacket's lapel, revealing inner folds that contained a myriad of blades and knives of every size. "Just a few work tools."

My eyes widened, and I swung my gaze to Barnabas who was now sealing the bite on Olaf's neck. Olaf was slumped against the wall, a dreamy look on his face, as Kaillen's expression turned to stone. A strum of his worry flickered to me on the mate bond. He'd obviously picked up on my sudden apprehension.

I grumbled. Of course, our bond went both ways . . .

I whipped back to Fallon just as understanding dawned. "Oh my gods. You're both hired killers?"

Fallon raised his eyebrows. "I prefer *assassin*. It has a better ring to it."

Barnabas wiped his lips, his tongue flicking out to nab the last drop of Olaf's blood, before he straightened his clothing. "Off you go," he said to Olaf. "And remember, you no longer have any ill feelings toward my friend. In fact, you feel you deserved to be caught for your misdeeds."

Olaf nodded dopily, then ambled out the front door.

My eyes widened as the worry strumming from Kaillen grew as he and the vamp sauntered toward us.

I leaned back in my seat, my lips parting in surprise as I raised bewildered eyes to my mate. "Assassins? Your best friends are *assassins*?"

Kaillen and Barnabas slid back into the booth as Kaillen eyed me coolly. That iron mask had descended over his face, but I still caught the scent of anise rising from him. He was *really* worried.

Barnabas brought a hand to his chest. "Oh my, you're not the judgey type, are you?"

I glared at the vamp. "No, just the surprised type. My mate failed to mention anything about either of you, other than your ability to rile him, before we arrived."

Barnabas laughed. "Ah, new mates who haven't known each other for long. This shall be fun." He rubbed his hands in glee. "Now, where is it that we're off to? I feel quite energized after that little meal."

But Kaillen ignored his friend and glowered at Fallon. "What did you tell her?"

Fallon lifted his shoulders as he drained his glass. "I just showed her my work tools."

"Lovely, so you now know we're independent contractors for hire." Barnabas scooted closer to me, but one growl and yank from Kaillen had the vamp backpedaling. "A thousand apologies my friend, but she is most delicious smelling and quite delectable to look at."

A tingling sense of unease drifted through me, and the anise fragrance from my mate increased.

My wolf growled, already sensing where my thoughts were going, but I couldn't help it. Once again, it became apparent to me that I barely knew Kaillen despite his claim that I knew him better than most.

Barnabas stroked his chin, his lips curving up in a titillating smile. "Does it bother you? What we do for work? I do love when women pretend to be squeamish about our lifestyle, but actually ache with need for a man like me who will—"

Kaillen's hand locked around his friend's throat. "Don't even finish that sentence. You're really starting to test my patience."

Barnabas raised his hands innocently as Fallon snickered.

"We need to get moving," Kaillen added, releasing Barnabas. He eyed me again as crimson fire rolled in his irises, before he addressed his friends. "Are you two up for helping us track down a group of supernaturals who keep trying to abduct Tala?"

"Will there be killing involved?" Fallon asked.

"Hopefully," my mate replied.

Fallon shrugged. "Sure."

Barnabas grinned. "I'll happily track down anyone if it means watching you fuck things up with your beautiful new mate."

Kaillen muttered something under his breath and stood. I got up too but didn't rush to his side.

A scowl tugged at Kaillen's lips.

Fallon was the last to slide out of the booth. With all of us standing, I realized how big each of them was. Fallon had to be at least six-four, maybe even six-five. He wasn't as broad as the hunter, but he was strong and lean. And Barnabas was a couple inches over six feet too.

Next to the three of them, I had to crane my neck up to make eye contact.

Kaillen inched closer to me, his hand drifting behind my back to press against my spine. I felt his questioning emotion through our bond, his fear that I was having second thoughts about him.

I gave him a reassuring smile, but it still struck me that there was so much I didn't know.

A low discontented growl came from him, and he nodded toward the door. "Let's get moving. If the two of you are joining us, we go to Culasberee now."

CHAPTER SEVENTEEN

"Culasberee?" Barnabas replied once we were on the sidewalk outside. "How wonderful. That's where *me ship* is."

I angled my head at the lilting accent that had just entered his tone.

"I know," Kaillen replied. "Which I'm guessing is another reason you'd be more than happy to join."

The vamp rubbed his hands together. "Me always likes to see *me beauty*."

"Here we go." Fallon rolled his eyes as the four of us headed to the corner of the cobblestone street, then dipped into a small bend just off the sidewalk that wasn't busy.

Fairy residents strolled by while Fallon stood with an exasperated expression and Barnabas tipped a pretend hat in a passing fairy's direction—a rather attractive female fairy.

Kaillen pulled a portal key from one of his many

harness contraptions. He probably had a bucket of them, just like Prisha did.

Since leaving the *salopas*, he'd stayed at my side, constantly touching me as though to reassure himself that I hadn't run away again.

Considering I had a habit of that, I couldn't blame him, but we were mated now. I wasn't running. Still . . .

"Are there other illegal activities that you get up to that I should be aware of?" I asked Kaillen quietly when Barnabas and Fallon fell into a discussion about ships—well, Barnabas did and Fallon seemed to be appeasing him, even though he didn't pretend to feign interest.

"What do you consider illegal?" Kaillen grinned cockily, but that subtle anise scent rose from him again.

"I know you're faking your confidence right now."

His smile wiped clean, and that licorice scent grew. "You know I'm a hunter. By definition, my job walks on the gray side of the law."

"I know that, but you just encouraged your friend to compel a supe and drink from him. That's not the gray side of the law. That's firmly in the *illegal* spectrum of practices that could get you both sent to the supernatural prison."

Barnabas glanced over his shoulder at my comment, but Fallon had good enough manners to pretend that he hadn't heard us.

I gave them my back and lowered my voice further. "And your friends are *assassins*. You can get away with your hunter stuff, since that in itself isn't illegal, but what they do is totally illegal."

"Are you saying that killing people for money isn't something you approve of?" A hesitant smile tugged at his lips.

"This isn't a joke."

"On the contrary, everything can be a joke."

"Kaillen . . ." I gritted my teeth.

He ran a finger across my cheek, grazing the skin just enough to elicit a tingle down my spine. His teasing expression evaporated, a graver one taking its place. "It's all they've ever known. They didn't grow up in a conventional manner, so they had to learn how to survive in the only way they could. Don't hold that against them."

I took a step back, breaking contact with his incessant fingers. I couldn't think clearly when he was touching me like that. "I'm not judging them. Honestly, I'm not. The way I think of them doesn't change just 'cause of what they choose to do for work, but it does make me think about what other stuff I'm going to get dragged into. You're talking to the nine-to-five lady who pays her taxes, remember?"

His devilish smile returned. "A very sexy nine-to-five lady."

I rolled my eyes but a smile tugged at my lips. "Are there more surprises I should know about? No more secrets, remember?"

His brow furrowed. "It didn't occur to me to tell you about their professions, but in hindsight, I probably should have so you weren't surprised."

Some of the worry in me eased. "That would have been nice."

The anise in his scent calmed, and he stepped closer to me. "Since I'm now an open book"—he smirked when I rolled my eyes—"I suppose I should tell you that we're now on our way to find an old seafaring friend of Barnabas's in Culasberee. Valahan has a nasty bite and an even fouler mouth, but he also owns a tavern near the port—The Crow's Nest—and is involved in black-market activity. If anyone's trying to escape via the sea while running from the authorities, Valahan will know."

"Okay." My stiff posture relaxed even more. "And are there any other potential surprises I should be aware of?"

The hunter cocked an eyebrow. "Maybe. Last time Fallon, Barnabas, and I were at The Crow's Nest, we beat six of Valahan's fairies in several games of poker. Last I heard, they weren't very happy with us."

"Why not?"

"We might have completely cleaned them out. I believe one now has problems with his wife because of it."

"Then maybe they shouldn't play poker. Losing money is part of the game."

He grinned devilishly. "I do enjoy that sharp tongue of yours." His hand drifted down to my lower back, as he leaned in to kiss my neck.

The feel of him, and the musk rising from his scent, made my heart thrum faster.

Barnabas called from behind us, "Do you two need a room? Or perhaps we should just move deeper into this lane so he can fuck you against a wall. I do love a good show."

Kaillen snarled at his friend, and I muffled a laugh, but thankfully the vampire's blatant interest in watching me have sex with my mate had dampened my arousal.

Still, I stepped closer to Kaillen and loved the feel of his heavy arm settling around my shoulders as he pulled me in. He did it as naturally as breathing. And that licorice fragrance had completely left his scent since we were once again on common ground.

"See, told you I could be an open book." He gave me a crooked grin.

I snorted a laugh.

"Ready to go?" Kaillen called to his friends. "The hunt has officially begun."

THE PORTAL KEY dropped us onto a field just outside of the port city of Culasberee. Dusk had arrived, and the fae sun was sinking lower to the horizon. Since there were no electric or engine-powered vehicles in the fae realm, it was generally much quieter and more tranquil than earth, and Culasberee was no exception.

The air was filled with foreign bird calls as the wind whistled through a nearby grove of trees, and faint music floated to us from some distant region in the city.

Even though the day was ending, the sweeping field surrounding Culasberee was awash with color—moss, butternut, sapphire, cotton candy. The field was like a beautiful painted canvas.

Colors in the fae lands were always brighter and more vivid than on earth, and an underlying scent of magic perpetually floated through the air. Thanks to my newly enhanced werewolf senses, all of the field's colors appeared sharper and magnetic somehow. And the fragrances erupting from the wildflowers, trees, and foliage tickled my nose with a million new aromas that I didn't even know how to begin cataloguing.

"Such a lovely city, is it not?" Barnabas quipped.

"It is," I replied as Kaillen drifted closer to my side.

Similar to the capital, the city's lanes were cobblestone and the houses had thatched roofs, but there wasn't a wall around Culasberee's perimeter, nor were there gates guarded by sentries. The city sprawled throughout a valley, unlike the rising mound the capital had been built on. Towering mountains rose along the valley's sides, and in the distance, the vast glimmering sea sparkled in the growing twilight.

"Is that the Bakken Sea?" I asked.

"Ah, I see we have a geographical scholar in our midst." Barnabas rocked back on his heels, grinning.

I gave him a side-eye as Fallon replied, "Yes."

"Did you know that it connects with the Tala Sea?" Barnabas winked. "Quite a lovely name for a sea, is it not?"

"It is indeed." I gave the vamp a saccharine smile.

Barnabas barked out a laugh.

"Do you think Jakub's still here?" I nibbled on my lip.

Who knew how many hours had passed in the fae lands since we'd heard that Jakub was aiming to escape from here—not to mention the extracurricular activities that had delayed me and Kaillen even further. Time moved differently between earth and the fae realm, which often resulted in tricky schedules when one ventured here, since a month in the fae lands could feel like a week on earth.

Kaillen lifted his nose and took a long inhale, closing his eyes.

"Do you scent anything?" Fallon asked.

Kaillen nodded, and a flash of fire rolled in his irises when he opened his eyes. "Jakub's been here recently. Let's move."

In the distance, mighty ships had docked in Culasberee's port, their towering white sails like bedsheets flapping in the breeze.

"So, Kaillen said we're meeting an old friend of yours?" I said curiously to Barnabas as we began walking toward the city, the long grass swishing around us. Since Kaillen's portal key hadn't taken us directly to the wharf, I guessed Culasberee had wards that didn't allow transfer directly into the city.

"Indeed." Barnabas winked. "He runs the dark side of port life. This area is commonly used by smugglers."

When we reached the city's perimeter, Barnabas inclined his head toward a line of domals and carriages.

Fallon prowled behind the vamp to the nearest carriage, and Kaillen and I followed.

The carriage dipped under the heavy weight when the

three men climbed on board, and the domal—a fae horse—looked over his shoulder and huffed.

Domals weren't able to use language, but they were more intelligent than their earthly counterparts, and they conducted their own businesses. A driver wasn't required.

"Off to The Crow's Nest at the wharf!" Barnabas called loudly once I'd climbed in. "We haven't a moment to lose."

The domal dipped his head after Kaillen placed payment into his satchel, and then took off at a brisk trot, his eggplant-colored coat reflecting an ebony hue in the dying light.

As the carriage jostled and swayed along the cobblestone lanes, Kaillen dipped his head toward Fallon and Barnabas.

"Jakub will inevitably be traveling with weapons and a trained team. From what we've learned so far, everyone employed by him sports the same tattoo." He described the constellation pattern to them, going into detail.

"That's unusual," Fallon commented, the yellow-haired fairy leaning back in the carriage as his legs sprawled out in front of him. "And foolish. It makes it too easy to identify them."

"I've thought the same," Kaillen replied. He slung an arm around me as the scent of salt entered the air. We were fast approaching the wharf. "But from what I've seen, Jakub is anything but stupid. There has to be a reason he tattooed his entire crew."

Barnabas stroked his chin, his indigo eyes flashing with interest. "And he's after you specifically, my dear?"

I inclined my head. "He believes I'm the key apparently."

"Key to what?" Fallon asked.

I shrugged. "If we only knew."

The fairy assassin's brows furrowed together.

"That's his brooding face," Barnabas said. "When Fallon gets that look, it's best to leave him be."

Fallon gave Barnabas a withering glare at which the vamp laughed.

"The Crow's Nest is just up ahead." Kaillen pointed down the lane we'd turned onto. The domal's swift trot hadn't lessened, and the mighty ships I'd seen from the city's other side now glistened like polished ivory in the fading twilight.

I wasn't sure what fae ships were made from, but the cream-colored exterior appeared smooth with darker colored lines scouring the seams.

"Bone ships." Barnabas leaned forward, his eyes brightening with interest. "The fae ships are much sturdier than the earthly ones. Almost makes me wish I was a sailor again."

"Again?" I cocked my head. "Have you been on many ships?" I asked as the domal pulled up to a tavern with a sign hanging over the door in faded paint informing us that we'd reached The Crow's Nest. The bar's windows revealed a boisterous party inside, and if the music, laughter, and noise of scraping chairs were any indication of what was to come, I was glad I'd worn sturdy boots.

We all stepped out of the carriage as Barnabas sighed wistfully. "I have. Before I was turned, I sailed the high seas on earth. Of course, the fun we had then is now a thing of the past."

"Being a sailor was fun? Seriously?" From what I'd learned in history class, it was a life of hardship. "How long ago was that?"

"Roughly four hundred years ago."

"Didn't you get scurvy or something before you turned to a vamp?" I asked as the four of us walked to the door. "Surely, that wasn't fun."

"Oh, it was plenty of fun if you were a pirate." He grinned, his fangs lengthening.

"Don't get him started." Kaillen slid an arm around my waist, and my wolf preened at the contact, practically purring to have her mate so close. "Once he gets started about the old glory days, he doesn't shut up."

"And whatever you do, don't mention the B word." Fallon pulled the tavern's door open.

"B word?" I scrunched my nose up as a zap of magic washed along my skin when we stepped over the tavern's threshold.

"Blackbeard," Kaillen whispered into my ear, then nipped my earlobe.

A shiver danced through me as Barnabas cussed. "That Blackbeard was a wily sonuvabitch who—"

A knife flew right for Barnabas's head.

The vamp dipped to the side, the movement graceful and executed with perfect ease.

The knife's blade embedded itself into the wooden post

behind him, then a high-pitched scream came from across the room.

"And I see that they're still quite upset . . ." Barnabas sighed.

Before I could process what was happening, six fairies leaped toward us.

CHAPTER EIGHTEEN

Kaillen shoved me behind him, but a fairy barreled into him, tumbling both of them to the ground as I shrieked and scrambled out of the way. Amazingly, none of the patrons in the tavern even glanced at us.

"You fuckin' twats have a lot of nerve showing your face here again!" one of the fairies yelled.

My wolf snarled, rage firing through her that someone had attacked our mate, but then I realized it was more like a brawl than an actual attack, especially when Kaillen laughed after the fairy punched him clear across the jaw.

"Don't be such a sore loser," the hunter admonished when the fairy swung again.

"My wife left me because of you swine!" he replied.

In one fluid movement, my hunter was on his feet, his eyes wild with excitement as the fairy came after him so hard that he shoved Kaillen against the wall.

My jaw dropped. "Are you hurt?" I called to him.

"No," he replied with a grin as the fairy landed a solid punch to his stomach.

But Kaillen returned the hit, while Barnabas and Fallon were doing the same. All six of the fairies, along with Kaillen and his friends, were duking it out like a boxing ring.

"Now, now, it's not my fault that you can't count cards —" Barnabas ducked when one of the fairies aimed for his throat.

A sprawling punch from Fallon had one of the fairies launching at me, but I released a rush of telekinetic magic, strengthened with a maximizer spell and combined with a binding one.

The fairy froze mid-air, before I sent him flying through a window, glass shattering everywhere, because seriously, this fight needed to stop. We had a madman to catch.

Fallon lifted his gaze, surprise flaring in his eyes, as he held one of the fairies in a headlock. "She can fight?"

"Better than you two losers can," Kaillen replied with a crooked grin as he punched another fairy right in the gut.

The fairy doubled over, sputtering, just as Barnabas pounced on him. The vamp sent him careening through the same window that I'd smashed a second before.

I could only imagine what the passersby on the street were thinking.

Fallon tightened his hold on the fairy he still held in a

headlock. "Concede. It's not our fault we beat all of you. It was a legitimate game."

The fairy sputtered and thrashed. "Fuck you, Fallon! I lost three months of pay!" The fairy tried to lean down and bite Fallon's forearm, but the assassin merely tightened his grip, and the fairy's face turned purple.

"You know it was all an unfortunate outcome," Barnabas said pacifyingly to the two fairies whom he towered over on the floor. Both had split lips and wore irritated glares. "Why don't you fellows put your pesky feelings aside, and we'll all sit down for a nice drink."

A taller fairy, with flaming red hair, who was currently beneath Barnabas's boot, glanced my way. His gaze raked over my frame.

A low growl came from Kaillen.

"Who's the new female?" Flaming Hair said curiously.

"She's *mine*," Kaillen replied.

"Yours?" Flaming Hair's friend—a Solis fairy from the looks of it, since he had wings, white hair, and crystalline blue eyes—leered at me. "Quite a looker. Did you hire her? 'Cause I wouldn't mind giving her a ride on my cock when you're done."

Kaillen snarled, then whipped into a blur so fast that I didn't have time to tell the Solis fairy that I was not in fact a hooker.

Barnabas dusted his fingernails off on his shirt, as Kaillen landed a nasty uppercut to the downed fairy. "I have a feeling that was the wrong thing to say to a newly mated werewolf," the vamp said under his breath to me.

"No kidding?" But while I would have loved to let the Solis fairy know that I wasn't actually a prostitute, when Kaillen finally reappeared, his chest heaving as gold and fire flamed in his eyes, the two who had been taunting me lay immobile on the floor.

"Are they dead?" I gaped as the other patrons continued to enjoy their drinks around us.

"Oh no," Barnabas replied just as Fallon released his hold from his fairy who slumped to the ground, apparently unconscious after being deprived of oxygen for so many minutes. "Just subdued. We don't actually have time for this. We have a villain to catch, remember?"

Kaillen drifted to my side, rage still swirling in his eyes.

"I'm sure he was kidding, friend." Barnabas patted him on the back. "He probably saw Tala's mating mark and wanted to get your goat."

Fallon let out a low whistle. "Kaillen's got it bad," he said in a low voice to Barnabas, but of course, I still heard it.

"As I also noted." Barnabas leaned his forearm across the bar top as the bartender, a tall willowy female fairy, sauntered over. "I need to speak with Valahan. Is he free?"

"Yeah, he just finished with a new client. You can head on back." She jerked her thumb toward a corner back door. "But before you go, what about my window?"

"I'll get it," Fallon said, stepping forward. He waved his hand toward the shards of glass that remained in the windowpane, and a gush of magic flowed from him.

The shattered glass on the floor floated into the air,

then reformed in the pane, sealing together, as if melting under an invisible flame, until the window was whole again, no debris to be found anywhere.

The bartender inclined her head in thanks to Fallon.

My eyes widened into saucers. All fairies had magic to some degree, but to be able to repair something that intricate? That took *a lot* of magic. The yellow-haired assassin had some serious magical mojo.

Barnabas ambled toward the back corner, as Kaillen pinned himself to my side.

A few of the patrons appraised me when we passed, their curious eyes skittering to the mating mark on my neck as we followed the vamp to the back room.

As we entered, Barnabas called, "Valahan, I need a minute."

A short and squat troll turned his way.

I drew up short. The troll's large yellow eyes turned to slits. "What do you want, bloodsucker?"

Barnabas pulled a chair out, swung it backward, then straddled it. "I'm looking for a fellow who goes by the name of Jakub. He's possibly traveling with a group. All of them have tattoos on their necks in the shape of a constellation. Do you know his whereabouts?"

Valahan's stench wafted toward me more as he shifted from his squatting position. I did my best not to gag . . . but holy mother of gods in all the realms . . . his scent was foul with a capital F. Like decaying corpse mixed with rotting meat and a side of fermented eggs.

I brought a hand discreetly to my mouth, to hide my

reaction, but Valahan's eyes narrowed. "Who's she?" he asked in a deep, disjointed voice that made me wonder if he ate gravel for breakfast.

Kaillen stepped in front of me, but his protective stance was fine by me. Being hidden behind his broad back and shoulders allowed me to have a gag or two.

Fallon looked down, pretending to inspect one of his blades, but I still caught the amused curve of his lips.

"She's mine." Kaillen crossed his arms.

I stifled an eye roll. Apparently, that was my new way of being introduced.

"Mated, I see?" Valahan commented, as he studied the mark on Kaillen's neck curiously. I had a feeling he'd never seen that mark on a male before.

Kaillen only grunted.

"Valahan?" Barnabas said in a smooth tone that reminded me of melted butter. "We're in a bit of a time crunch. What can you tell me about Jakub?"

The troll held out his hand, the large appendage twice the size of a dinner plate. "A thousand rulibs."

My eyes bulged. A thousand fae rulibs was the equivalent of ten thousand US dollars.

Barnabas sighed as Kaillen whipped a pouch from his harness and threw it at the troll. *Say what?* Kaillen was so rich that he owned fifty thousand acres of land in Montana and carried the fae equivalent of thousands of dollars in his pocket like it was no big deal? Just how wealthy was my mate?

"The information, please?" Barnabas asked in that sweet tone again.

"He's with a large group," Valahan replied. "All of them have those tattoos. They just left port an hour ago."

My breath caught.

"Going where?" Kaillen asked.

"Beats me." Valahan shrugged. "I don't care where the scum go after they leave my city. All I care about is that they pay their dues to pass through."

Kaillen grumbled as an excited gleam grew in Barnabas's eyes. "And which direction were they headed?"

"West." Valahan opened the pouch my mate had given him, his thick fingers counting the coins.

If Jakub and his men had gone west, then they'd gone out to sea, just as Commander Klebus had feared. My stomach bottomed out. There was no way we could catch him now. We were too late.

Barnabas gave a small bow, and the four of us left the back room as the troll continued riffling through his new riches.

"Do you have to look so excited?" Fallon said in a monotone voice as we all headed toward the tavern exit.

"Oh, don't begrudge me for it." Barnabas waved his hand.

"Begrudge you for what?" I asked as we stepped outside into the cool night. I was twisting my hands, because our lead for Jakub was officially gone, and who knew when the next one would arise.

"To what awaits us, my dear."

Fallon groaned, and Kaillen just shook his head.

"Am I missing something? What awaits us?" I asked while I wondered why nobody else was looking concerned that Jakub had escaped.

Kaillen hooked an arm around me and propelled me toward the boardwalk.

"Why, the adventures on the high seas, of course," Barnabas replied as his eyes gleamed like amethysts in the starlight. "Fallon gets seasick, so he's never been much of a fan, but if Jakub is escaping via the sea, then there's only one way to catch him."

My eyes widened. "We can still catch him?"

Fallon groaned. "Yeah, on a boat. We get it."

I nearly squealed. "Oh, that's right, you said you have a ship here!"

"Indeed I do." Barnabas waved toward the ship at the end of the boardwalk. It was a sleek vessel with a myriad of sails. "Tala, meet the only lady I've ever loved."

I stared at the inscription on the back of the boat and burst out laughing. Barnabas hadn't been kidding. The name of the boat was indeed, *The Only Lady I've Ever Loved.*

A twinkle formed in Kaillen's eyes. "I hope you don't mind sailing?"

CHAPTER NINETEEN

The nighttime sky loomed above us as Barnabas's ship sailed through open water. We'd sailed so far out to sea that I could no longer see land, which meant the night sky dominated the view.

During the day, the fae lands' sky was a pale green with white and pastel-colored clouds, but at night it was a sea of black with luminous stars, three moons, distant planets, and a strip of the cloudy galaxy. It was even more beautiful than earth's night sky.

Barnabas stood at the helm of his ship, singing quite boisterously, while Kaillen had planted himself at the bow. My mate's shoulders were tensed as he conducted whatever sorcerer mojo he used while hunting.

"Southwest!" Kaillen called over his shoulder to the vamp. "Angle us slightly to the south." He closed his eyes, his nose lifting again.

"Aye-aye, matey!" Barnabas veered the ship to the port-side, and the sleek vessel cut through the water like a shark.

I approached Kaillen tentatively. His brow was furrowed, his eyes closed. A part of me wondered if I should disturb him or not, but I was so intrigued by his hunting skills that my feet moved of their own accord.

Even though I approached him silently, my wolf's skills coming in handy as the ship rocked beneath my feet, he still reached out a hand for me while his eyes stayed closed.

My fingers threaded through his, my wolf rumbling in contentment at the contact. A low answering vibration came from Kaillen through our bond, as though his wolf had a similar response.

I sighed. Even though our wolves had thoroughly taken over in that way, I was coming to accept it.

"Am I bothering you?" I asked quietly. "I don't want to mess up whatever you're doing to find Jakub."

Kaillen squeezed my hand, his palm warm and rough. "You could never bother me."

Smothering the warm feeling that statement provoked, I stood silently at his side as he continued channeling his magic into hunting Jakub-Dipshit.

The wind flapped the sails as the vessel rolled beneath my feet. While I'd never spent much time on the open water, despite living on Lake Michigan, I was coming to realize I enjoyed it.

A heaving sound came from the back.

"Poor Fallon," I murmured, glancing over my shoulder to see the fairy leaning over the railing. My own stomach became queasy listening to him. It was the fourth time he'd retched. I'd tried to help him earlier, but he'd been so stoic and had dismissed my concerns. Now, though? I had a feeling maybe he'd changed his mind.

"Be right back." I squeezed Kaillen's hand as my mate's brow furrowed again.

"South more," he called to Barnabas over the singing.

The vamp winked at me when I passed, his baritone song pouring from his lips like he'd been made to sing at the Sydney Opera House.

I ventured toward Fallon, as the ship dipped. Salty wind caressed my cheeks, and the night sky shone like a dome above us.

When I reached the fairy's side, I extracted a potion from my belt. "This will help. You should really take it."

The fairy wiped at his mouth, his complexion ashen in the starlight. He eyed the potion warily. "What is it?"

"A potion I try not to leave home without. It's one of my own remedies to be used when any sickness prevails. It won't make you immune to the sea forever, but it should help for the next forty-eight hours."

His eyebrow quirked, and I could tell he was trying to look nonchalant and tough, but he totally just looked sick and miserable, and judging from the green tint that had entered his complexion, he was also about to hurl his guts out for the fifth time.

"You don't have to take it, but I'd advise you to." Especially since we had no idea what lay ahead if we caught up to Jakub.

He took the potion and uncorked it before sniffing. "Is there pallfenroot in here?"

"Yep, it's one of a few fae ingredients along with a few from earth, but it also has a hefty dose of magic added into it that does the trick."

He gave me a side-eye. "And this won't make me sicker?"

"No. It'll make you better. Promise."

He let out a breath when another wave rocked the boat hard, then downed the contents in one swallow while holding onto the railing. He made a face, as if he were going to throw up again.

"Sorry." I twisted my hands. "Did I forget to mention that the taste isn't pleasant?"

He gave me a weighted look. "It's repugnant."

"You'll still thank me in a few minutes."

I turned before the fairy could respond, knowing he probably wanted to compose himself as the potion took hold.

I made my way back to the helm where Barnabas was in his glory days as Kaillen had called it.

The vamp's animated singing hadn't abated. If anything, he was singing louder. I swallowed a laugh when I actually listened to the words.

Oh, the earth we sail, and the waves we tide.
  She's got big tits on those swells we ride.
  We thrust and pull o're the water's tithe.
  And dream of our lovelies as they writhe.

"Is that a song from your sailing days?" I tried to keep a straight face when I reached him.

Barnabas grinned, his fangs shining like silver as he paused his song momentarily. Kaillen stood at his side, having apparently abandoned his position at the bow. My mate shook his head in exasperation. "Don't encourage him."

But if the vamp heard him, he didn't let on. Facing me fully, his hands stayed on the ship's wheel as he grinned. "Oh no, that's not one of me sailing ditties from the years past. That's one I made up on this fine night as we venture yonder across this vast realm. Argh!"

"Barnabas, enough already." Kaillen pinched the bridge of his nose, and I swallowed another laugh.

"Are your songs always that perverted?" I asked when the ship dipped into another swell.

"Oh, most usually. I do fantasize regularly about women's breas—"

Kaillen slapped a hand over the vamp's mouth. "My mate doesn't need to hear about your wet dream material."

Barnabas side-stepped, expelling Kaillen's palm. "Oh, I think she would enjoy it. In fact, I think that's why she asked." He smiled broadly and waggled his eyebrows.

Kaillen's eyes rolled skyward just as Fallon came lumbering over from the back of the boat.

"Feeling better?" I asked. The pea-green hue had left his face, and he stood straighter, not looking at death's door anymore or like he was going to curl over and spew his stomach contents onto the bone-white deck.

"Much." He joined his friends at the helm, then eyed me again. "You really made up that potion?"

"I did. I own a magic shop in Chicago, and I craft all of our spells, hexes, brews, potions, and everything else we sell. It's kind of my specialty." I jolted the second that comment left my lips. I'd just declared to someone I barely knew the strength of my power. And to think only a month ago I was still hiding it and would have given all of the credit to Tessa.

Fallon lifted his brows just as Barnabas hissed, "And I believe we've caught him at last."

All of us straightened, our gazes cutting to the horizon where Barnabas had his eyes trained.

In the distance, something glinted off the waves, like a diamond reflecting moonlight.

"Is that really him?" My heart picked up a staccato beat as my wolf got to her feet, hackles rising.

Fire glittered in Kaillen's irises. "That's him."

A stone settled in my stomach, as Barnabas launched into a new song about sex-deprived sailors and sirens who lured them to their deaths.

We grew closer to Jakub's ship glittering on the horizon. I assumed once we were in hearing distance of Jakub and his minions, that the vamp would curb his obvious enthusiasm about being on the open sea, but I couldn't be sure.

Kaillen lifted his hand, a spell shooting from his fingertips. His illusion magic descended over us, a veil glimmering over the ship like a dark shroud.

A deadly burn of satisfaction coursed through me that we were closing in on Jakub's tail, and he probably had no idea. Because for the first time since my life had been thrown into upheaval, I was no longer the hunted.

Now, I was the hunter, and I was coming to collect my prey.

"HOW ARE we going to play this?" Fallon asked as he sharpened a blade with a stone. His weapon was long and lean, with a curve at the end. A slight mist wafted over the blade every time it slid over the rock, making me think it was spelled.

"We do it like in the glory days," Barnabas replied. "We slam into his vessel, jump aboard, and then battle every last one of his crew until we claim victory and the spoils of their riches."

"What are their riches?" I asked.

Barnabas stroked his chin. "Well, that I cannot answer. Argh!"

Fallon shook his head. "Seriously, all he needs is a parrot on his shoulder and an eyepatch."

"That could be arranged," Kaillen replied dryly.

We were fast approaching Jakub's ship. The vessel Jakub-Dipshit traveled on was larger than *The Only Lady I've Ever Loved*, but it was clunky, which had allowed Barnabas's sleeker boat to catch up with him easily.

Surprisingly, Jakub's ship wasn't veiled under a spell,

leading me to think that he knew the SF hadn't been able to pursue him. Or perhaps he was so incredibly arrogant that he didn't think anyone could stop him.

My blood boiled just thinking about that insufferable ass. If the man who'd tried to capture me in Philadelphia was indeed Jakub, then he had another thing coming if he thought he could escape.

"How many do you think are on board?" Fallon sheathed his blade, the slice of his knife ringing through the night.

"Valahan said that he traveled with a group of supernaturals." Kaillen cinched down the straps on his harness, then checked his cargo pant pockets. The man was a literal walking nightmare. He had so many blades, potions, and magical devices strapped to him that I wondered if he even knew where all of them were.

"Even though there are only four of us, we have the element of surprise. I daresay that this shall be an easy capture." Barnabas turned the wheel again, and the ship's sails billowed in the night wind.

"When do you think we'll reach them?" I inched closer to Kaillen, and his hand automatically went to my lower back. I melted into the feel of him, loving his warmth and the strength that radiated from him.

His strong fingers massaged my muscles, and the scent of musk and iron rose from him.

"We shall be ramming their ship within the hour," Barnabas replied. "I still enjoy seeing *The Only Lady I've Ever Loved* utilized in the way in which she was designed."

"Meaning what?" I asked.

Barnabas gave me a cocky smile. "Meaning me ship's bow is designed to slice through the likes of that one." He pointed toward the behemoth that Jakub was sailing on.

Excitement hummed through my veins, and a part of me wished that Prisha was here. She would've been as excited as me at the upcoming battle, because there was something about the beauty of revenge that made a fight so much sweeter.

The musky scent off Kaillen grew, and he leaned down to whisper in my ear. "You're giving off the most delicious aroma right now."

I shifted closer to him, my wolf practically purring at the close contact. Desire pooled between my legs, and the aroused scent off my mate skyrocketed. "What scent is that?"

"Sex and violence. I have to say, it's quite delectable." He nipped at my ear, causing me to shiver.

"Do you two need a room before we end that prick once and for all?" Fallon asked, a slight twitch to his lips. No one would have guessed that the fairy had been puking his guts out an hour ago. He was now the picture of lethal grace as his legs dipped with each roll of the ship while he stood steady and sure.

Kaillen arched an eyebrow at Barnabas. "Does this ship have rooms?"

I whacked my mate in the stomach, which got a chuckle from him.

"I find the storeroom below to be quite useful for that

sort of activity." Barnabas gave me a wink before turning his attention back to the sea.

Kaillen's hand drifted lower, cupping my ass as his musky scent grew. "Should we try it out?"

I gave him a look. "You can't be serious. You're acting like a horny teenager who's just snuck out of his parents' home and will take any private space he can find to bang his girlfriend."

"And that's a bad thing?" His expression stayed completely deadpan.

I laughed, then pulled him down for a kiss. "No, but the next time you take me, I want to scream so loudly it will echo through this realm. But I don't particularly want to do that with your friends so close."

Two new musky aromas wafted from the direction in which the assassins stood. I knew they'd overheard me, which made a flush stain my cheeks.

A low growl rumbled from Kaillen as his eyes narrowed in his friends' direction.

Fallon held up his hands in surrender. "You know I mean no disrespect, but when a woman talks like that, it's hard not to . . ." He shrugged helplessly toward the growing bulge in his pants.

"Are you sure you're not interested in a three-way?" Barnabas asked me with a cocked eyebrow.

Kaillen let out a terrifying growl and lunged for him.

The vampire side-stepped out of the way at the last second, but then hurried around to the opposite side of the ship when Kaillen swiped out to grab his throat. "Only kidding. You can't blame me for trying to rile you when it's so easy to now."

A new aroma wafted up from Kaillen. It wasn't one I'd detected before. It smelled of jasmine and night, and my wolf took notice.

The hunter drifted back to my side once his friends' attention had wisely returned to Jakub's ship which was now less than a quarter of a mile away. He locked an arm around my waist, hauling me closer, then dipped down and inhaled my scent.

Goosebumps tingled down my spine as I arched to give him better access to the sensitive area beneath my ear. "Can I ask what emotion smells like jasmine and night?"

A low rumbling snarl vibrated in Kaillen's chest. "It's a scent unique to male werewolves even though other species can also feel that particular emotion."

"And what emotion is it?" A small gasp left me when his lips pressed against my skin. I curled a hand around the nape of his neck and was seriously contemplating the storeroom in the hull of Barnabas's ship even though a part of me was mortified that I was mentally going there.

"It's when a male werewolf is feeling possessive and protective about his mate. While many male species can feel that way toward their women, the way a wolf feels toward his mate is a bit different. That's why it has its own scent." He nipped at my skin again, his teeth grazing along that sensitive area.

I gasped and gripped his shirt to pull him closer. That undeniable urge to drag him to my bed was swimming through my veins and making my head spin. "I want you."

"The feeling's mutual, my love." The evidence of his arousal pressed against my stomach. "Are you sure you don't want to try out the room below?"

As tempting as that was, my gaze drifted toward the other ship. With each second that passed, it loomed closer. "Afterward. When Jakub's dead, and this is over once and for all, I'm going to ride you so hard you'll see stars."

The possessive emotional scent off Kaillen strengthened a hundred-fold as an answering growl worked up his throat. "A fight and then a fuck? You certainly know how to please a man."

I pulled him in for another kiss. His tongue swept in to dance with mine, and his taste, feel, and scent were nearly driving me mad. Gods, these instincts and reactions to him were beyond compelling. I felt drugged, as though I *needed* him in order to breathe.

Somehow, I managed to pull back, taking a shuddering breath. "I do aim to please."

Kaillen's hands tightened around my waist.

"Excuse me, lovebirds," Barnabas said dryly. "I'm afraid you've missed your opportunity for a quickie in the hull. I think that despite the illusion spell, our nemesis has sensed our impending arrival."

My gaze snapped to the sea, then widened when I beheld Jakub's monstrous ship.

It was turning, its front angling to point toward us.

Similar to Barnabas's ship, a large spear protruded from the bow.

"Don't fail me now, *The Only Lady I've Ever Loved.*" Barnabas lovingly caressed the wheel, then began snapping orders at Fallon and Kaillen.

The two whipped into action. Cold night air blew against my skin the second Kaillen stepped away from our embrace.

Barnabas's fangs lengthened as the energy around Kaillen and Fallon soared. My own magic hummed in response, as if knowing what was coming, while my wolf began to pace in my belly, snarls rumbling in her chest as her hackles rose.

"I need to hit them before they fully turn." An excited gleam filled the vampire's eyes as he steered his vessel toward the oncoming ship, not looking the least perturbed about the inevitable crash. "Brace yourselves, mateys, this one might hurt."

CHAPTER TWENTY

Shouts and scents of casting magic came from Jakub's vessel just as Barnabas issued another order to Kaillen and Fallon. *The Only Lady I've Ever Loved*'s sails snapped under the hauling ropes and levers, just as an explosion of magic launched from Jakub's ship.

Our nemesis's incoming spell crackled against the illusion shield that Kaillen had cast, and in a shower a sparks, the illusion vanished just as our ships collided.

Since Jakub's vessel wasn't fully facing us, Barnabas had the advantage. His bow's deadly point rammed the larger ship's hull in a splinter of bone and wood.

The crew aboard the vessel sneered and scowled, their movements frantic as they darted into action. My eyes widened when I took in their vast numbers. Ten, twelve, no twenty . . . there were too many to count.

A flood of magic barreled toward us, cast from someone on the ship I couldn't see.

"Tala!" Kaillen roared over the screech of crushing wood and bone as Barnabas's ship began to bob back. "Watch out, we're—"

I was thrown forward as a huge wave rocked *The Only Lady I've Ever Loved*. A spray of ocean water shot across my face, salt stinging my eyes as I cast a spell at lightning speed, erecting a shield around myself before throwing it toward Kaillen and his friends. Another flare of magic fizzled over my shield, but it held and protected me, Kaillen, Fallon, and—

Barnabas was gone.

The clang of clashing swords filled the air as I blinked and my sight cleared. Barnabas was already on the other ship, sword in hand as he dodged and swayed in a dance of beauty and stealth. A deranged smile had plastered itself to his face, and I had a feeling he was reliving his pirate glory days.

I downed my shield as Kaillen gave me a fierce nod. "We all charge as one!" he bellowed.

I dashed toward Jakub's ship, potion in hand, as Kaillen and Fallon flew past me, all three of us leaping from *The Only Lady I've Ever Loved* in one giant arc to the larger vessel.

The crew aboard Jakub's ship all had weapons out or spells flying. My hair blew in front of my eyes when I dipped and rolled as a vampire lunged at me with a two-foot blade. I came up behind him, kneeling on the deck, and grabbed a splintered piece of wood from a pile of ruined rigging. Calling upon the speed and strength of my wolf, I swiveled around and drove it up and into the vamp's chest.

His eyes widened in surprise just as his body turned to ash.

A ferocious growl came from behind me, then the scent of casting magic as Kaillen became of blur of fire, magic, and spells. He moved so fast that I couldn't see him, but his scent and the tug of our bond alerted me to the location he was darting toward.

I whipped around, searching for Jakub, but amidst the chaos all I saw were fighting fairies, snarling werewolves, battling sorcerers, raging half-demons, and hissing vamps. But one thing I did notice? *All* of them had the constellation tattoo on their necks. Only now, their tattoos were glowing.

A sudden melody came from the sea, a beautiful song of promise and love. My body instinctively tugged toward it, my feet itching to move to the rail and throw myself overboard into the watery darkness that would envelop me in a silken paradise.

Dammit. The sirens had arrived, obviously sensing the blood and battle.

I whipped out another shield spell to protect myself from the sirens' call, just as one of Jakub's crew members stumbled toward the railing and flung himself overboard. A dopey-looking grin stretched across his face as he plummeted downward. Hisses and the sound of tearing flesh followed below. *One sucker down, dozens to go . . .*

The flash of a sword swiped toward me from a half-demon just as a fairy came at me simultaneously.

I dipped, narrowly avoiding the half-demon's blade, as my awakening power slithered out of its cave and caressed my insides. It no longer barreled out of me, but stress apparently still provoked it.

Sweating, I cast a binding spell on the fairy as they both tried to catch me. Concentrating on my awakening power, I beckoned more of it from its black void. It'd been days since I'd last used it, but the intensive two weeks of daily training with Kaillen were paying off.

My awakening magic responded as though it were an extension of myself. It raced through my limbs as its razor jaws gnashed and flowed toward my unsuspecting victims, like a ferocious lion going in for the kill.

I blasted a maximizer spell combined with werewolf strength at the half-demon. The punch knocked him unconscious. *Huh.* Didn't know I could combine werewolf strength with my witch magic.

A wave of burning hot fire descended on the half-demon, and a fluttering of internal awareness told me it'd come from my mate. Kaillen's black flames disappeared as soon as the half-demon turned to ash. I assumed that was so the ship wouldn't burn beneath our feet, leading to an unpleasant death thanks to hungry sirens waiting below . . .

Kaillen and I made eye contact briefly before two more crew members descended on him.

My binding spell on the fairy shattered, and in an instant, he leaped to my front with his weapon in hand.

I bent backward, my body arching as his blade swung toward me as he tried to corner me by the rail, and it struck me that he wasn't trying to kill me but instead he was trying to capture me. I bent my knees and flipped in a backward somersault, landing on the balls of my feet just as I flung my awakening power toward the fairy.

Tiny strands of magic intermixed with zapping power flew out of me as my invisible tentacles wrapped around the fairy like an octopus's arms. My power bit into him, and my awakening power's teeth serrated through his inner magic, shredding his insides to ribbons.

His feeling of surprise hit me first. Then his fear. I sank my claws deeper into him, hacking through everything that made up his essence. He cried out as his magic spewed from him like a volcano. Fairy magic flooded my pores.

My wolf whined at the intrusion of a foreigner's energy, but I reassured her for a split second before pushing her back as I concentrated on extending my power.

More tentacles slithered from me to every opponent on the deck as sweat trailed down my skin and soaked my clothes. My power moved so fast and speared each opponent so quickly, that I didn't have time to corral their magic as it poured into me.

Those strange octopus-like arms latched onto one supernatural after another. *One. Two. Three. Four* . . .

My entire body trembled at the exertion of sinking my magical teeth into so many at once. A wave of dizziness swept through me, but one by one, our opponents were beginning to fall.

But where was Jakub? I scanned the deck again. Still no sign of him.

Fallon's brow furrowed when a fairy he'd been battling abruptly fell to his knees, his features anguished. Only Kaillen knew what was happening as Fallon turned to a new opponent as he and Barnabas continued hacking and cleaving their way through everyone in their paths.

The assassins moved with deadly grace, their strikes solid, their movements coordinated with cool precision. Fallon's face was a mask of efficient purpose, while Barnabas still wore that maniacal grin.

Our enemies were annihilated as my awakening power continued to ensnare and capture, but this was different than training. I was moving too frantically, pulling too quickly. I'd lost the control I'd learned in training, and I couldn't contain their magic as it barreled into me.

"Tala!" Kaillen called. "It's too many!"

My body began to sway, but my awakening power knew no bounds. It flung and pounced as a primal feeling of revenge swept through me despite my fatigue.

Sweat poured from me in rivers as all of the supernaturals I'd latched onto moaned and writhed, collapsing one after another. Their magic siphoned to me, filling me with brimming strength and heat, yet I still didn't know how to wield it.

My knees buckled.

So much magic. So much power. It flooded me as I took all of their rage and hate, their lust for the battle, and their feelings of terror as they realized that they were losing control, and that they no longer owned their magic, but *I* did.

Fallon and Barnabas stopped cleaving supernaturals in two when they realized their opponents weren't falling from their strikes, but instead from an invisible force wielded on shadowed wings and misted claws.

Kaillen and his friends surveyed the damage as a colossal amount of magic hummed through my veins and flooded my senses. It was too much. I couldn't contain it. I needed to release it, needed to get it out of me, needed to—

"Your ancestors would be proud. Your power is quite impressive." A detached clinical-sounding voice flowed toward me from the back of the ship.

I clumsily twirled around, since I felt drunk on the raging power flowing through my veins. "Where are you?" I hissed.

I surveyed the area, barely able to do more in my debilitating position as power vibrated through my body. I directed all of my attention on the source of where I thought the voice had come from.

"I didn't expect you to pursue me but am pleased you did," Jakub continued. "It's interesting that you thought you could catch me, if that's what you were attempting? But I'm glad I'm here to witness this, to know beyond any doubt that you truly are the blood descendent. The key."

Kaillen snarled and lunged, but Jakub-Dipshit was nowhere to be found. I couldn't see him, yet I could *sense* him. Something prickled along my skin and tingled my nerves.

He's hiding under a cloaking spell. That realization snapped me upright, because it meant he could be anywhere.

I staggered around, searching for any hint of Jakub's presence as Kaillen and his friends did the same. Instinctively, we formed a circle, our backs to one another so that we were all facing outward.

I nearly buckled as the last of the crew members died from my power. "Why can't we see him?" I managed. "We're all strong. We should be able to see through whatever cloak he wears."

"Because I'm commanding more power than you," Jakub answered in that cold tone again, except he was closer this time.

I swung toward his voice, and the power that I'd harvested from the fleet of supernaturals surged against my skin.

"Tala," Kaillen said, and then groaned, as the strength of my caged power barreled toward him on the mating bond. His growl came just as something cold caressed my skin.

Jakub.

A powerful zap of magic snaked over me, and my eyes widened when I recognized the feel of a portal key about to activate.

I rocked myself back, knowing that if I didn't escape Jakub's grip, he would steal me away by using the portal key I'd sensed, and the two of us could be anywhere in seconds. I would be alone. Trapped. Potentially at his mercy.

I cast a curse lightning fast, hoping I'd casted it on him. If my curse hit its mark, it would link me to him so my magic could find him and tether us. Then I would know where he was even if I couldn't see him.

Something brushed against my curse's power, but it was there and then gone. I had no idea if my curse had taken root because the power from the dead supernaturals was surging inside me, stirred up by the absolute panic I'd felt when Jakub had tried to whisk me away.

I groaned, but I couldn't stop it. Couldn't contain it.

I spun toward where that last sensation from Jakub had come from, just as all of the power brimming inside me rushed to the surface.

"Watch out!" I cried.

An explosion of magic, as wide as the slowly sinking ship, shot from my chest. Radiant energy rocketed out of me, the gathered magic of all of those I'd killed pouring from me in one vicious and uncontrolled blast. It rose like a tidal wave, higher than the masts, wider than the ship. It was as though a tsunami of energy blasted into everything in its directed path.

The ship's side turned to fizzling embers when my explosion hit it, and all of us were jolted off our feet as the remaining floor beneath us gave a great, groaning *creak* as half of the ship fell away.

"She's sinking!" Barnabas clamped a hold of my arm just as my legs gave out.

He jumped us farther up the deck as water swirled around our ankles and the entire ship tilted upward, sinking so fast that it was a miracle he was able to retreat us at all on the heaving vessel.

The call of the sirens increased, their deadly beautiful song carrying through the night on a dark melody. Their curved claws scraped along the bottom of the tilted ship, beckoning us closer.

Shining eyes peered up at me from the darkness as their pearly skin caught the moonlight. Their luminescent scales reflected beneath the water as their powerful tails kept them moving with the ship while it heaved and groaned.

Razor-sharp teeth appeared between the sirens' lush lips as they continued to sing their enthralling song, coaxing us toward the water.

Go. Must go to them. Touch them. Kiss them. Hold them. So beautiful.

I wanted to fall forward and plummet into the sea, to be swept up in their embrace. Another giant lurch came from the ship, and a rush of water flooded its hull.

Somewhere in the back of my mind, I knew that my magic was gone. The foreign magic that my awakening power had gathered had been detonated. My shield spell had been obliterated, and I had nothing left. Nothing but that alluring song which called to me and beckoned me closer.

"We need to get off this ship, now!" someone yelled.

An arm clamped around my waist and then I was moving upward. Kaillen's cedar and citrus scent flooded my senses, and I tried to thrash against him, to return to the enchanting sirens as water flooded the deck below us amidst the sinking ship.

"Where is he?" Fallon asked in clipped tones while he scrambled up the near vertical deck to the railing's edge.

I was vaguely aware that they were all climbing the deck's tilting surface. Kaillen threw my limp, useless body over his shoulder so he could use his hands. "Don't know," he grunted.

"Jump now! She'll be under within the minute!" Barnabas called sharply.

Night air caressed my cheeks as Kaillen catapulted us through the air, and then we were landing on Barnabas's ship.

Kaillen rolled us across the deck, maneuvering me so his body took the brunt of the fall. Bone-white floorboards gleamed in the moonlight as Kaillen lay me down on the deck, my body supine as he hovered over me.

"Tala? My love?"

I blinked as the sirens' angry hisses and thrashes grew quieter. Then came the sounds of gurgling and creaking before a steady spew of water shot into the sky from Jakub's sinking vessel.

The ship we'd been on only a moment ago disappeared from view as it sank into a watery grave, and then all that was left was Barnabas's ship rolling gently on the waves. Any evidence of the battle we'd just waged had disappeared beneath the silvery water.

The sirens' song abruptly vanished as they returned to the depths of the sea.

My head cleared, and I blinked, then blinked again as Kaillen peered down at me. A golden glow and crimson fire waged in his irises as he smoothed back my hair and cupped my cheek. "Tala?"

"I'm okay," I finally managed even though weariness flooded my limbs, and a heavy sensation cleaved my thoughts.

He growled. "Bullshit you're fine. You just used your awakening power and depleted yourself."

My eyelids grew heavy. I struggled to keep them open, but I wanted to know, needed to know . . . "Is Jakub dead? Did my blast kill him?"

"I don't know."

"Can we sail?" Fallon's question came to me on the breeze as he and Barnabas inspected the damage done to *The Only Lady I've Ever Loved*.

"She'll hold till we reach port," Barnabas replied, but that cocky swagger had left his step. Part of the mast was cracked, and one of the sails had been shredded when Barnabas had rammed into Jakub's ship.

"Get us back to land!" Kaillen barked. Prickly energy surrounded my mate, and low rumbling growls came from his chest as I lay weak and cold in his arms.

"But what about Jakub?" I persisted. "Do we know if he's dead?" I felt inside me for the curse I'd cast, but I was too weak to activate it and see if it had indeed tethered me to Jakub.

"If your blast didn't kill him, then the sea will," Kaillen

replied. "No supernatural can swim across an ocean if they're not part siren."

"What if he's on this ship with us?" Fallon asked. "And is still hiding under his cloaking spell?"

I shook my head. "He'd have already taken me if he were. He tried to take me earlier with a portal key."

"He did?" Heat poured from Kaillen as murder shone in his gaze.

The ship heaved beneath me, and I rolled, too weak to stop myself. Another terrifying-sounding growl came from my mate as he gathered me in his arms.

His warmth soaked into my cool flesh. I reveled in the feel of him, the scent of him, as a niggling sense of doom descended over my mind. We hadn't heard Jakub speak again after my blast of foreign power. Surely, that explosion had killed him.

But what if it hadn't? What if he'd escaped using his portal key?

That was the last thought I had before darkness claimed me.

CHAPTER TWENTY-ONE

A finger caressed my cheek, and emotions strummed toward me—lust, love, tenderness. My eyes fluttered open to see Kaillen hovering over me.

My wolf rumbled in contentment as she stretched and also woke.

"Hi," he said quietly.

Bright sunlight streamed behind him, and I lay on a soft warm bed in a small room I didn't recognize.

My hand automatically came up to cover his as he continued making lazy movements along my skin. Those emotions continued to strum into me, and I realized they were from the bond.

Love.

My breath caught at the feeling, but I squeezed my eyes closed. Kaillen loved me. *Or did he? Was that his wolf talking too?*

But I shoved those questions aside. I would never know.

"Where are we?" I asked.

"An inn. We're back in Culasberee. Barnabas sailed us here after you passed out."

I sighed as everything from last night returned to me. The battle. Our escape. My fear that Jakub was still alive. "Is Barnabas's ship okay?"

A wry smile lifted Kaillen's lips. "You expelled so much magic you passed out and Jakub nearly abducted you again, yet your first question is whether or not Barnabas's ship is okay? If Barnabas knew you'd asked that, he'd swear his loyalty to you right now."

I muffled a laugh. "Very funny, but seriously, is his ship okay?"

He stroked my cheek again. "Yes, his ship's fine. It has some damage, but nothing that can't be fixed."

I stretched. "Good, I'm sure he'd have been devastated if it wasn't." I gave another stretch and was amazed to find that I didn't feel sore or more tired after that epic use of my powers. "How long was I out for this time?"

He eyed the clock on the bedside table. "Eight hours."

I followed his gaze. It was late morning. Nibbling my lip, I leaned back onto the pillow, and the lust strumming through the bond grew.

Kaillen watched as I worried my bottom lip, heat growing in his eyes.

I smiled. "Should I be disturbed about what you're

thinking right now, given that Jakub could still be out there?"

"You should always be disturbed about what I'm thinking, even if Jakub's not in the equation." He leaned down to kiss my neck.

My body arched, and already that incessant pulsing need began in me. *Want. Want. Want.* I groaned, but it did little to quell the pooling of desire in my belly.

"What is it?" He grazed his teeth across my earlobe, and I shivered.

My fingers threaded through the hair at the nape of his neck. "This pull I have toward you. I feel like a toddler, and you're this toy that I just have to have."

He chuckled. "I'm okay with that. I've always wanted to be a boy toy."

I snorted. "Is that how it feels for you, too?"

"Pretty much."

"Did you feel that at all before your wolf caught my true scent?"

He paused, then looked me in the eye. "You feel really insecure about that, don't you?" A flush stained my cheeks, but when I tried to hide under the covers, he pulled them down. "Tell me."

I sighed. "Yes, okay, I do. I know that we're mated now, and that what we feel is how it's going to be from now on, but I still can't let go of the fact that this is all manufactured by our wolves."

"But you wanted me before your wolf did, quite desperately if I remember right." He gave me a cocky grin.

I swatted his chest, and he nipped my lower lip.

"Yes, yes," I said in an exaggerated tone. "The big bad hunter had a bod that I couldn't resist. Ha, ha. So funny."

He just grinned at me.

I ran a finger along his chest, and his muscles tightened. "So you knew I was attracted to you before my wolf was born, but how did *you* feel toward *me* before your wolf got in the equation?"

He leaned down to continue his onslaught to the sensitive area on my neck where he'd marked me. "I told you. You intrigued me."

"But were you attracted to me?"

"Any unmated male would be attracted to you. You're not only gorgeous, but you have a killer body." A low growl rumbled in his chest, and that jasmine and night scent rose from him.

So he didn't like the thought of another male wanting me. Okay, well, that I could live with.

I sighed. "Fine."

He paused, and looked up, his amber-hued eyes studying me again. "What do I need to do to make you feel secure?"

I shook my head. "Nothing. It's just me. I need to get over it."

"In that case . . ." A wicked smile curved his lips. "How about I show you just how attractive I find you?" Gold flared in his eyes as he pressed his very firm, and very impressive, erection against my side.

My insides fluttered. "I suppose that would be okay," I replied breathlessly.

~

WE GOT up an hour later after screwing like bunny rabbits not once, but three times, then joined Barnabas and Fallon for lunch.

Barnabas was lounging in a reclining chair at a quaint café outdoor seating area just around the corner from the inn. He sipped a hot beverage, steam rising from the top, as Fallon dug into a plate of mutton and a mashed root vegetable indigenous to the fae lands. Both nodded in acknowledgment when we passed by on the sidewalk as we headed toward the café's front door.

Kaillen and I ordered plates of food at the counter before joining his friends in the outdoor section. Bright sunlight streamed overhead, and a warm breeze caressed my cheeks, making me not in the least sad that I'd left Chicago's cold weather behind me.

"So what's the story, morning glory?" Barnabas asked after we were seated. The vamp's lounge chair sat under a shaded area, so that all portions of the his skin were concealed from direct sunlight. Even though Barnabas wouldn't burst into flames from the sun at his age, he would have developed some level of sunlight sensitivity by now—something all vampires who were hundreds of years old suffered from. "Are we done chasing the dimwit?"

"Is he dead?" I asked, not missing a beat.

"Probably, unless he can swim across an ocean," Fallon replied and took another huge bite of his mutton.

"If you'd been hired to kill him, would you consider your job done?" I persisted.

That comment made both of them pause mid-bite and mid-sip. Kaillen grinned and sat back.

"No," Fallon and Barnabas replied simultaneously.

"And why not?" I asked.

"No proof of death." Fallon shrugged and resumed eating.

"What he said." Barnabas jerked his thumb in the fairy's direction.

"If we'd hired you to kill him," I continued, "what proof of death would you have presented us with?"

"His head," they replied in unison.

I grimaced. "Eww."

Fallon cocked an eyebrow. "You asked."

"It would have been presented discreetly and cleanly in a sealed non-spillable bag," Barnabas added. "But back in my day, such a thing didn't exist. Now, you can ziplock those heads right up, making travel with proof quite pleasant."

"Traveling. With a severed head. Pleasant." I made a face. "Right, whatever you say."

Barnabas's fangs lengthened, and he grinned devilishly. "Perhaps you'd like to join me on my next job so you can experience such a pleasant encounter firsthand?"

"Pretty sure the lady isn't interested." Fallon shoveled another bite of food into his mouth.

"What he said." I pointed at Fallon, then frowned, not from the thoroughly unpleasant images I was getting of traveling with a decapitated head, but because we were all in agreement that it was too early to call Jakub deceased.

Ugh. Everything still felt so unresolved. And while I knew that Jakub could be dead, I still didn't feel fine saying everything was over and done with.

My frown deepened. "I did attempt to place a curse on him. If it took root and I activate it now, we would know for sure if he's alive or not."

"But if he *is* alive, and you activate that curse, then he'll have a clear link to *you* too," Kaillen countered. I'd told him about the curse this morning, and it'd been pretty obvious right away that the hunter wasn't happy about it. "That's a risk we don't need to take."

I faced my mate. "Even if it confirms whether or not he's still living?"

Kaillen scowled. "Let's see if we can find out another way first. I don't want him to have a direct tie to you."

"In all likelihood, your blast killed him." Barnabas took another sip of his drink. "Having said that, though, no, I wouldn't rest easy if this were a job."

"Exactly, and Jakub had a portal key. What if he used it before my blast hit him?" I added, strengthening my belief that he'd escaped. "Or he had some other type of magic that could transport him? Kaillen can transport himself from anywhere."

"But that's only on earth," my mate replied, before grabbing our drinks and food off the floating tray that had come to us. He placed two plates in front of me. My order held an entire fried fae bird on one plate, and a heaping portion of crisp greens along with the same root vegetable Fallon had ordered on the other. *Le sigh.* I still ate like a horse.

"Speaking of that blast." Fallon let out a low whistle. "Your power was quite remarkable."

"You noticed that too, huh?" I dug into the white meat, similar to chicken, and savored the crispy skin and herbed flavor.

"You seem surprised by that," Fallon replied.

"I am. I've never expelled it like that before," I said between chews. "So it was new to me that I'm capable of that."

Barnabas finished his drink, not blood from the looks of it but a tea of some kind, and leaned forward. "How do I put this delicately?" He tapped his chin. "May I ask what you are? Your scent is that of a witch, but also of a were-wolf, but your power is off the charts, even more so than the most powerful witch I've ever met."

I gave him a passive smile. Funny how I'd been asking that same question of Kaillen not too long ago. I took a huge bite of what was similar to mashed potatoes but a hundred times more flavorful.

Once I'd swallowed, I hesitated briefly about revealing what I truly was, but then realized that if Kaillen trusted Barnabas and Fallon—when my mate was guarded around almost everyone—then I could trust them too. Besides, I was beginning to find this newfound life in which I didn't hide who I was to be quite freeing. "I'm a witch and now also a werewolf, and perhaps something else too, but we're not entirely sure what."

Barnabas's brows slanted together. "*Now* a werewolf? Is that why Kaillen has a mating mark? Something men don't normally have?"

"It's a long story," Kaillen cut in. He'd ordered a steak and was already halfway through it. It had to be at least fifty-six ounces, but since his bites were the size of my fist, he was powering through it. "But yes, that's the reason I have a mark, although I'm sure it's a story Tala doesn't want to tell right now," he added gruffly when Barnabas opened his mouth again.

The scent of jasmine and night wafted up from Kaillen, and when I caught how he was glaring at Barnabas and Fallon, daring them to ask anything further, my stomach dipped.

I looked down, so I wouldn't do something stupid or mushy. But a warm feeling still gushed through me at how quickly Kaillen always acted to protect me. Few people had ever done that, because usually, it was the other way around. Me protecting Tessa. Me helping our employees. Me smoothing things over with our customers. Prisha sometimes showed feelings of protection over me, but it was different with her. She was a woman who commiserated with me more than anything. She never had a look of such violence on her face as Kaillen did now.

Using my knife, I cut more bites of the white meat, anything to distract myself from this quaking feeling of whatever it was growing in my chest. Because I was so used to being the strong one who never faltered, it had never occurred to me that with a partner like Kaillen, the responsibility could go both ways.

A tug came from the bond, as if questioning. I sent a soothing caress back to him, one of thankfulness and . . . love.

An immense burst of satisfaction flowed from him into me.

I cleared my throat and blinked rapidly. "Anyway, back to Jakub." I gave Kaillen a shy smile.

My mate placed his hand on my lower back—just a simple touch. A simple gesture as if to say, *I'm here.* The bond pulled at me again, and I cleared my throat for the second time. *Keep it together.*

I finished the fae bird, then faced his friends clear-eyed, *thank the gods.* "Was it just me, or did any of you notice that the tattoos on everyone's necks were glowing last night?"

"I saw that too," Kaillen replied.

"Same," Fallon chimed in.

"I also observed such an occurrence," Barnabas added.

"But why would they glow?"

Kaillen frowned. "Magic would do that."

"So the tattoos are spelled?" Fallon asked.

"That's what I'm thinking too," I replied.

"Spelled to do what?" Barnabas asked.

I shook my head. "No clue." Frustration again bubbled up inside me. "Since we can't know for certain why those tattoos glow, I guess the next question would be, how do we find out if Jakub died or not?"

Barnabas eyed Kaillen who'd also just finished his plate.

The hunter relaxed into his chair, his hand still on my lower back, only now he was making lazy circles, massaging and soothing my muscles and *OMG* . . . I was growing aroused.

I squirmed in my seat, and a smile tugged on my mate's lips as his friends' nostrils flared. Fallon politely kept his gaze off of me, but Barnabas gave me a knowing side-eye.

A warning growl rumbled in Kaillen's chest, and the vampire wisely whipped his attention away.

So embarrassing.

"Do you still sense Jakub?" Barnabas asked Kaillen.

"Not in the way I normally do after I've tracked someone." Kaillen frowned but worked his hand up my spine, and my entire body melted toward him, tingles of desire pooling between my thighs.

"So he could be dead?" Fallon cocked his head.

"Possibly, but like both of you, I wouldn't consider this job done without proof," Kaillen replied.

I nodded, even though I felt like jelly. Since I was damned near having an orgasm at an outdoor café, I forced myself upright and away from my mate's alluring touch. "So now what?"

"Now we wait," Barnabas replied.

My eyebrows shot up. "Wait?"

"It's what we would be forced to do if this was a hired job." The vamp inched back on his chair as a ray of sunlight hit his ankle. "I've had jobs that I've been hired for take years to resolve when unfortunate situations happen such as the one last night. Without proof of death, I can't demand payment, so I wait. Sooner or later, the living always show back up, and when they do, I swoop in." He grinned wickedly.

"Do you do the same?" I asked Fallon.

He inclined his head.

I worried my lower lip, not liking the idea of waiting, but without any further leads of what had happened to Jakub, what other choice did we really have?

I could activate the curse. I could see if I'm linked to Jakub.

But I brushed those thoughts off. That was too risky right now. Kaillen was right.

"Do you think there's any way we can find out more about the tattoos while we wait?" I asked Kaillen. "Tessa was going to charm one of the SF members at her safe house and ask him to do research in the SF's libraries. Maybe I could also ask her to see if they can find anything about the tattoos."

He nodded. "It's worth a try."

"So, back to earth?" Fallon asked.

I shook my head. "No, Jakub's wanted on earth. That's why he's here. My guess is, if he's still alive, he's still here somewhere in the fae lands."

Fallon shrugged. "So we'll stay here and see if we can flush him out."

"Exactly," I agreed.

That jasmine and night aroma emanated from my mate again. I could hardly blame Kaillen for feeling protective.

The four of us stood to leave, and while I hated not knowing what had happened to Jakub, we had at least learned one thing—the constellation tattoos glowed, which told us they not only identified Jakub's crew but also served a magical purpose.

But *what* purpose? Exactly what kind of magic did those tattoos harness?

CHAPTER TWENTY-TWO

After I wrote a letter to Tessa, asking her to request that Archie also look into glowing constellation tattoos during his library research, I sent it via a fae courier to the SF so they could deliver it to my sister. Following that, we retreated to our room at the inn, and I plopped onto the bed, frustration making me irritable.

"So what do we do now?" I asked Kaillen. "Jakub fled earth because he's a wanted man, yet if he's still alive and part of the European mafia, he probably has an endless supply of supernaturals working for him, so who knows how long he'll be on the run."

The mattress dipped when Kaillen settled beside me. "We'll figure this out."

"When? In weeks? Months? Years? How long will it be before he tries to abduct me again, if he's even alive? This is beyond infuriating. I'm currently running for my life, I've abandoned my store, I haven't spoken to or seen my best friend in days, Tessa's hanging out in a desert, and for what?"

"Something tells me you're angry and frustrated."

"Did you pick up on that?" A small smile curved my lips at his teasing tone.

"A bit. It might have been the word *infuriating*, and the anger that's coming from the mate bond."

"Oh, right. I don't even have to tell you now. You can feel it."

"Something all mated males are thankful for." When I cocked my head, he added, "Women can be difficult creatures to read at the best of times, but when your mate's upset, it can be even more perplexing. I think that's why nature gave mated males the bond. That way, we can understand you better so it's easier to please you."

I snorted. "Please me?"

"Yes, please you. Don't you feel that for me?"

I frowned, realizing we were getting off track, but I was too curious to stop this tangent now. "Kind of? I don't know. I want you happy, but I don't feel the need to please you."

"Hmm." A discontented rumble came from him.

"Is that what you feel for me?" I asked incredulously.

"Perhaps."

I burst out laughing. "Why do you look so upset about that?"

"Because it's not something I'm used to feeling." He pinched my side. "Before, I didn't care if I pleased a woman or not, outside of the bedroom."

My nostrils flared.

"Sorry, TMI." He touched me soothingly, that ashy scent rising from him.

Calming, I wrinkled my nose. "Sounds like you were an ass."

"I could be. Until you." He chucked me under the chin.

Even though a warm feeling slid through me at the thought that I was a special snowflake to the hunter, that returning sense of disappointment also followed. The dude loved me because of his wolf. If not for his furry companion, he probably would have been an ass to me too. I knew I seriously needed to get over that, but I also knew that it was probably going to bug me for the foreseeable future.

"Anyway," I said with a sigh. "Back to the matter at hand. How shall we catch and destroy Jakub-Dipshit?"

"Ah, that violent side of yours that I love so much is making an appearance again." His brow furrowed. "That's a good question. I may be able to track him again, but without anything that he owned or touched, it will be harder."

"What do your hunter senses feel now?"

"Not much. It was hard enough last night to find him, but now I don't have a lead. Before, we knew that he was heading toward Culasberee, so my senses sharpened once we were in his vicinity. If I'm going to find him again, I'll have to collect a few ingredients to scry for him since I don't have anything he owned."

My curiosity grew since it was the most Kaillen had

ever spoken about his ability to hunt. "Where do you get your ingredients?"

"I have a few distributor contacts."

"That sounds time consuming." I knew all too well how hard it could be to procure needed items for spells, hexes, potions, and whatnot.

"It can be."

"So if you get those items, how long would it take to scry?"

"Can't say. It all depends on how strong I can make the connection again."

"Is there a possibility you won't be able to find him?"

A line appeared between his eyes when his brows pinched together. "That's always a possibility."

Nibbling my lip, I frowned too. What had seemed like a guaranteed capture last night was beginning to seem less and less likely. "So now what?"

"I think it's best if we wait for Fallon and Barnabas to return before going to collect supplies. I wouldn't put it past Jakub to amass an army to claim you . . . if he's still alive." Golden light flared in his eyes, and that protective scent rose from him again.

Barnabas and Fallon had used a portal key to travel back to the capital. Both lived there and needed to grab a change of clothes and some supplies before joining us again. Since Kaillen and I had packed lightly, we had what we needed for the time being.

"This sucks." I leaned back onto the bed and draped a hand over my head.

Kaillen inched closer to me, a wicked smile curving his lips. "I know what we can do while we're waiting."

A laugh escaped me despite all that had happened. "Oh, I can only imagine what you have in mind." Just the thought of the hunter settled between my thighs made tingles begin in my belly.

His nostrils flared, and he threw me a devilish smile. "While my ability to arouse you at any time of the day makes me disturbingly happy, that's not what I had in mind."

I pushed up onto my elbows and unbuttoned the top of my shirt. "Really? Then what did you have in mind?"

He watched my fingers before he locked his jaw. "I was thinking we should train. You detonated an incredible amount of power on that ship, but it was uncoordinated. You need to learn how to control it better."

"True." I undid another button.

A musky scent rose from him, then a muscle flexed in his jaw. "What are you doing?"

"What does it look like?"

"That you're trying to seduce me."

"Such a wicked mind. I'm merely changing in preparation for training."

He chuckled. "Doubtful."

"Fine. Maybe changing isn't what I had in mind."

"We should train," he said hoarsely when my shirt parted, exposing my abdomen and the swells of my breasts.

I leaned up and nipped his lip. "We'll make this one

quick. Promise," I said, purposefully using words and actions that he'd used on me in his man cave.

With a groan, his arms were around me and he had me flat on the mattress.

That insatiable need for him rose up inside me again. *My mate. Mine.*

Apparently, Kaillen felt the same, because in a blurred movement, my clothes were off, and then he was sliding inside me. He started slow, his strokes long and grinding. I grasped him to me, giving in to the erotic feel of him until we were both panting, our need growing. His thrusts became faster and more frantic. I moaned, my body coiling around him.

We came together, our climaxes vibrating so strongly that I felt his through the bond and I knew he felt mine too. I had no idea sex could be like this, but I knew as we lay spent and panting in one another's arms that there could never be another. Kaillen was my mate. I was his. And even though so much else was chaotic in my life, for the first time since meeting the hunter, I was beginning to make peace with where we were, even if the manufacturing part still bugged me.

I may never know if a relationship between us would have been possible before, but that was then, and this was now. It was time I let it go.

He smacked my ass as I spread like jelly on top of him. "Up, woman. It's time to train."

I rolled to the side, as he slid out from beneath me to stand naked in the room while hunting for his clothes.

Unabashedly, I admired the view. "Why are you so insistent on training now?"

He hiked his pants up. "Because magic leaves residue. Jakub's proven capable enough that he may be able to sense your magic and find you again. If he does, you need to be ready to defend yourself."

"You mean, like the way you were able to sense him after coming into contact with him?"

"Yes."

I pushed to sitting, and the hunter's attention dropped to my bare breasts and parted thighs. I lazily picked up my shirt and lifted it over my head. Taking a cue from my sister, I did it languidly, giving him a thorough show of my back arching, my stomach tensing, and my breasts straining against the material until it settled.

When I finished, I peered up at him. Fire and gold danced in his eyes.

"You were saying?" I asked innocently.

Musk poured from the hunter, and with a curse beneath his breath, he turned so he no longer faced me, but I still caught the bulge that had grown in his pants, and I knew that he suffered from the inevitable pull and need that came with the bond.

"I'll meet you downstairs," he said striding toward the door.

"Really?" I asked, not believing that he was actually leaving.

"Really," he replied dryly. "If I don't leave, I already

know that I'm going to spend the rest of the afternoon fucking you."

"Is that a bad thing?"

His nostrils flared as he stood at our room's threshold. "Train first. Fuck second."

The door slammed behind him, and a thrill ran through me. Well, if my hunter wanted to spend an afternoon training in which his magic entered my body and stroked my power from the inside out, then I supposed I could appease him.

After all, it was delicious foreplay.

KAILLEN FOUND a quiet area in the inn's courtyard, so we settled ourselves on the grass. Similar to earth, the grass was green. Well, mostly. Blades of sapphire, marigold, and pink also intermixed with the emerald stalks, so when the sun hit it, the grass turned into a dancing array of subtle rainbow colors.

I'd just connected my forbidden power to Kaillen, readying for a new training session, when the feel of the hunter inching along our bond caressed my insides. The tantalizing way we bonded birthed a sudden idea in me.

I sucked my magic back inside me, my wolf growling her displeasure. Yep, Mrs. Wolfy had perked right up at the feel of her mate's energy strumming toward her.

Kaillen opened his eyes and cocked an eyebrow.

I closed the distance between us, placing my hands on

his thighs. "What if I suck magic from you *and* Barnabas *and* Fallon?"

"Why would you do that?"

"You said that Jakub may be able to track me if he has a hold of my energy, and we know that if I activate the curse, he'll definitely be able to find me. So what if I enhance my magical footprint by feeding off all of your powers? That will not only increase my magical footprint—perhaps making him come for me—but I might also be able to see past his cloaking spell by using your powers."

His eyebrows drew together. "But you couldn't see through his cloaking spell on the ship, and you were feeding off fifteen supernaturals."

"True, but that was during battle when I was a bit frantic. I'd lost my cool, and I wasn't controlling it or corralling it. It was wreaking havoc on my insides, which I think is why it blasted from me. But if I could corral it and wield it, perhaps then I'd be able to see him."

His hand curved around my waist, almost absentmindedly as he considered my idea. "But if you were to increase your magical footprint to attract him to you, then Jakub wouldn't be running from us, he'd be hunting you again."

"I know, but if we're prepared for it—"

A low growl rumbled in his chest. "That would put you at risk by making you the prey."

"I'd be the bait, not the prey. I have no intention of being prey ever again."

Golden light flared in his eyes. "That's taking a substantial risk. We wouldn't know when Jakub would show or how many supernaturals would be joining him."

"Doesn't magical residue fade with time?" He nodded, so I added, "In that case, most likely, he'll act soon. So if I lure him to me by increasing my footprint, there's a good chance he'll show when we want him to."

"What if he brings forty or fifty supernaturals to fight with him? You passed out last night after killing fifteen."

"But I'd lost control. I don't intend to let that happen again. That was my first use of my awakening magic during battle, and now I know what to expect."

He scowled.

"Why are you upset?"

"You want to use yourself as bait after having *one* experience of wielding that much power."

"Well, isn't that why we're here in the courtyard right now, so I can learn better control?"

"One training session isn't enough to learn that new ability."

"I'm a fast learner."

"It's reckless."

I cocked my head. "Perhaps it is, but the longer Jakub evades us, the more likely it is he'll get away or show up when we least expect it, and what about the fact that the SF still isn't here? That tells me that they haven't been allowed into the fae lands to conduct an arrest yet, otherwise, they'd be crawling all over this town. So, it really comes down to us. Are we willing to take a risk to try to stop him, or are we going to sit back and hope that he doesn't succeed in abducting me again when we least expect it? You have to remember that he's still after me. What if he takes me tonight while we're asleep?"

A hint of crimson flames rolled through his eyes. "I don't like it."

"Is that you talking or your wolf?"

His head tilted. "I don't know."

"I'm guessing it's your wolf. Tell Mr. Wolf to cool it. I need to talk to you, the hunter, right now. 'Cause you're a pretty analytical supe who's rather adept at the chess game when it comes to getting what he wants."

"Whatever are you referring to?" A sly smile tugged at his lips.

"Perhaps a little stunt you pulled that had me moving to Ontario."

"You have to admit, I played that well."

I snorted. "Yes, yes, you're brilliant. Sorry, dear. Have I not stroked your ego enough?"

He laughed and pulled me closer. "Have I told you that it's not just your violent side I love but also your wit?"

"You may have mentioned that before."

His tongue darted out to taste my skin.

A pulse of desire quivered in my belly, but I shoved him back before we could get sidetracked again, and I had a feeling that was what he was trying to do. He didn't like this plan because it put me at risk, but I was done being hunted.

"A delicious scent has just begun wafting off you," he purred.

"Plug your nose. I mean it. We need to sort this out."

He grumbled but wiped his expression clean.

I settled more on the grass in front of him. "So if we use me as bait and bring Jakub to us while I'm channeling all of your power, then we'll have the upper hand."

His nostrils flared, that golden hue brightening around his irises.

I cocked my head. "You call me a *colantha* for a reason, remember?"

A muscle tightened in his jaw, but he gave a curt nod. "I'm listening."

"With knowing the area, we would have an advantage."

"True."

"And since we've already encountered Jakub several times, we already know what to expect."

"Possibly true. He could have more surprises up his sleeve."

"Unlikely. Each time he's tried to abduct me, he's either hidden or sent someone else to do his dirty work. And he always uses those blue cuffs. Only now, I'm immune to them. Are you?"

"Not yet. I was too busy hunting for my brother to pay a visit to the SF."

"Oh, right, but *I'm* immune. So that right there gives us the upper hand. Even if Jakub were to capture me, I could break out of his cuffs."

His nostrils flared again, and the muscles in his jaw began to tick, as that iron fragrance entered his scent.

"Why are you getting mad?"

"Because I'm thinking about him cuffing you and capturing you . . . it does things to me."

"Well, keep your panties on. He hasn't captured me yet."

"It's hard. I'd rather have my panties off around you." A suggestive curve lifted his lips.

"You wear panties? I didn't realize you were a cross-dresser."

He snorted. "I'm more of a boxer briefs kinda guy if you hadn't noticed, but I can call them panties if you prefer. I'll even wear them if that's your thing."

"Black lace?"

He shrugged. "If that's what you're into. Speaking of black lace . . . When are you going to wear that little nightie I found—"

"We're getting off track again." I sighed and forced my attention away from our incessant need to banter. "So even if things went south, I can break out of the cuffs, and even if things were to go *really* south—as in Jakub actually abducted me—you could still track me. The blood bond makes that possible in this realm too. Right?"

"It should. The bond means I can track you anywhere, even across realms."

"Super handy, but still a total violation of my privacy. Just sayin'."

He smirked. "Would you like to be able to track me? I could have a tracking hex placed on me to your specification. Would that appease you, my love?" He leaned forward and nipped my neck.

A burst of goosebumps skated down my spine.

"Speaking of tracking . . . If I also activate the curse, in addition to increasing my magical signal by pulling on the three of you, I'll not only know if Jakub's alive, but I'll also be tethered to him. It would ensure he could find me, and he'd probably come for me if he could feel me that strongly."

Kaillen grumbled. "If you activated it, then he would have a lifeline straight to your location."

"Which would make it *very* easy to draw him out. This could end tonight."

He seethed, but I pressed on.

"So do we have a deal? I use myself as bait, feed off of your powers to increase my magical footprint and my ability to see through his cloaking spell, *and* activate the curse tonight to capture Jakub?"

Kaillen was quiet for a long moment.

"Please? Will you try it for me?"

His jaw ticked again before he said, "Fine. We'll try it, but if I see any inkling that you're in true danger, I'm using a portal key and getting you out of there immediately, and then you're banishing that curse."

"Deal. You have my permission to be a possessive, dominant werewolf and whisk me to safety if needed."

He leaned forward, until I tilted back. "Why do I detect a hint of sarcasm in your tone?"

My eyelashes fluttered. "Whatever are you talking about?"

A low growl rumbled in his chest before he hauled me back up. "If we're doing this tonight, then we're training all afternoon. Until I feel confident that you can successfully wield my power enough to see past Jakub's cloaking spell, I won't allow it."

"*Allow* it?"

"You know what I mean," he growled.

I sighed. "Yes, I do. Okay, in that case, we better get training."

CHAPTER TWENTY-THREE

K aillen and I trained for six hours. It took that long for the hunter to feel appeased enough to consent to my plan. But I'd improved, even in that short timeframe. Each time I had his magic in my grasp, I used it to my advantage, before returning it to him. We also practiced with cloaking spells. He hid multiple objects under very heavy spells, and then I used his power to see past them. Most of the time, I could, and even though it wasn't easy and I was far from perfect at it, I did have one advantage now. My wolf.

In Ontario, when Kaillen and I had been training daily, I would have succumbed to the fatigue from what we'd done today. But each time exhaustion had threatened me this afternoon, my wolf surged forward, offering me her strength, resilience, and enhanced healing properties. I hadn't used her during the battle, since I'd pushed her down, but now she was insistent, and I could see why.

Having her work at my side, allowed me to continue training beyond what I'd been capable of before, *and* she healed me. The fatigue vanished, and I was able to train the same maneuver again and again.

A huge dose of gratitude filled me each time she helped me so willingly, and I was beginning to see what Kaillen meant about a symbiotic relationship. Because of her, I truly felt ready to face Jakub again.

After receiving a text from Fallon saying that he and Barnabas were back in Culasberee, Kaillen and I ended our training, cleaned up, and ventured to the café around the inn's corner again for a meal before setting out to capture Jakub. I was running on fumes after that rigorous training session, so eating was a must before I activated the curse and lured Jakub to us.

Most of the seats were filled as the inhabitants of Culasberee were out enjoying family dinners or drinks with friends, but we managed to find an empty table.

As soon as we all sat, I said, "I want to capture Jakub tonight by using all of your powers to enhance my magic to lure Jakub to us, and with any luck, your magic will also allow me to see through his cloaking spell."

Barnabas gave me a delighted smile. "Well, that's quite the introduction."

"I know. Sorry for not giving you a heads-up earlier."

Fallon shrugged. "We took longer in the capital than intended."

Kaillen sat at my side with a protective arm around my shoulders while a scowl twisted his features. My mate had been in an irritable mood all afternoon even though he claimed to be onboard with my plan. But I knew his instincts were screaming at him to lock me up so nobody could hurt me. It was only sheer will on his part that had stopped him from doing so.

Barnabas leaned forward in his seat. "So you really want to draw that little spineless sorcerer to us? I have to admit, that's ballsy." Given the vampire's grin, I could tell he approved.

"We can't guarantee he's little," Fallon replied, totally deadpan. "We never saw him."

Barnabas scoffed. "Surely anyone who hides behind a cloaking spell is little." He angled in his seat to face Kaillen better. "Have I told you that I like her?"

The hunter grunted. "Once or twice."

"Well, let me just say it again. I think she not only smells mouthwatering, has a delectable body, and is quite possibly the most gorgeous—"

"No need to continue." Kaillen bared his teeth as crimson fire began to roll in his irises. In the café's dim fairy lights, his dark hair shone ebony as the scent of jasmine and night rose from him. "I get it. You like my mate. For your own self-preservation, I would advise you to stop reminding my wolf of that. He's a bit on edge right now."

Barnabas conveyed a mockingly innocent expression. "Many apologies, my friend."

I rolled my eyes and forced myself not to sigh in exasperation as the vamp once again got his kicks from riling my mate.

Kaillen's only response was another rumbling warning sound.

"It's just too easy," Barnabas said under his breath to me when Kaillen's fingers curled around my shoulder.

I was pretty sure Kaillen was two seconds away from leaping across the table and smashing a fist into his friend's face.

"You might want to tone it down a notch," I said quietly to Barnabas, and then raised my eyebrows when Kaillen hauled me closer to his side, the scent of night-touched jasmine so potent I was swimming in it. At least, *my* wolf was content.

She preened and rumbled in happiness and urged me closer to my mate.

Fallon watched the entire exchange with a smooth face. The fairy was nothing if not an expert at hiding his emotions. The entire time I'd known him, his smell had stayed muted. I again wondered how he did that or if he truly didn't experience many emotions.

"What about you? What do you think?" I asked him.

Fallon inclined his head, his yellow hair as bright as a banana. "I'm game to lure him in."

"And you're both okay with me feeding off your magic? I'll give it back to you. I just need it to increase my footprint and see through Jakub's cloaking spell when he arrives."

They shared an intrigued look.

"Will it kill us?" Fallon asked.

"No," I replied. "I'll return it before that happens."

Fallon shrugged again. "Sure, why not."

The vamp stroked his chin. "I would love to."

I clapped my hands. "It's settled then."

Barnabas rubbed his hands together just as a tray floated toward us and our drinks and food appeared. The spelled serving platter began dispersing the plates and glasses to us as the café's magic sparkled in the air.

Barnabas lifted his glass. "We dine, then we lure that little prick to us, then you stroke our magic . . . I mean *use* our magic," he added when Kaillen growled. "And then you kill him with our help if needed. I can't wait." He saluted everyone. "And I get dibs on his blood."

My eyes widened. "You're going to drink from Jakub?"

"Of course." Barnabas gave me an affronted look. "Why would we let all of that luscious blood go to waste? It's much better than this stuff." He sniffed at his glass, which contained blood that was probably a few days old from a willing donor who'd been paid for the donation. "It's best warm and directly from the source." He smiled, his fangs lengthening again.

"If you say so." I raised my beverage, as did Kaillen and Fallon.

We all clinked glasses, then I dug into my rack of lamb that had been seasoned with mint—the herb imported from earth. But the meat had other seasonings too. A tangier fae spice rolled across my tongue and made my mouth water even more, but my belly was growling so painfully that all of my concentration fell on attacking my food.

I knew that if I wanted to capture Jakub tonight and be finished with his games once and for all, I'd need to be strong and alert.

Good thing I'd ordered four plates of food.

"WE'LL LURE HIM HERE." Kaillen stood at the top of a cliff overlooking the sea. Starlight graced the sky, the three moons easily visible in the cloudless night. "It won't be easy for him to escape once he arrives."

A warm breeze caressed my skin, and for the first time since I'd hatched this plan, a sense of foreboding filled me.

"Tala will be exposed on the cliff," Fallon pointed out.

"Which is what I want," I replied. "Jakub thinks I'm the key to something. The more it looks like I'm vulnerable, the more he'll be tempted."

"And if he whisks you away using a portal key?" Barnabas asked.

I stiffened. It was the concern Kaillen had too. "Kaillen and I have a blood bond. He'll be able to find me."

Kaillen paced along the rocky ledge, dust and pebbles skittering from beneath his soles. "If you think he's going to transport you, back off. While I'll be able to track you anywhere, there's no guarantee I'd be able to penetrate whatever place he imprisons you." He raked a hand through his hair as dark energy poured from him.

I gave the vamp a look, as if to say, *don't bring up the risky stuff*. It'd been hard enough to convince Kaillen to allow this plan to move forward. I didn't need the vamp planting more seeds of doubt in my mate's mind.

Barnabas shrugged and rested a hand on the hilt of a sword. Yep, the vamp had graced himself with a weapon from the Middle Ages. He said it reminded him of home. I had to admit, he wielded the heavy monstrosity like a champ, the skill no doubt learned in his pirating days.

"How long do you think it'll take for him to detect you?" Fallon stood casually with his arms crossed.

"If my awakening power pulls on the three of you, and I activate the curse to Jakub—if it hits its mark—not long. My magical footprint will be really high."

"Do you think he'll know that he's being manipulated?" Fallon asked.

"Not if I don't fully activate the curse. If I only partially activate it, he'll feel me, but I won't be able to feel him. He'll know it's one-sided."

A snarl tore from Kaillen.

I raised my shoulders apologetically. Giving Jakub direct access to me was a concern I had, too, but it was a risk I was willing to take. This ended tonight.

"I want you both ready to intervene the second he shows." Kaillen scowled. "He's already failed three times in trying to capture Tala. He'll no doubt try to make this attempt a guaranteed win . . . if he's still alive."

"Should we get on with it then?" I pushed wispy strands of hair away from my face. A long braid trailed down my back, and form-fitting pants hugged my legs. I'd worn comfortable clothes that would allow me to easily move and fight. *Battle gear* was what Prisha would have called it.

Thinking of my friend made an ache form in my chest. It felt like years since we'd properly spent time together, and I hadn't spoken to her since before my first shift. *Just as soon as this is over, Prish, you and I are going out on the town together.*

Kaillen crossed the distance between us in a blurred move. He towered over me, his inherent citrusy cedar scent rolling to me on the wind. Burning crimson fire stoked his irises, and the energy rising from him was palpable. "You do know that I've never felt like this before, right?" he said quietly. "I'm honoring your wishes, but my wolf is trying to make me shift as we speak. He wants you in his den, properly cared for and safe."

I peered up at him, and my stomach flipped at the fiery possessiveness in his eyes. "And what do *you* want? Do you want to lock me up too?"

A groove appeared between his brows. "I don't know anymore. It's all tangled up—my feelings and my wolf's feelings. I'm inclined to say that I want you locked up too, but I'm not sure if that's because my wolf is trying to rule me right now."

An ache formed in my gut, but I pushed it away. Kaillen loved me, even if neither of us had declared those words to one another yet out loud. But our feelings for each other would always involve our wolves. It was simply the way it was. "Hopefully at this time tomorrow, you and I will be enjoying a late dinner, plenty of drinks, and your large bed back in Montana."

The gold in his eyes brightened. "Naked?"

I snorted, unable to help myself. "If you insist."

A wicked smile streaked across his face. "Oh, I insist." His arm encircled me, and he hauled me closer before he leaned down and inhaled along my skin. "My beautiful, *colantha*. I would slay dragons for you."

My neck arched, my pulse fluttering rapidly at his contact. "Hopefully, that won't be necessary."

He kissed along the column of my throat, his lips firm and urgent. I knew he wanted to do more. Wanted to bend me over, claim me again, and plunge his length inside me. I knew all of that because those were the feelings sparking through me, and our wolves were so intertwined it was as though they were one.

"Make him suffer," Kaillen whispered.

I smiled. "Still a demon, I see."

"Always." He pressed one last kiss to my jaw before claiming my lips, and even though his kiss was quick, it was full of heated promise.

"Are you two lovebirds done yet?" Barnabas called. "Your scents reek of sex, and considering I'm downwind, I'm getting a hefty dose of it."

"You know he's enjoying it, right?" Kaillen grumbled before pulling back.

"I kind of figured."

Kaillen's nostrils flared when he cast a look at his vampire friend. Sure enough, Barnabas was grinning while

Fallon stood stoic, the picture of a battle-hardened warrior.

"Make him suffer, but also make it quick," Kaillen said with one last squeeze around my waist. "Don't give him a chance to take you."

"I won't."

He finally released me and joined his friends.

I took a deep, steadying breath as salty sea air whipped around me. In a blink, Kaillen and the assassins had vanished under a cloaking spell. I squinted, straining to see them, but my mate must have conjured a huge amount of magic because I couldn't detect a thing.

"Impressive," I murmured under my breath.

Giving them my back, I faced the sea and closed my eyes. The time had come to take matters into my own hands. No more running. No more chasing.

I was bringing Jakub to me.

CHAPTER TWENTY-FOUR

I whispered the spell to activate the curse that I hoped I'd placed on Jakub. If it'd been successful, a tiny threaded connection would activate between us. It would be enough that Jakub would be able to sense me and know my whereabouts, but I wouldn't know his. And then the question was, would he take the bait? Or would he know that I was trying to manipulate him?

Magic sparked in my chest, my witch powers humming and activating. A surge of heat encased my limbs as a tiny flutter began in my belly, then spread through my chest and arms.

My heart beat harder as the curse activated, linking me to an unseen force on the horizon. It felt as though a spool of thread grew from me, as if spinning and stretching across the galaxy. It flowed and flowed, unwinding its imperceptible ribbon of awareness. And when it reached its recipient, a distant consciousness strummed toward me.

Oh my gods . . . he's truly alive.

The curse tugged, anchoring to Jakub and connecting us with invisible arms, but I backed off, letting it stay tethered to me but withdrawing my awareness. One-sided it needed to remain, as vulnerable as that made me.

I bit my lip, wondering if Jakub had sensed me. I knew this could be a long process, that I could be out here for hours waiting for Jakub to show, and if he didn't, I would be forced to fully activate the curse and chase him down. If I fully activated the curse, though, Jakub would also be able to feel me coming. It would be a cat-and-mouse game of potential endless chasing. Not ideal.

I forced myself to settle into a seated position on the cliff, as that tiny little string that connected me to the asshat stayed flowing and humming in my core. I closed my eyes and tapped into my awakening magic, hoping its use would be felt by Jakub-Dipshit and he'd come calling.

The deep dark cavern beside my forbidden power stretched and yawned. I dipped my awareness into it, coaxing and beckoning that new magic forth.

It slithered upward, those octopus-like tentacles writhing and lengthening as it asked to do my bidding.

My concentration turned inward further as I used that new power to search the area around us. Despite the cloaking spell that Kaillen had placed over himself and his friends, I sensed their forms. I couldn't see them or hear them, yet I was *aware* of them. But I hadn't been aware of Jakub on the ship, which meant that he had to be incredibly strong and powerful.

I felt for my mate, and he was easy to find. It was as if my new power told me that three heartbeats lay just beyond the cliff in that thin forest.

I stretched my magic farther, searching for other life forms as I let my awakening magic swell and rise, the energy around me growing and beckoning. Animals and plant life registered in my senses, but it was different with those creatures. They didn't have the higher power of thinking that supernaturals and humans did. So while my awakening power was aware of them, it didn't latch onto them.

A growing sense of invincibility began to consume me as I shifted my power back to Kaillen and his friends and let it grow.

I let my power swell and rise, not pulling on the men so much that they were weakened, but activating my power enough to make myself a beacon of energy, a tidal wave of might, while also having their magic on standby for when Jakub showed. *Come and get me, Dipshit.*

And as my power consumed me, I realized just how strong I was. Kaillen had hinted that this was what I was truly capable of. That I was a supernatural like none other on earth, and the memory of combining my awakening and forbidden powers with my witch magic and werewolf strength again entered the forefront of my thoughts. I'd only just scratched the surface of all that I was capable of.

My wolf rumbled within me, agreeing that I was truly unique and a force to be reckoned with.

A fierce smile spread across my lips. I would be ready

for Jakub if he showed. I knew I could take him on. Now it was only the matter of if he had the balls to face me.

I sat like that until the breeze cooled, yet I didn't let my focus drift, and because I was now using my wolf, I didn't grow tired.

So I left the void to my awakening magic open, those tentacles ready, but I didn't fully latch onto my mate or his friends. I connected with them just enough to tempt Jakub while conserving my powers for the epic battle ahead.

I shifted from where I sat, dust and pebbles moving beneath me.

Something changed in the wind, to the energy in the realm.

My back straightened, as my nerves prickled. A new consciousness drifted toward me, subtle at first, as if the recipient was trying to remain inconspicuous.

Every fiber in my body stood to attention as the newcomer approached on lethally quiet steps.

A tug on the mate bond came next, and a hint of Kaillen's anxiety strummed to me. He'd sensed something too.

My lips parted as my chest rose shallowly. That new presence drifted closer, not concrete, though, as if the bearer was here but not quite.

It was similar to how it had felt on the ship, when I'd sensed that Jakub was near, yet I couldn't pinpoint his location.

He's here.

I fully activated my awakening power and pulled on my

mate and his friends. Their power surged into me, and I felt their response, groans of invisible pleasure as I stroked their magic and caressed their insides.

I opened my eyes and gazed out over the vast sea as my power rose. Moonlight glittered off the water and the rolling waves, as blazing starlight filled the sky.

Jakub's presence drifted toward me, until it felt as though he were only a few feet behind me. *Now.*

But just as I was about to turn, a sharp tug suddenly came on the mate bond, and then came the feel of Kaillen and his friends' magic drifting away.

What the hell? I swung around, readying myself for battle even though the energy I'd been commanding had been siphoned away, but—

Nothing was there.

The only thing that greeted me was darkness and the quiet forest beyond. My wolf's powers kept my vision sharp. Even in the moonlight, objects were clear and focused. Nothing was out of place, yet I could have sworn that Kaillen had just sent me a warning. And why the hell had their powers abruptly cut off?

I sent a questioning emotion along the mate bond back to him, but he didn't respond.

Uneasiness filled me. I tugged again on the mate bond, calling to Kaillen, but he didn't pull back. Yet, I could still *feel* him with my awakening power. His body was still there, but he was strangely quiet, and his magical essence, along with Barnabas's and Fallon's, had dimmed.

Oh gods.

I tried to pull at their magic more, to enhance my strength, but it was sluggish and slow, not readily coming to me. *Shit.*

I pushed to my feet in a blur of werewolf speed. My wolf strained and growled inside me as my gaze darted to the trees, then to the sea, but I still couldn't sense where Jakub lay, or understand what had happened to Kaillen and his friends.

My heart beat harder. *Dammit.* It was like on the ship. Jakub had to be wearing that enhanced cloaking spell again. I'd thought maybe with Kaillen's and his friends' powers siphoning to me, that I might have been powerful enough to see through it, but with their powers now quiet . . .

I searched again for the three of them with my awakening magic. Kaillen hadn't moved. Neither had Barnabas nor Fallon. They were still there, exactly as they'd been previously, but what had happened to them?

I felt along the mate bond again, my unease turning into panic. *Kaillen! Answer me!*

Silence.

My pulse fluttered as my feeling of panic grew. Something was horribly wrong.

I jerked around as I searched and strained for Jakub, but I couldn't see him, or hear him, or feel him. *What the hell did he do?*

I took a step toward the trees as my wolf urged me to find my mate. She whined and clawed, beckoning me to go to him.

"Did you really think you could trick me that easily?" a cold, detached voice flowed toward me.

Every hair on my neck stood on end. *Jakub.*

I froze. "Where are you?" I no longer tried to pretend that I had the upper hand. I clearly didn't.

I swung around in a circle, searching and hunting for him, but all that responded was a sigh which sounded as though it were coming from a void.

"Did you really think that I wouldn't know you'd cursed me?"

I twirled around in another circle, and took a step away from the forest. I wouldn't lead the dipshit to my mate.

"What do you want with me? Why do you keep hunting me?" I readied my witch magic, curling my power into a tight ball of crackling telekinetic and binding spells just waiting to be unleashed.

"So many questions. And they will all be answered soon." A cold finger traced down my cheek, and I flinched, lurching back, but I wasn't fast enough.

Pain lashed around my left wrist as something clamped a hold of me. I hurtled my readied magic toward the left, and it shot out of me in an explosion of power.

But Jakub didn't materialize. My magic shot through the realm, the spell weakening and then dying in a cloud of dust when it never landed on a recipient.

"Kaill—!" But then the world was tumbling and falling beneath me. I was thrown through a void, everything dipping and flowing as my stomach shot into my throat and my voice was cut off in my chest.

A portal key.

Jakub had used a portal key on me.

A functioning part of my brain realized that just as I landed on something cold and hard. The breath knocked out of me, my stomach aching from the sudden impact, right before my head cracked against concrete and everything went dark.

CHAPTER TWENTY-FIVE

"Time to wake up, Ms. Davenport."

I opened my eyes as that cold, clinical voice floated from above me. Blinking, I stared in confusion at the smooth concrete floor spread out around me. I pushed to sitting, amazed that my temples weren't throbbing. Blood smeared the floor where my head had cracked against it, but then I remembered that I was part werewolf now. I healed fast.

Heart speeding up, I assessed my surroundings. Tall concrete walls and one door completed the room. No windows. I was in a prison cell.

Shit. Not good.

My breaths sped up more when I remembered Jakub on the cliff's edge, invisible yet *there*. And what had happened to Kaillen, Barnabas, and Fallon? Why hadn't they responded?

I frantically felt for the mate bond again.

A sob of relief filled me when I felt that Kaillen wasn't dead.

Knowing that calmed a part of me as I searched the cell for anything that would give me clues to where I was, but nothing about this place had any identifying marks.

Okay, stay calm. Kaillen isn't dead. He's still alive. He'll find you.

My eyes widened, and I tried to keep my heart from beating out of my chest, but panic was on the verge of blazing through me. This was literally our worst fear come true.

A quiet zapping filled my ears. Bites of magic pulsed on my wrists. A glance down confirmed that I was wearing the glowing blue cuffs. I'd been so consumed with my mate that I hadn't even realized I was bound.

I laughed almost hysterically. *Well, Jakub-Dipshit's certainly not original.*

But I didn't have time to process that before the corner door opened. A man stepped into the cell. Medium build. Dark-brown hair. Wide mouth.

He was the same supe who'd been in Philadelphia. This man *had* to be Jakub. Rage filled me as my hands balled into fists.

Jakub stopped in the doorway and stood completely immobile. His cool, detached expression didn't waver. "I was growing impatient. You were unconscious for nearly two hours." As before, I detected that strange accent from him.

I nearly scoffed. I probably would have been unconscious all day if not for my wolf. Inside me, she growled, hackles raised.

"Where am I?" I demanded.

"Where you should have been when my sorcerers took you from Ontario."

Philadelphia again? The cuffs' magic pulsed along my skin, but hopelessness didn't fill me. I'd been spelled with immunity by the SF. I could break out of these cuffs, but I had to bide my time. I had to do it at the right moment when Jakub least expected it. "What do you want?"

"You," was all he replied.

"Why me?"

"Because you're the key." Despite the fact that he'd finally caught me, there was no excitement in his voice. No triumph. Just cool clinical interest, as if I was an experiment and he was collecting my data.

"You're one sick bastard, aren't you?" I kept my voice even, as though being cuffed in some freakin' concrete prison cell was no big deal.

But my goading didn't have its intended effect. I saw no anger in him. No bruised male pride. The only reaction Jakub gave was a slight incline of his head.

I shivered. Something about this man was . . . off.

I jutted my chin up. My wolf snarled inside me again, rage making her physical form heat and swell. She lunged against my control, trying to force the shift. Visions of tearing out Jakub's throat with our teeth filled my mind, but I pushed her down. Right now, I couldn't lose control. Now of all times, I needed to maintain my human form.

I held up my hands in the glowing blue cuffs. "Now that you have me, what are you going to do with me?"

His detached expression remained. "Why don't you follow me and find out?" He crooked a finger in my direction, and something shoved against my back, as though invisible hands pushed me from behind.

I whipped around to look behind my shoulder, but nothing was there. Yet the force remained. Whatever magic Jakub commanded was incredibly strong, because the force at my back was like a telekinetic spell on steroids.

"What you're sensing is merely a taste of all that's at my fingertips," he called over his shoulder. There was no arrogance in his tone, no boastfulness, merely a cold hard fact that he was enlightening me to.

"What are you?"

"I'm sure you've often asked yourself the same."

I struggled against the force pushing me, but even though I planted my feet on the floor, using my newly enhanced werewolf strength, it was useless. I was no match for it.

"You can fight me all you want, but it will be futile. I am the master here, and you will be one of my puppets, just as the others are."

"What do you mean by—" The question died on my lips when the force pushed me into a large open room.

My throat turned dry as my eyes popped wide open.

The room was a perfect concrete circle, maybe a hundred feet in diameter with a soaring domed ceiling. No windows. No color. Just concrete. And around the room's perimeter was a circle of *cages*.

Just like in the nightclub.

Inside each cell was a supernatural. Fairy, vampire, werewolf, siren, half-demon, the list went on. Every single supernatural species that existed was in one of the cages. There were men and women, young and old.

Shit on a stick. This really isn't good.

I knew I was staring at the twelve missing supernaturals that the SF had been searching for. A flash of something Tessa had said came to me, from when she'd been a captive in Jakub's collection. *"There'd been other supernaturals, too, across from our cells, but they'd been there longer than the three of us, and they were—I don't know what they were doing to them, but it left them . . . It changed them."*

My heartbeat ticked up more as I assessed the twelve supes' vacant expressions. "What did you do to them?"

Jakub gave me a perplexed look, as though it were obvious. "They've been harvested."

I began to tremble, my entire body vibrating, but not in fear. Fury strummed through me that this psychopath felt he had the right to do this to others.

It took everything in me not to lash out at him and kill him once and for all, but I couldn't, not yet. I needed to know what his endgame was, why he was doing this.

So instead, I felt inside myself again for the mate bond, hoping I could feel if Kaillen was coming, if he'd sensed where I was and I could know if he was on his way.

But then his one fear came back to me.

He'd been worried that I would be transported to a building that he couldn't penetrate. I eyed the concrete walls again and swallowed hard.

I felt inside for him and gave a frantic tug.

An immediate tug came back, nearly violent in its pull. My relief was so swift that I nearly slumped to the floor from it. I sent a soothing response toward him, as best I could, just so he wouldn't panic like I had when our connection had gone quiet before.

"What did you do to Kaillen on the cliff?" I asked Jakub.

Jakub cocked an eyebrow just as the sound of stomping feet came from the hallway he'd dragged me from. Twelve supernaturals marched out, each of them carrying a long sharp-pointed metallic spear. All twelve of them sported the constellation tattoo, and their tattoos were glowing.

They moved quickly and efficiently around the room, each of them placing their spear on the floor in front of each cage. When they finished, they bowed at Jakub. Actually *bowed*, like he was some freakin' high lord.

The submissive gesture halted them long enough for me to see their faces and expressions. Like the caged supernaturals, Jakub's men also held distant gazes, as though they no longer commanded their own senses.

My brow furrowed. "What did you do to them?"

Before Jakub could reply, his men left, leaving me alone with the dipshit. The spears all stayed on the ground, pointed toward the center of the room.

"Tell me!" I demanded again when Jakub didn't reply.

"I take what I need from them when I need it," was all he said.

"Are the supernaturals working for you part of the European mafia too?"

He cocked his head. "You know where I hail from?"

"Answer me!"

"That is not your concern."

A prick of fear strummed through me, but I shoved it aside and focused on distracting Jakub, on delaying whatever he had planned. "What did you do to Kaillen on the cliff?"

"He's still alive if that's what you're wondering." *I know.* "But I couldn't have him interfering, now could I?" Jakub added.

That invisible force shoved me again, this time toward the center of the room. I pushed against it, thrashing and flailing as fury exploded into my gut that he was treating me like a doll.

Jakub waved a hand and all twelve cages opened, their doors swinging on silent hinges as the vacant-looking supernaturals came to attention like zombies in their cells.

Frantic breaths rose my chest, but I squashed any panic down as I dove into that deep dark cavern inside me and reached for my awakening power. Even though I wanted to discover Jakub's endgame, if Kaillen couldn't get here in time, then waiting was no longer an option.

Jakub needed to die. I needed to escape. And this place needed to be destroyed.

I grasped my awakening power just as the force holding

me in place positioned me in the center of the room and held me there. My eyes widened when I realized I stood in the center of a circle. Etched into the concrete floor were constellation symbols and circles.

My heart beat harder when I looked at the spears. They looked like . . . arrows. Heart ticking up even more, I frantically took in the catatonic supernaturals marching toward those spears from their cages. All of them had constellation tattoos on their necks.

The moment the twelve catatonic-looking supernaturals picked up their spears, their tattoos began to glow, telling me that our theory of the tattoos somehow holding magic was even more likely.

Around me, the constellation symbols carved into the floor hummed and then flared to life, a turquoise hue rising from them.

"Why do I have a feeling I'm in the middle of a ritual?" I asked, yet despite trying to keep the panic from my voice, it cracked.

Jakub's only response was a cool flick of his eyes my way.

The tentacled power inside me rose and slithered, just as another tug came from the mate bond, stronger and filled with so much wrath that I knew Kaillen had sensed my panic. Hope burned through me along with renewed determination. Kaillen was alive and searching for me. I just had to hold on until he arrived.

I called forth all of my new awakening power just as the bond inside me grew stronger, burning in awareness as my mate bore down on my location like an army from the dead rising with vengeance. I felt Kaillen's power, his rage, his wrath, and his growing presence, and I *knew* that he was getting closer.

With a huge flare of magic, I whispered a maximizer spell and called upon my wolf's strength.

She was more than happy to assist as I wrenched my arms apart and broke the cuffs.

Jakub's eyes widened as the cuffs snapped off of me just as I threw my tentacle power in his direction, slamming everything I had into killing this bastard once and for all.

But the twelve catatonic supernaturals moved simultaneously with me. They lifted their spears and blasts of magic came from each of them, shooting down their spears just as my power arced out of me, aimed directly at Jakub.

The second the magic from the spears hit me, my awakening power changed course. Instead of clamping a hold on Jakub and serrating through his essence like a ravenous shark, it veered downward, right into the constellation pattern beneath my feet. My awakening power slammed into the glowing turquoise symbols as a cold smile spread across Jakub's lips.

It was the only emotion he'd shown all night.

Power flowed through me from the twelve supernaturals down their spears, and it heightened the magic inside me as more of my awakening power zoomed through the symbols. The symbols glowed brighter and hotter, my heart slamming against my ribs as the energy in the room changed. It grew, yawning open, as though a great chasm had been cracked beneath my feet.

I tried again to throw my power at Jakub, to stop whatever madness was being born, but a *new* tentacle of power —a foreign one—slithered upward through a crack beneath my toes. My heart thundered because I was staring at another supernatural's power that was *just like mine.*

It felt distant, yet familiar, and I watched in horror as a power very similar to my own climbed up my legs to my body before caressing my awakening magic's octopus-like arms.

My breath seized at the feel of it. It felt as though a mother were stroking her child.

Disbelief flowed through me as those foreign tentacles grasped my power and pulled it from me, yanking and clawing as if finally latching onto the child it'd always wanted.

Jakub watched it all, his small smile still in place. He didn't utter a word, didn't applaud, yet I felt his burning interest.

Erupting light cracked the floor even more, and even though the concrete crumbled beneath me, I didn't fall or move. The power flowing from the spears—from the catatonic supernaturals who held them—kept me in place as my awakening magic connected with whatever void and foreign tentacle power had been created beneath me.

I grasped again at my awakening power, trying to pry it from whatever was holding it, but it wouldn't let go. It was as though the newcomer and I played a game of tug-of-war, only I wasn't the biggest or strongest.

Screaming from the exertion, I desperately tried to coax my power back inside me again, but even though I used my wolf's strength, those invisible *other* tentacles turned into claws and sank into me, as though determined not to let me go. I swallowed a yelp as searing pain lashed through me.

The magical spears and symbols glowed even brighter, so blinding they rivaled the sun. All twelve captive supernaturals looked strained and haggard, as though whatever magic they were using to create this ritual was running them dry, but they were all so strong and so powerful, as their magic continued to zoom toward me.

An abrupt memory slammed into me, of what Sinister Fairy Dude had said to Kaillen back in that New York nightclub.

"If nothing else, you'll be an important spear in Jakub's collection."

Shock hit me. This was why Jakub needed powerful supernaturals—to channel their magic into me for whatever it was he was creating. *This* was why he was collecting them.

The crack beneath my feet widened more, and then a burst of light flooded the room as a plethora of stars and galaxies exploded into focus beneath me. A universe appeared.

Panic flared inside me, then roared to the surface. *No, no, no, no, no, no.*

Something burned into my neck, and I gasped and raised my hands to my skin as though trying to ward it off, but the burn only increased as an ancient sense of awareness filled me.

And then I was moving, going down, down, down. Moving at light speed as I plummeted through a cosmic void of time and space.

My awakening power shot to the surface as those claws that had been holding me turned into talons. They sank into me so deeply that I screamed in pain.

I barreled through time and space, dipping and swaying, here and there, yet nowhere all at once.

And then I came to a slamming stop. I found myself staring down at a vast unknown world, hovering above it. Then I moved again, careening through the atmosphere as though I was a jet flying high over its surface. My heart pumped painfully as I gazed at the barren valleys, soaring desert mountains, trickling rivers, and dry fields. It was a world awash with colors of beige and grays, bleak and desolate. A new world. A new planet. Not of my universe. Not of the fae universe. But something different. Something undiscovered.

Cities appeared on the horizon. Ancient-looking cities of stone and brick.

Where am I? It was the only thought I had before that light-speed movement yanked on my form again, and I lurched back, going up, up, up. Time and space flew around me, here, there, everywhere at once.

And then I was back in the center of Jakub's room.

I blinked, then blinked again as a cacophony of screams, roars, and casting magic blazed around me.

There was a war raging in this room. SF members were locked in battle with dozens of Jakub's men. The clang of metallic weapons hitting spears reached my ears, then came the scent of casting magic and the sight of flaring potent spells. It all waged around me, as though I were in an untouchable void in the middle of it all.

That portal to an unknown universe still lay beneath me, but it wasn't open as it had been a second prior. However, I felt that it could be, if only the collectives activated their spears again. But amidst the chaos, the collectives were either fighting or dead, and I knew that it was their loss of power that had returned me to earth instead of keeping me on that alien planet.

Crawling on all fours, I moved as far away from the crack in the floor as I could. I tried to stand, to get to my feet, but my mind spun, and my legs felt like jelly. All of my magic was gone. Whatever Jakub had done with the spears and me as the conduit—his key—had drained me.

My heart hammered in my chest as I caught a flash of dark hair to my right and then a face etched with rage came into view. *Kaillen!*

He battled Jakub one-on-one as both cast spells at one another. Immense power blasted from their hands. The two of them fought so fast that it all became a blur.

Despite my efforts to try to reach my hunter, I was too weak. I remained near the center of the room, still feeling that tug from that other world—to wherever I had been transported to and had gone—but I pulled back from it, keeping my awakening power buried deep in the void inside me as it began to recharge.

But those alien talons continued to search and hunt for me, sneaking through the crack in the floor every now and then, before retreating when the width halted their progress.

Some instinct deep inside me knew that I needed to detach myself completely from that other world. That I had to close whatever portal had been created to it. A glow still lit the floor, the constellations etched into the concrete still bright and shining, but the symbols no longer flared like the sun, and a part of me knew that was because the cataclysmic power from the twelve supernaturals had disappeared.

But we couldn't leave the portal open. I didn't know how I knew that, but I was certain terrible things would happen if we didn't close it. So I summoned everything inside me. I called upon my witch powers, my forbidden magic, my awakening power, and everything from my wolf as I tried to smother that void in the center of the room.

My vision swam dark as I put everything I had into it.

The crack in the floor began to close, little by little, and the universe that had shined back at me slowly faded.

That's it. More. More. More.

But just as the floor began to seal, something shot out of it. That foreign octopus tendril burst through it, heading right toward me until it speared my chest at light speed.

The power inside me instantly extinguished, and I

screamed as something in me shattered. It felt as though my body had cracked in two, as if a giant hammer had been sent from the heavens and smashed down onto me with the power of the gods.

My inner magic cleaved in half. My soul wrenched apart.

"Tala!" a roar came from someone in the room.

My wolf vanished, her single yelp the only sound I heard from her before she was gone, completely obliterated.

And then my awakening and forbidden magic rose up inside me, humming through my belly, the chest and cave they'd been stored in within my body shattering into a million pieces. My otherworldly powers flowed together, combining and writhing until they swallowed me whole.

My eyes flashed open as everything in the world grew still.

Power flowed through my veins like lightning. My heart sang. My mind calmed. And a deep instinct came to me from the beginnings of time. It surged to the surface and wrenched that foreign hold off of me that had still been trying to drag me back into the void.

And then I was free.

Power surged out of me into every single supernatural who was battling my mate and the Supernatural Forces. My awakening magic clamped down onto them, sinking its teeth through their magic, their souls, right through their bones until their forms exploded in a rush of magic and power.

I gasped as the entire room fell silent.

Every SF member stood shaking, all eyes turned on me as disbelief and horror etched into their expressions.

My entire body trembled as I took in the scene around me.

The room was awash with blood and gore. All of the supernaturals that had held the spears were dead, their mangled bodies mutilated and broken.

What have I done? I frantically looked among the dozens of SF members staring at me.

"Kaillen?" But I didn't see him, didn't hear him. I searched inside myself for the mate bond, frantically clawing for it, not knowing if he was among the living or the dead.

But I felt nothing. *Nothing.* Not a whisper or a hint of that delicate thread which had linked me and my mate.

The bond was gone.

And that could only happen if one's mate was dead.

CHAPTER TWENTY-SIX

"Tala!" Commander Klebus's sharp voice called to me as though down a tunnel, yelling and screaming at me to open my eyes. Her demanding yell pulled me back to the surface and I peered upward to see the vampire hovering above me, her cobalt eyes blazing. "Tala, we need to get you out of here and to a healing center."

I lay limp on the floor, a turquoise glow still illuminating the symbols all around me. The portal. It was still open.

But that didn't matter. None of that mattered anymore. Kaillen was dead. My mate was gone.

"No, no, no. He can't be gone. He can't be dead," I mumbled.

He's gone. He's gone. He's gone.

"Tala?" another frantic voice called from the edge of the room.

My eyes shot to where the voice had come from—that hauntingly beautiful voice that should not be possible.

Kaillen shoved past the SF members in his way and strode toward me with a look of absolute confusion and devastation covering his face.

My eyes widened, my heart thrumming erratically in my chest.

He's not dead. He's still alive.

I shot to my feet, strength flowing through my veins as hope surged within me. I bypassed Commander Klebus's outstretched hand and ran toward him, my arms automatically opening.

I threw my arms around Kaillen, immense relief flooding me, as my otherworldly powers continued to hum and flow inside me.

"You're alive! You're still here!" I held him close and thanked the gods that he hadn't been killed.

I couldn't make sense of time and day, space or matter. It was as if the past five minutes or hour or day, or however long I'd been trapped in the portal's void and gone to another realm, had all been squashed into milliseconds. All of the events had become one big jumbled mess, like a kaleidoscope of chaos.

"How are you still alive?" Kaillen looked down at me as crimson fire burned in his eyes, yet that devastated look remained. "I felt the bond snap. I thought you'd been killed."

I nodded. "I thought you were dead too. I felt the mate

bond break as well, and I thought that you . . ." A sob shook my chest.

His eyes shuttered as his gaze roamed over my face. I waited for my wolf to whine in eagerness and happiness that her mate was okay, but she remained silent.

I shook my head. It was all so much. "Where's Jakub?"

"We have him captured." Commander Klebus nodded toward a man on his knees in the corner. "He's the only one you didn't . . . kill." Her throat bobbed in a swallow. "He'd been trying to escape but Mr. King stopped him."

Jakub was cuffed and kneeling on the floor, four SF members surrounding him. All of them had their particle guns aimed at his head.

Jakub's cool eyes locked onto mine, yet despite the vulnerable position he was currently in, he didn't look dismayed. Instead, triumph filled his eyes—a true emotion, the first real one I'd ever seen him wear—before that cool clinical smile lifted his lips.

I shuddered.

A finger traced along my neck, and I snapped my attention back to Kaillen. As soon as I peered up at him, his finger dropped. He shook his head as he glanced at my neck again, confusion twisting his features.

I tried to tug on the bond, tried to sense what he was feeling, but then remembered it was gone. So I sniffed, trying to detect his emotions, but all that filled my nose were the remnants of casted magic and burned flesh.

Frowning, I stared up at Kaillen as a sick sense of dread filled my belly.

"Where did you go?" he asked as a storm of confusion, despair, and disbelief waged in his eyes.

"Go?"

"You disappeared for a while during the battle. And when you reappeared, the mate bond broke."

"I . . . I went . . ." I felt inside me again for my wolf, for her presence, but all that loomed back at me was a tidal wave of those otherworldly powers, unleashed and humming through me.

A moment of panic filled me. *Where are you?* I called to her.

Silence.

"Where's my wolf?" I swung around in a circle, as if I could find her outside of my body, waiting or hiding, which was absolutely ridiculous. "I don't feel her or the mate bond." I whirled back to Kaillen and stared at him imploringly. "Where? Where did she go?"

A grim expression overtook his face. "I don't feel her either."

I shook my head frantically. "I don't understand. What's going on?"

"I don't know. I don't know what's happened, Tala." A look of anguish contorted his features. "My wolf—" His throat bobbed in a swallow. "He's mourning right now, howling inside me. He knows your wolf is gone. He knows she died."

My heart cracked "She died? No, that can't be." I shook my head frantically. "And what do you mean that your wolf's in mourning? *I'm* still his mate, and I'm right here."

"But your wolf isn't. She's gone, Tala. I can feel it."

My hand flew to my mouth because as much as I wanted to deny it, I could *feel* that he was right. When I reached inside me to find my wolf again, nothing greeted me. *Nothing.*

That acceptance hit me like a freight train. My wolf was gone. Dead. Vanished. My beautiful, strong she-wolf . . . the wolf I had initially rejected, yet had grown to cherish in such a short time, was *dead.*

"No, *please* no." A wail tore from my throat.

Kaillen looked down at me, his chest rising as anguish distorted his features. "My wolf . . . he doesn't believe you're his mate. He doesn't recognize you anymore."

"What?" The shocked whisper flew from my lips, and that was when I felt it. *Saw* it.

Kaillen was looking at me with anguish and confusion, but not with love. Not as he had only hours ago.

Cold hurt and devastation slammed into me. "Kaillen?" I whispered, unable to keep the pained ache from my tone. "No. Don't say that. It's not true!" Tears streamed down my face, but he made no move to comfort me or hold me.

"There are a lot of unanswered questions here." Commander Klebus cut in, breaking me away from Kaillen as she began issuing orders. "We need to get you to a healing center and checked out, and we need to get everyone out of here, and that—" She gazed toward the cracked floor, and with a gasp I took in the waving turquoise portal door that had grown around it. "That needs to be contained."

Her lips pressed into a thin line. She looked pale, her golden skin ashen, as if whatever had occurred in this room haunted her to the depths of her soul.

"What's happened?" I called to Kaillen again, needing to touch him, feel him, be reassured by him, but his confused expression remained. "Kaillen!"

He shook his head as his shoulders tensed. "I don't know. I *don't know*, Tala, but I need to get back to the fae lands. Barnabas and Fallon were also knocked out by whatever Jakub did to us. I left them, to rally the SF and find you, but I need to check on them."

He strode toward the exit of the room, pulling his yellow crystal from his pocket as he went.

And that was when I *knew*.

Whatever had been born between Kaillen and me had been shredded in a matter of minutes or hours. Whatever Jakub had done, whatever power had erupted inside me and transported me to that distant world, had also eradicated our bond, had killed my wolf, had destroyed whatever remnant of myself had been planted firmly in this world. The person that Kaillen's wolf had sensed as his mate had died, and now, whoever I was, *whatever* I was, his wolf no longer recognized as his mate.

To his wolf, his mate had died.

And everyone knew how male wolves reacted when their mate died. They closed off, they retreated into mourning, they no longer wanted any woman of any kind.

I felt inside me for my wolf again, hoping against hope

that she was still there, that I could find her if I simply searched hard enough, dug deep enough.

But my search proved fruitless.

She had truly vanished.

A sob shook my chest. Only days ago, I'd been wishing she'd never been born, but now? Now it felt as though I'd lost a piece of my soul.

"Kaillen?" I called after him again, my voice pleading. "My love? It's still me. I'm still Tala."

He stopped at the edge of the room and turned back to me. Crimson fire rolled in his eyes, but that golden flare was gone. His eyes dipped to my neck again, his expression impossible to read. His brow furrowed, and a fleeting sense of confusion washed over his features for the millionth time.

"It's gone," he eventually said with finality. "The bond that sealed us is gone."

CHAPTER TWENTY-SEVEN

Three days later, I stood in my bathroom and stared in the mirror at the tattoo encircling my neck. Stars. Constellations. Foreign symbols. They ringed my skin in an intricate design of alien purpose and power. Whatever had awoken in Jakub's concrete warehouse had permanently marked itself into my very essence.

I tilted my head, studying the mark. It was different to the single tattoo on Jakub's men, and my tattoo didn't seem to serve the same purpose. As we'd learned since capturing Jakub, the constellation tattoo had been a way to combine Jakub's magic with the magic of those that worked for him. An ancient spell had linked them through the tattoo, allowing Jakub to harness his men's power and wield it. It was what had made him so powerful. And when Jakub had activated the tattoos' spell—which had made the tattoos glow—Jakub had been sucking magic directly from his men, which explained his inexplicable power when we'd battled him at sea.

My gaze drifted to the bottom of my throat, and my breath stuttered. The crescent shaped moon that had once ghosted my skin had vanished with my wolf.

I snapped my attention back up and looked at my eyes. My sapphire-blue irises, sparkling with stardust, stared back at me. Vibrant, humming power swirled in their depths—another world shining through them, as though night and galaxies were reflected within a bottomless chasm.

I stood rigidly, still in disbelief at what I was seeing. So much about myself had changed.

Shuddering, I snapped my attention away from the mirror and retreated to my bedroom. Tessa and I were back in Chicago, and had been ever since hell had been unleashed on my life.

Hurrying to my closet, I grabbed a pair of socks. I had another appointment at the SF this morning that I shouldn't be late to. Commander Klebus was already pissed at me for going after Jakub alone. I didn't need to give her another reason to be irritated.

But even though I'd gotten an earful initially, she'd also reluctantly agreed that without Jakub whisking me to his hidden Philadelphia warehouse, the SF never would have found it. Jakub had hidden his lair under so many illusion spells that even the SF sorcerers hadn't been able to detect it. But my mate had been able to find it through our blood bond. It was the only way the SF and Kaillen had found me and Jakub's building.

My heart stopped. *Kaillen. My Mate.*

A humorless smile lifted my lips. I supposed I should start referring to Kaillen as my *former* mate now.

I swallowed the lump in my throat and whipped a shirt over my head, my fingers trembling when I straightened the hem. I then began hunting for my shoes.

I'd been at the SF office nearly nonstop since the entire ordeal in Philadelphia, in which a new portal had been created, I'd been transported to some other world, I'd unwittingly killed dozens of supernaturals, and the SF had put a stop to Jakub once and for all.

And while those deaths were haunting me, causing me numerous nightmares while I slept and feeling indescribable guilt when awake, I felt even worse because killing all of those supernaturals wasn't what was haunting me most.

Instead, it was the death of my wolf and broken mate bond. There had been moments in the past few days where that realization had hit me so suddenly that I couldn't breathe. It'd felt as though I were drowning as I gasped with the knowledge that the wolf I'd grown to cherish in the short time I'd had her, and the man I'd fiercely loved, were both gone.

Klebus had seemed to sense the despair in me. She'd worked hard to find me answers to what had happened. From what the SF had learned, it was my otherworldly powers activating to their full potential that had destroyed my wolf, as though the connecting portal's power—those *other* octopus arms I'd felt—had sensed my wolf and obliterated her foreign presence. And once she was gone, it'd given my otherworldly powers even more room to grow.

Klebus hadn't commented yet that I'd been a female supernatural with a wolf inside her—although I could tell that she had put two and two together as it explained how I'd broken the blue cuffs while I'd been at Tessa's safe house. The commander obviously knew something had happened between Kaillen and me to create my wolf, but she had yet to ask, and I had yet to volunteer it.

I had a feeling my pain was written across my face for her to see, and even her shrewd non-beating vampire heart had been moved by it enough not to pressure that information from me.

But despite all that I'd lost, and how hard we'd fought to stop Jakub—we hadn't.

The SF database had indeed confirmed that Jakub and his cohorts were members of the European mafia. It was why he'd had so many supernaturals at his disposal since that organized crime ring was huge. And it also explained how he'd still achieved his goal even though we'd eventually caught up with him. Because inside that concrete room in Jakub's hidden warehouse, a shining and brand-new turquoise portal waited. A portal to a world nobody had ever heard of, yet was a world I was somehow tied to and Jakub had known existed.

Commander Klebus had told me on day two that opening the portal had been Jakub's goal all along. During one of his interrogations, he'd told her "they" were still coming, and that he would be rewarded for what he'd done. As if that'd made his capture by the SF worth it. As though that justified those twelve innocent supernaturals' deaths—deaths that now rested on my consciousness and had caused me numerous nightmares.

But following that admission, Jakub had stopped answering the SF's questions. Commander Klebus said that now he was simply waiting.

But waiting for what?

My hands felt clammy as I tied my shoes.

It still tugged at me, that visit to the other realm, as though something was beckoning me to return to that concrete circular room and venture once more to that desolate planet.

I shook my head, shrugging off these strange new instincts. It shouldn't be possible. It should all have been a dream, but it wasn't. And inside me, as much as I was trying to fight it, a deep instinct had awoken, and my forbidden and awakening magic now breathed like fire in my veins, no longer contained or caged, but free and so much more powerful.

I fingered my new tattoo again, then slipped a jacket on.

A part of me knew that my awakening magic and forbidden power had been born from that world I'd visited, that they were remnants of an ancient time from long ago. It was why Jakub had called me the key. He'd known that the powers inside me had been the way to open the gateway to whatever that realm was I'd visited. Because my powers had most definitely come from there.

I'd felt it and seen it, when those tentacles had reached through the void and clamped onto me, as though a mother were welcoming her child home.

I shuddered just thinking about it.

"Are you ready?" Tessa called to me from the living room. A second later, she appeared in my doorway, her expression solemn. She also had her jacket and shoes on. "You know, he stopped by again this morning, asking to speak with you."

My entire body stilled as I pictured Kaillen at our front door. "You told him I was busy, right?"

She twisted her hands. "I did, but he still knew you were here."

I lifted my eyes to my dresser's mirror and gazed one last time at the exploding stars in my eyes. "He made his choice," I said simply. "A clean break is the best way to deal with this."

Tessa took a deep breath, pain evident on her face.

I knew that my heartache was written all over my expression. Despite trying to hide it and pretend that I was fine, she could see everything.

But it was, what it was.

After Klebus had taken me out of Jakub's warehouse, Kaillen had returned to the fae lands to check on Barnabas and Fallon. Apparently, Jakub had been able to sense them in the forest, with whatever powers he'd harvested from his zombie supernaturals that had given him such extreme magic. He'd knocked all three of them unconscious with his stolen power, not an easy feat to do to someone such as

Kaillen, but that was why their power had diminished in those final moments and I hadn't been able to use it to see Jakub through his cloaking spell.

But the hunter had woken first, healing faster than his friends, so he'd transported back to earth to rally the SF before they'd stormed Jakub's warehouse while Barnabas and Fallon remained unconscious in the fae lands.

I didn't fault Kaillen for returning to check on his friends right after what had happened in that warehouse, not at all. But what hurt so damned much—what hurt so intensely that I couldn't breathe every time I thought about it—was how he'd looked at me in that room. With such finality and grief. As if he agreed with his wolf and thought his mate was dead, even though I'd been standing right in front of him.

Not surprisingly, Kaillen had disappeared after returning to the fae lands, and I hadn't heard from him in those first twenty-four hours. No response to my texts. No calls. I'd initially tried to reassure myself, telling myself that he was still in shock, that it would wear off and he'd realize that his wolf just needed to learn that I was still here. I wasn't dead.

But then day two passed and nothing came. So I started telling myself that he'd gotten caught up with his friends' care. Maybe something bad had happened to Barnabas and Fallon, and Kaillen was so consumed with ensuring they were safe that he couldn't get in touch with me.

I'd managed to keep it together because I'd convinced myself of those beliefs, but then Commander Klebus had told me that Kaillen was back on earth and had been since only a few hours after leaving Jakub's warehouse. She'd seemed surprised about my concern for Barnabas and Fallon, stating they'd been conscious and fine when Kaillen had returned to check on them.

And how had she gotten a hold of him? His phone. When she'd called him, he'd answered. In other words, he was responding to other people. Just not to me.

My throat closed up again just thinking about it. The rational side of me told me not to hate him. Because his wolf truly thought his mate was dead. I was no longer who his wolf craved, so of course, Kaillen no longer felt the same for me.

It was exactly as I'd always feared. His feelings had been manufactured by his wolf, and now that his wolf no longer wanted me, the hunter didn't either.

That deep, unfathomable pain opened up inside me again. With trembling fingers, I grabbed my brush and tore it through my hair one last time before I faced my sister. Tessa and I were no strangers to loss. We'd lost our parents. We'd lost our distant relatives. We'd lost home upon home growing up. Yet we'd survived.

And I'd survive this too.

But one thing I couldn't survive? Seeing that look on Kaillen's face again. That look of anguish, grief, and confusion. No. That, I wouldn't subject myself to again.

"Don't you think you should talk to him?" Tessa asked gently as we walked into the living room toward the front door.

"Why, so he can reject me again?" I grabbed my purse off the table by the door. "His wolf thinks his mate is dead. You know what it's like for male werewolves once their mate dies. They never love again."

"But you're still alive!"

"Try telling his wolf that."

Her brow furrowed, sympathy clouding her expression. "Why would he stop by to see you last night, and then again this morning, if he didn't care about you at least a little bit?"

My lip quivered, but I pulled it into my mouth and bit hard, using the pain to distract me so tears wouldn't form in my eyes. "Didn't you say that he had all of my bags with him this morning?"

"Yeah, but—"

"Then I think it's pretty obvious why he came. He wanted to return my stuff."

Tessa gave a single nod, sadness still evident on her features.

I sighed. "Let's go. It's gonna be another long day at the SF."

She linked arms with me, and I leaned on her. Leaned on her so hard. Because for the first time in my life, I wasn't the strong one. I was splintering apart inside, my inner soul shredding bit by bit, and I needed her to keep me together, to keep me from breaking until enough time had passed and my heart could heal.

She locked the door to our apartment behind us and pocketed her key. I whispered the spell to activate our new ward. True to his promise, Azad—Prisha's father—had cast iron wards around our apartment's entire perimeter while I'd been in Ontario.

In my purse, my cell phone buzzed, and I pulled it out to see a text from Prisha.

> I'm swinging by as soon as you finish at the SF today. Just let me know when you're done. I'm there.

My lip trembled again as I replied with a heart emoji. It was the only response I could muster as my soul tore a little bit more. Prisha knew how fragile I felt at the moment. The concern in her eyes, as she and Tessa had hovered around me last night when I'd learned that Kaillen had stopped by, had nearly undone me. I may no longer have a mate, but I had the most fiercely loyal friends and family that a girl could ever hope for, and I loved them so much it hurt.

The ward around our apartment settled into place, and we set out. Halfway down the stairs, Tessa's phone buzzed. She pulled it out and frowned. "Archie just got in touch."

My feet made loud stomps on each stair. Without my wolf, I was no longer a silent predator. A deep ache filled me again. My wolf was gone—*dead*—and I missed her so fucking much.

I shook my head as I tried to snap myself out of my grief. "Who's Archie?"

"He's the SF member from my safe house who was going to search in the libraries for me, remember?" She opened his text and began reading it, then stopped, a gasp escaping her. "Tala!"

She grabbed my arm and stopped me halfway down the last flight of stairs. "Read this." She shoved her phone into my hand.

My brow furrowed as I read Archie's text.

> I have findings to report. I found a spellbook in the libraries that speaks of an ancient spell that can create glowing tattoos on a recipient that allows their magic to be siphoned.

> And I also found two documents in the libraries about the Bone Eaters. They weren't easy to find. I had to enlist the help of a gargoyle scholar, but apparently there are a few ancient documents that speak of a group called by that Bone Eaters name. They're supposedly from a lost realm, an ancient civilization that once roamed earth yet heralded from a different universe, like the fae realm does. But several thousand years ago that realm was lost and their kind disappeared along with the terrible magic they commanded. Nobody has seen or heard of them since.

I stilled, then read it again. *Different universe. Terrible magic. Disappeared.*

An uneasy feeling skittered through me, and my heart began to pound.

With a trembling hand, I gave Tessa's phone back to her. "Come on. We need to go. We'll think about that later." I resumed my walk down the stairs but tripped and had to grab the railing to stop myself from falling. But despite holding onto the railing, it felt as though I was plummeting down, down, down.

What the hell do those findings mean?

Once outside, Tessa pulled up her rideshare app. Everything inside me felt numb until we pulled up to the SF's office.

Shelley showed us to the conference room that we'd spent the past couple days in meetings with Commander Klebus and other SF officials.

Commander Klebus stood when we walked in, her expression haggard. Even though vamps didn't need sleep, I could tell this investigation was beginning to take a toll on her. It was doing that to all of us. I mean, seriously, another realm had been opened up in Jacob's warehouse. That was shit you couldn't make up.

"How are you doing today?" she asked, her tone surprisingly gentle.

I managed a brittle smile. "Just super. You?"

She sighed. "Probably the same as you."

I gave a short laugh, and she did the same. Yep. This sucked all around for everybody.

We settled onto our chairs and spent the rest of the day going over everything, piece by piece again. They also wanted to conduct more tests on my otherworldly powers as they tried to grasp what exactly it was and where it originated. Throughout it all, I kept thinking about that text from Archie. *Different universe. Terrible magic. Disappeared.* When I finally told Klebus about it, she cocked her head, looking as perplexed as me but stated she would look into it.

It was only near the end of the day, when I was so tired I felt as though I could fall asleep standing up, that they finally dismissed me.

"We'll see you tomorrow," Commander Klebus said as she walked me to the door.

"How much longer will she need to do this?" Tessa asked as she linked arms with me.

"Only another day or two. If we can't make any headway on answering our questions about that portal, we'll try a different route that doesn't involve your sister."

In other words, they'd begin investing more time in Jakub's warehouse, even though nobody wanted to go near the actual portal. I didn't know exactly what the SF was doing with it, but I knew that it was guarded twenty-four seven by a dozen SF members. If anything came through it, they would know.

Tessa and I walked down the hall, almost reaching the front, when a familiar figure stepped out of a room.

"Tala, how are you?" Carlos gave me a small smile, then reached for my hand.

His fingers enclosed around mine, his werewolf's nature to touch and show affection so apparent that my throat tightened. My ex-boyfriend had shown no hesitation in touching me even though I'd changed, yet Kaillen . . .

I managed to smile, and then squeezed his hand in return.

"Another long day?" he said quietly.

"Very."

He squeezed my hand again. "Can I do anything for you?"

I quickly shook my head. I still hadn't had *that* conversation with him. The one in which I firmly told him that we didn't have a future together. Quite frankly, even the thought of expending any kind of energy in something that emotional made me want to curl up into a ball and sleep forever, but I knew sooner or later I'd have to. Just not today.

"No, I'm okay. Thanks though." I squeezed his hand again, then let go.

As Tessa led me toward the front, I felt Carlos's gaze on me linger.

In the entryway, Shelley bid us goodnight before we stepped out the door to wait for our ride. I pulled my phone out to let Prish know I'd be home soon, just as a blazing yellow portal swirled in front of me.

I dropped my phone, the sound of it clattering to the ground filling the air around us.

Kaillen stepped out of the portal, his hair tousled, three days' worth of beard coating his cheeks. I quickly stepped to the side and awkwardly picked up my phone. I kept my attention on the ground, though, so I wouldn't have to see him enter the SF office to meet with Klebus or whoever he was here for.

But he didn't move. His feet stayed planted to the spot as his portal disappeared behind him. "Tala?"

The sound of his deep voice made tears prick my eyes, so I blinked rapidly.

He stepped closer, the energy off him soaring when I continued to gaze at my feet.

"Tala," he said more gruffly. "Please look at me."

Tessa mumbled something about forgetting her purse inside, even though her purse was hanging from her shoulder, before she disappeared back through the front door, leaving me alone on the sidewalk with the hunter.

"Tala," he growled, the sound pained.

I finally did as he asked, raising my eyes to his.

His breath sucked in when our gazes locked. I could only imagine the plethora of exploding stars and power shining from my irises.

But this was who I was now, perhaps had always been. I couldn't hide it or stop it.

To his credit, he didn't look away. He held eye contact, not backing down.

"You've been avoiding me," he finally said. His jaw locked, his expression impossible to read.

I scoffed softly. "I think it's actually the other way around."

He tore a hand through his hair, his chest rising in unsteady breaths. "I know. I'm sorry about how I was initially. It's been a weird few days."

"No shit." Bitterness crept into my tone.

Pain flitted across his expression. "My wolf thinks his mate died."

"As I'm aware."

"It's been affecting me."

Pain needled my heart. "As I'm also aware."

He took a step closer, then reached forward until his fingers touched mine.

My breath stopped.

"I . . . don't know how to act, with a wolf howling forlornly nonstop in me, but I—" His throat bobbed. "I know that I don't want this. I don't want to never see you again."

It felt as though my throat were closing in, but I managed to swallow and reply hoarsely, "But your wolf doesn't want me anymore. You can't fight that."

A low growl rumbled in his chest. "No, he doesn't *not* want you. He's simply very confused. He still recognizes your scent, but he also knows the wolf inside you died. He's—" He took a deep breath. "He's pretty fucked up right now, but that doesn't mean that *I* don't want you, even if he's confused."

My heart stopped. "*What?*"

"I said that *I* still want you."

Surely, I'd heard him wrong. Grief was obviously making me hallucinate. "But male wolves don't ever want another when their mate dies—"

"*Fuck* all of that." He lifted his hand to cup my cheek, his eyes blazing crimson. "I meant it when I said that you intrigued me from the beginning. It wasn't just my wolf. And even if he never comes around, he's not in control. *I* am."

I swallowed the thickness in my throat and shook my

head back and forth. *How? How could this be?* "*You* still want me?" I repeated, only because I was still certain I'd heard him wrong. "You actually want me even if your wolf doesn't?"

"Yes."

My stomach shot into my throat as hope surged in me so brightly that I knew it shone through my eyes. My biggest fear, my worst nightmare had come true. I'd thought Kaillen didn't want me, that everything he'd felt for me had been manufactured by his wolf, but here he was, at odds with his wolf, and he still wanted me. He was *fighting* to keep me.

A tender look crossed his features, and his thumb traced along my cheek. Heat flared in his eyes when his gaze dipped to my mouth, but something else did too. A warring emotion. A battle within.

He abruptly looked away and snarled, but I could tell that his snarl wasn't directed at me. No, it was meant for his wolf, who was probably howling at him to stop because in his wolf's confused world, his mate was dead.

Some of the hope inside me withered. Even though Kaillen—the man—stated that he wanted me, his wolf was in mourning and conflicted. And his wolf side would always rule him to some degree, whether he liked it or not.

"Is it as bad as I think?" I asked hesitantly as I swallowed the dryness in my throat.

The hunter let out a deep breath and dropped his hand. "Yeah. It's been . . . hard. But dammit, Tala, I'm not letting you go." Scarlet fire rolled in his eyes again, and I knew his demon was battling his wolf at this very second. "I know I avoided you initially after everything went down, but that was then, and this is now. I've had a few days to get my head around it, and I know one thing. I want you. I'll fight for you if I have to. I'll fight my wolf. I'll fight the SF. I'll fight that new fucking realm. I'll fight whoever tries to stand in my way. I'm not letting you go."

My stomach dipped at that fierce declaration, and I tentatively touched his waist.

For the briefest moment, he stiffened.

I hastily let go, my heart ripping at the thought that what we'd had before when our wolves had been a part of us was over, but dammit, I could be stubborn too. I wasn't going to give up on Kaillen just because his wolf now had some issues. But I also knew it wasn't going to be all roses, and that it could very well end in disaster.

But I was willing to try.

I gave him a small smile and kept my hands to myself, even though I itched to touch him and pull him close. "Maybe we should take this one day at a time."

I tried to broaden my smile, tried to show him that I understood that some things were beyond one's control, and if it became too hard for him, too unbearable to constantly be battling his wolf, that I wouldn't hold it against him. I wouldn't hate him for conceding to those instincts.

He closed the distance between us, drawing me to him in a fierce, possessive embrace, even though another low grumble came from him that I knew he directed inward. "A *colantha* to the bone." He leaned down, running his nose along my neck. He paused, then did it again. "You still smell like you."

"That's because I am still me."

"But I can also sense that you're different."

I squeezed him back, the sensation of his arms around me still feeling so *right* despite all that had happened. "I'm still me, Kaillen," I replied softly.

"I know." He inhaled my scent again, and something in his stance loosened, as if his greatest fear—that I was no longer me, no longer the woman he knew—had vanished. "Your scent is stronger now, though. More powerful."

My lips tugged up in a smile. "Haven't you heard that I was the key to another realm, and apparently, I command power from that lost world?"

"I believe I did get a memo about that."

I lifted my face to his, wanting him to kiss me more than anything, needing to feel his mouth on mine, his taste on my tongue, his body beneath my fingers. I'd been to hell and back, and the one thing I needed right now—*craved*—was him. Just him. Not his wolf. Not his demon. But Kaillen, the man.

Another low grumble came from him, and he pulled back just an inch.

The hope in me diminished when I saw him battling his wolf again. I stepped out of his arms and ran a shaky hand through my hair. "It's okay if—"

"Tala!" Tessa shrieked as she barreled out the door.

Kaillen and I both whipped our attention toward her.

A look of horror covered my sister's face as she came to a skidding halt beside us.

"What's wrong?" I darted a glance over her shoulder.

She panted, looking more panicked than I'd ever seen her. "I was talking to Private Merrick in the back when an alarm went off in Klebus's office." Tessa's eyes widened to saucers as her harsh breaths continued. "I overheard her talking to someone, and I think it was the SF members guarding the portal." She gripped my hands tightly, her fingers biting into my skin as my otherworldly powers swirled inside me at the mention of that void. "She said to *keep them contained*, Tala."

"Keep who contained?" Kaillen growled.

"I think someone has come through the portal," Tessa hissed.

The cold late-autumn wind bit into my cheeks as I whipped my gaze back to Kaillen. His scowl grew as a deep rumble vibrated in his chest.

"I think they've been summoned, Tala," Tessa said quietly to me. "I think this was what Mom warned us about."

"The Bone Eaters?" I felt myself pale, as Kaillen's expression turned fierce.

But I had a feeling Tessa was right, because it all made sense. All of the missing puzzle pieces clicked into place. Our mother hadn't wanted me revealing my power because she *knew.* Somehow, someway, we had ancestors from that lost realm, and she knew that I'd inherited their power—otherworldly power that could summon them back to earth, if only a connection was created. And I'd made that connection. I'd felt their power when they'd tried to suck me back to that world.

"They can't have you," Kaillen said in a low growl.

"Maybe not," I replied. "But they've finally been summoned, and I have a feeling whether or not I like it, they're here for *me*."

BOOK FOUR
SUPERNATURAL CURSE

We've finally uncovered the depths of Jakub's plan, but that discovery came with consequences none of us expected.

Despite his wolf's growls in my direction, Kaillen's determined to prove his love. So the two of us delve into my family's long buried past to discover the truth of who I really am.

But things don't go as planned, and our struggles uncover an impossible choice. I can either stay on earth and accept that my hunter and I will never be mated, or I can embrace my destiny and say goodbye to the only man I've ever loved.

ABOUT THE AUTHOR

Krista Street loves writing in multiple genres: fantasy, sci-fi, romance, and dystopian. Her books are cross-genre and often feature complex characters, plenty of supernatural twists, and romance in every story. She loves writing about coming-of-age characters who fight to find their place in this world while also finding their one true mate.

Krista Street is a Minnesota native but has lived throughout the U.S. and in another country or two. She loves to travel, read, and spend time in the great outdoors. When not writing, Krista is either chasing her children, spending time with her husband and friends, sipping a cup of tea, or enjoying the hidden gems of beauty that Minnesota has to offer.

THANK YOU

Thank you for reading *Cursed of Moon*, book three in the *Supernatural Curse* series.

If you enjoy Krista Street's writing, make sure you visit her website to learn about her new release text alerts, newsletter, and other series.

www.kristastreet.com

Links to all of her social media sites are available on every page.

Last, if you enjoyed reading *Cursed of Moon*, please consider logging onto the retailer you purchased this book from to post a review. Authors rely heavily on readers reviewing their work. Even one sentence helps a lot. Thank you so much if you do!

Printed in Great Britain
by Amazon

45196117R00209